BEHIND THE FAN
BOOKS
REGENCY ROMANCE

KATE ARCHER

The League of Meddling Butlers

Book Five

A Perplexing Regency Romance

ISBN: 9798267317962

Prologue:

Mr. Matthew L. Browning was unendingly surprised that *The League of Butlers* had not yet said aloud that they required a President, and that President was him. Though he did not have the official title, he was quite certain that if any of the members were to pose the question "Pray, gentlemen, does anyone know who leads us?" the answer would be a resounding chorus of voices crying out, "Certainly, Mr. Browning leads us."

And why should he not lead? He served at the pleasure of His Grace, Hugh Finstatten, the Duke of Greystone. The Finstattens were an eminent family with one of the oldest pedigrees in England. The very air in the house was rarified. The furniture, the carpets, and even the curtains, had watched over generations of Finstattens. Unlike some newer arrivals to the *ton*, the Finstattens gloried in a threadbare carpet or frayed curtain because it represented history. Long, long history. They had no need to run out and purchase the latest paper-hangings or re-cover the drawing room sofas in a stripe. The faded blue paint on the walls would continue to peek around the picture frames and the faded Stuart-era red brocade on the sofa need not be changed.

The family peered down their nose at those who strived to be au courant. The Finstattens were both the past and the future and did not require a striped sofa to announce it.

As befitted the duke, he resided in the largest house on Grosvenor Square. Two houses had been made into one when the old duke had run things. That had been Mr. Browning's rather genius idea when he'd got wind of Sir Frederick wishing to sell the house next door. Mr. Browning fondly recalled the old duke's adoption of the idea each time he gazed at the exterior of the residence.

The old duke had since traveled to the great beyond to be reunited with his duchess, and young Hugh Finstatten had stepped into his father's illustrious shoes. It was a passing of the baton that had gone on for centuries.

If there were anything at all niggling at the edges of Mr. Browning's mind, it was perhaps that fate had elevated Hugh Finstatten to the dukedom unfortunately early in his career. He had not had sufficient time to take in and model all the gravitas of his father. That had left His Grace to his own devices and under the unfortunate influence of his friends.

The duke, now twenty-seven years on this earth, did not make his way through the house in any stately duke-like manner, but rather raced through it to charge out of the house and leap onto his horse in a rather hair-raising operation. Worse, when he got on that horse, he was almost certainly off to some activity that could end the line of Finstattens permanently. Horseraces, regattas, boxing, carriage races, swordplay, if there was a thing in England that could kill the duke, Mr. Browning was sure he was doing it. He could also be sure that the duke's closest friend, Sir Edward Bromley, was encouraging it.

Gone were the stately dinners Mr. Browning had once presided over. In were loud and raucous parties with his friends that went on until dawn.

Mr. Browning did not consider Sir Edward a very suitable influence and he had more than enough information to have formed that opinion. The last party had gone on until the sun was well up. After the revelers had finally taken their leave and the duke was abed, he'd ventured into the drawing room to assess what the housemaids would be faced with. Among other atrocities, a neckcloth was somehow draped over the frame of the painting of a revered forbear, the third Duke of Greystone.

He'd not needed to examine the small monogram on the inside of the cloth to know who was responsible. For the first time in his career, Mr. Browning had been forced to utter the words, "Jimmy, fetch a ladder from the stables so we might remove Sir Edward's neckcloth from the face of the duke's ancestor."

Out was a dignified newspaper and coffee at White's. In was, well he was not certain what went on at The Devil's Den. It was an unfortunately named club that counted the duke as a longstanding and apparently popular member.

The butler soothed himself by remembering that the duke had turned twenty-seven over the summer while managing to remain in the land of the living, and that meant the family's ancient tradition was to save them all. Throughout the centuries, the men of the Finstatten line married during their twenty-seventh year. Nobody remembered why or how it was so, Mr. Browning suspected some old duke had determined that it was deemed old enough for a suitable maturity and young enough to produce multiple heirs.

Wherever the tradition had come from, the old duke had been determined that it be carried out. On his deathbed, he'd made his son swear he would honor it.

That made it a set thing. Young Hugh Finstatten might have terrible friends, but he would not break his word to his father. A wife would settle him, and a son would assure the line.

Of course, it was a bit worrying that the duke was not happy about the obligation. Mr. Browning had overheard him telling the utterly irresponsible Sir Edward that if he could not find what he was looking for, maybe he should just hunt up a lady who sought a marriage of convenience. Then Sir Edward, ever a fountain of bad ideas, suggested he find himself a widow. According to Sir Edward, young ladies just out in society were too needy and would want the duke by their side all day long.

Though Mr. Browning had overheard those alarming ideas, he'd not heard what, exactly, the duke was looking for in the first place. Nobody seemed to know. All Mr. Browning had heard from His Grace was that the ladies of the *ton* struck him as "too cold." And then there been some mention of uncomfortable sharp points and he'd not had the first idea what that meant.

The League expected Mr. Browning to manage His Grace's

marital match, and all he had to go on was that what was not wanted was a lady "too cold" or having the mysterious "sharp points."

As if all that did not hang heavy enough upon his shoulders, there was Lady Lucinda Gaddington to consider. The duke's sister was ten years older than he was. She was long wed to the Earl of Gaddington and one would have imagined the duke's house would rarely see her presence. That was, sadly, not the case. She came in and out as if she still lived there and she was just as bossy as she'd been as a child, which had been exceedingly bossy.

Just then, Mr. Browning heard an audible sigh. He realized it had emanated from himself as he recalled what a tyrant that lady had been all her life. There had been times in her youth when Mr. Browning had the urge to throw a vase at her head and then offer his notice and imminent departure without a reference. There were times when he began to believe it might be worth it, just to make her stop complaining. Somehow, he'd restrained himself. He supposed he would credit a stiff brandy on occasion for making that possible.

When Lord Gaddington had offered for her, the old duke had insisted he would not abide a long engagement. No particular reason was given, but Mr. Browning presumed it was because the duke did not want Lord Gaddington to get too close a look at the temperament of his lady love. It had been glorious day indeed when she left the house in Gaddington's carriage. He always kept hope in his breast that the old duke had not overheard the raucous celebration below stairs that had followed.

Now that the young duke was obligated to wed, Mr. Browning had no doubt Lady Gaddington would be all but moving in to dispense her very decided opinions on every glance His Grace made in the direction of a lady. He wondered if he should quietly move all the vases in the house to the attics to lessen the chance of him accidentally throwing one at her head.

Mr. Browning had not communicated any of these difficulties to *The League*. At least, not as of yet. He must certainly tell them something, but he had not decided what.

Whatever he communicated, it must be couched in elegant and stately terms. He was, after all, the Duke of Greystone's butler and *The League's* de facto leader.

Chapter One

Grosvenor Square, 1806

Hugh Finstatten, the latest Duke of Greystone, had thought it would be a laugh to crew for Sir Edward Bromley, or Seddie as he called him, on *The Contessa*. Lord Bedwick's annual regatta would be held in a few days and the members of The Devil's Den were determined to put forward some competition to the Duke of Barstow, who'd won it several years in a row.

At least, Hugh had thought crewing might be a laugh when he'd heard about it last evening. Seddie had talked him into it at the club. Of course, he'd been in his cups and had found everything in the world amusing.

The cold light of day introduced less amused feelings. Seddie had dragged him out of his bed at dawn with his head pounding. The rogue had already been to the stables to inform them that Hugh's horse was to be saddled. Then he'd sped down to the kitchens to upset his staff by insisting they required eggs, rashers, rolls, and coffee as fast as it could be made. Hugh did not precisely know what went on in the kitchens so early in the morning, but he suspected that it was a time for the staff to have their breakfasts and otherwise enjoy their leisure. Or maybe Seddie had dragged them from their beds. There was no way to know until Browning told him in grim terms later.

Hugh had seen the look on Browning's face, who had no doubt been roused by the irate cook. They were not, generally speaking, an early rising household and his butler was clearly not entertained by the dawn hour. Or entertained by Sir Edward.

Or entertained by the notion that they were to set off on the Thames on Sir Edward's boat.

Poor Browning was often looking grim over something or other, and particularly over Sir Edward. It had always been so and Hugh was very used to it. He would be far more surprised if Mr. Browning suddenly broke out in laughter.

At least his valet had been left abed. Hugh was perfectly capable of dressing himself and Richards was not worth waking up so early. The fellow would just have his revenge by tying his neckcloth too tight and then pretending it was a mistake.

He went downstairs and found Seddie already at the sideboard, helping himself to sausages. He must be called Seddie, as it would be awkward to call him Sir Edward and even more awkward to call him Edward. The name was some combination of sir and Eddie and they'd settled it long ago. After all, Seddie did not call him Your Grace, but rather Finstatten.

When they'd been boys, they'd come to blows on the subject of names. Hugh had pointed out he was a marquess and should be addressed as a lord while his friend was as of yet a nobody. Seddie turned out to be remarkably good with his fists and they'd both ended bruised from head to toe before a settlement was agreed on. He had no idea why they had not settled on using Seddie's last name, Bromley, as they had on Hugh's last name. But then, they had been eight and not exactly brimming with sense.

At the moment, his friend was all enthusiasm and speed at this ungodly hour. He'd filled his plate, turned round, and then laughed raucously at Hugh. "What on earth are you wearing?"

Hugh looked down. He was dressed very usually, though he could not be entirely sure of the colors. At least, not the colors other people saw. He was colorblind, just as his father had been. Richards usually sorted that out for him, but Richards was still abed.

"Perhaps I might go above stairs and choose another waistcoat, Your Grace," Browning said.

From that, Hugh presumed that his waistcoat the coat did not match. He shrugged, as he really could not tell. He'd not even known he could not see colors as other people did until he was seven or eight. They were playing Taw and Seddie had told him he was blind as a bat when he could not determine which marble was yellow and which was green.

No sooner had breakfast been on the sideboards than Hugh had been rushed through it. Browning came back with another waistcoat and got him into it, and they were on their horses.

It was a chill, grey morning with spits of freezing rain stinging his cheeks. Heavy clouds scudded across the sky and an ill wind tugged at his hat. Some of the branches on the trees of the square showed a glaze of ice. His horse was entirely disgusted with it. Hugh was entirely disgusted.

They reached the river, and it seemed the Thames was entirely disgusted too. The water was a dark, cold grey and the waves, buffeted by the wind, were a deal higher than one would hope.

"We cannot go out in that," he said.

"Nonsense," Seddie said. "It's perfect. Challenging conditions will prepare us. Then on the day, conditions are bound to be better and we'll have the edge because we will have already been through the worst of it."

Hugh was not certain he followed the logic. Seeming to see his hesitation, Seddie handed him a flask of brandy. Perhaps it was not the most ideal solution to his hesitation, but it did indeed soften the unpleasantness of the situation.

He followed Seddie to a twenty-two foot sloop tied up on the pier. Hugh looked around, but they seemed to be quite alone. "Where is the boat man?"

"What boat man?" Seddie asked.

"The boat man. The captain. The man who will oversee the operation."

Seddie laughed. "The boat did not come with a man attached to it. I suppose it would have cost a deal more if it did. I'm the captain."

"Wait. You *bought* the boat? I assumed you rented it."

"Rented it? Finstatten, if one is to do something, one must go all in."

"So you bought a boat for a regatta. Then what? What will you do with it after the regatta?"

This appeared to be a question that had so far failed to present itself to Seddie's mind. Then he smiled. "I know what we'll do."

Hugh was a bit concerned at the use of "we'll."

"Remember when we tried to build a boat to sail down the Orwell?"

Of course, Hugh did remember that. It had seemed like an exciting idea at the time. The day before, they'd trekked the half mile to the river and went fishing. They'd come home empty-handed but while they were there, they'd talked of how glorious it would be to just set sail, captains of their own ship. They might even dare to sail all the way into the Channel. They'd been in an old and unused outbuilding that was their headquarters of sorts when they speculated on it. Their eyes had settled on the stacks of old wood piled in a corner. Then they'd got a hammer and nails and set to work.

On reflection, Hugh did not imagine the boat would have remained afloat for more than a minute, considering it was just planks hammered together that looked more a square box than a rounded hull. On top of that, they had still to come up with an idea to plug all the gaps, how to move it to the river when it was done, and what to use as a sail. It was all for naught, as they'd never got that far. Somehow the duke got wind of it and put a stop to it. He and Seddie had been delivered of a stern lecture, mostly to do with the height of the waves when the tide and wind ran against each other and how they would have ended two foolish boys drowned.

"You see what I hint at?" Seddie said. "We could go the other way. We somehow get the boat into the Channel, we could probably hire somebody to figure that part out, and then we sail up the Orwell as easy as you like."

There were several problems with Seddie's idea. First, whenever he used the word "somehow" there was almost always an insurmountable problem ahead. Second, whenever he claimed something was "easy as you like," there was almost always an insurmountable problem ahead.

"Perhaps we ought to discover how skilled you are at sailing the Thames before we head out to the English Channel," he said drily.

"Right you are," Seddie said, all enthusiasm. "Do not worry about a thing, I've read all about it."

He'd read all about it. Marvelous.

After boarding the boat, Seddie struggled to get the sail out of its canvas bag, which Hugh did not think a propitious beginning. Finally pulling it all the way out, four pieces of wood, all four of equal length, fell out of the bottom of the sail bag.

Seddie stared at the collection of wood for a moment. Then he said, "That's right. I read about these. They're battens. They go in holes in the side of the sail."

"What are they for?" Hugh asked.

"I don't know, they just go there. I presume they do something."

They spent the next ten minutes searching for holes. One

was finally found, which gave a clue as to where the other ones were. They still did not know the purpose of the battens, but they did fit exactly into the narrow slots so they supposed they'd got it right.

They were about to try to get the sail up when they realized the steering mechanism was lying at the bottom of the boat. Seddie pretended he'd realized it all along and made a great show of explaining that the rudder had to be attached to the tiller and then the whole thing attached to the back of the boat. That was another half hour in drizzling cold rain.

That done, getting the sail up was another palaver. Seddie stared at the sail, and then the mast, and tried to remember what he'd read about it. They finally figured it out. They got the sail up the mast and then the bottom of it tied to the boom. The sail flapped back and forth as Hugh untied the rope at the front of the boat.

"You are at the bow of the boat," Seddie said to him, very unnecessarily. "Best to start picking up sailor lingo. I am at the stern. I could also call it aft. I don't know what the difference is."

Seddie untied his rope and they both pushed off.

At first, they merely drifted away from the pier. "Easy as you like," Seddie said. "Let's head out and see what this boat is made of."

Seddie turned the tiller to head them out on the Thames. The boom swung at Hugh and he ducked. "Aren't you supposed to warn me about that?" he asked.

"Right you are," Seddie said. "When I say coming about, that's the time to duck."

And there they were, sailing the Thames on one of the worst days possible. As it *was* a terrible day, they had the river mostly to themselves. A few intrepid barges made their way up and down the river, staying as near to the banks as was practicable. It was probably just as well, as Seddie probably would have hit something if the river was more crowded.

The Contessa heaved upon the waves and the creaking of the planks underneath Hugh's feet were not reassuring. He could not tell if the tide was coming in or going out but wherever it was going, it was going with gusto. The wind whipped the sails and Hugh would be very surprised if they did not need repairs by the end of it.

He practiced letting the sail out and trimming it to try to figure out what worked. If he pulled it in too far it just started flapping. If he let it out too far they did not move as fast. He finally figured out that the trick was to pull it in until it flapped a little and then let it out until the flap disappeared.

In between that operation, he ducked the boom, trying to keep up with Seddie's wildly changing shouts and directions. He was certain Seddie had overestimated his sailing skills and had not a hope of winning Bestwick's regatta. Among others, he'd be up against the Duke of Barstow who'd won it several years in a row. Furthermore, he was very glad they'd never set sail on the Orwell all those years ago, considering what he was looking at now.

They turned to head downwind. They had gone that direction several times and Hugh had noticed that letting the sail all the way out was the way to go. Downwind was not as frenetic as they were not tipping to one side of the other. Hugh let the sail out, sat back, and felt he could relax for a moment.

Now that the wine of the evening before had been entirely blown off by the icy winds of the Thames and they were on the easy downwind, the problem hanging over his head crept back into his thoughts. He was twenty-seven. It had seemed such a far-off thing. Until it was not. He must wed this season. His father had very craftily waited until he was laying weak in a bed to wrench the promise from him. It was one of the family's traditions and the family's traditions were everything. As his father had said often, the Finstattens did not move with the times because the Finstattens were the times.

Of course he'd given his word. He would never have let the old soldier down. Now he must carry it out.

He'd have to find a lady he would not mind being around for extended periods. Seddie seemed to think a lady-wife could just be deposited somewhere, but Hugh did not think it was a very practical idea. He did not think he would like it even if it was practical. He also thought Seddie did not at all mean that idea for himself. He'd been chasing after their neighbor, Lady Genevieve, for two years.

No, Hugh would not be leaving his lady behind anywhere.

Who was she, though? It was not as if he was against marriage. Quite the opposite—he was all for it. He found it a wonderful idea to have a lady by his side. He was anxious for a family. He looked forward to creating traditions that were all their own and not a Finstatten tradition somebody had thought up when Henry VIII was king.

He'd kept his eyes open the last few seasons. But he'd not seen anybody he liked. The ladies who were held up as the diamonds of the season were all too angular and sharply pointed, too cold somehow, if not in their appearance, then in their manner. They seemed somehow bony to him, and not very sturdy, as if they could snap in half like a branch. He could not be comfortable with such a lady. What was hailed as elegant just felt devoid of feeling, what was stately seemed too tall. He did not like flirtatious banter or pretensions of boldness. He did not like gossip and affectations of being shocked. It all seemed... formal and uncomfortable. It was as if a gentleman could never relax or ever really know what was in a sophisticated lady's thoughts and he did not like it.

He felt as if he would know his future wife when he saw her, and hopefully she would know him too. But he'd just not seen her yet. Yes, he was certain he would know. Romeo and Juliet had known. They'd come to a bad end, so that part of the play could be ignored. The point was, they had known. Perhaps he was too sentimental, and perhaps he kept that part of his temperament very under wraps, but he really did believe he would know. Else, how was he so certain that he'd *not* met her yet?

He was sure he would find her, but this time constraint of the tradition was difficult. What if he could not find what he was looking for in time? Would he have to wed a lady he did not care for?

"Coming about!" Sir Edward shouted.

Already? Hugh ducked. The boom swung to the port side and he hauled in the sheet line. The last he remembered was the boom wildly swinging back in his direction, headed for his face.

~ ~ ~ ~ ~

Finella Fernsby, the eldest daughter of Baron Dunston, was not unaware of her various deficiencies. Her father was the very first of the Barons Dunston, so the title was sparkling new. Deficiency number one. She had lost her mother early and so had not had a womanly figure leading her forward to her maturity. Deficiency number two. As they were so new to the peerage, she did not have the benefit of all those things, like jewelry, that might have been passed down through the generations and spoke of history and a firm footing in society. All she had was a small gold cross from her father. Deficiency number three. But the biggest deficiency of all, the deficiency that would be immediately apparent to the *ton*, the deficiency she could not hide, was her person.

She was short and had curves where there should be none. Or if not none, then not so prominent. Her cheeks were a little too plump. Her arms were not long and lithe. The current fashion was not meant for her, the high waists of the style of dress did nothing for her. At home, it had not been so painfully obvious. At least, not to her. Most of the time. But in Town, gracious, the place seemed filled with statuesque and sophisticated ladies. Reedy sylphs whose clothes hung elegantly, whose very person cried elegance and sophistication.

As her carriage came into London, she'd begun to note them everywhere, going hither and thither. Then, the coachman had stopped the horses to allow a cart to pass on a narrow bit of road and she'd seen two ladies come out of a shop. Finella had been near enough to be hit on the head by how different they were from herself. They were goddesses. Their dresses hung with not even a ripple as the fabric did not encounter any bumps on the way down. Even their hands, which had waved so gracefully to a waiting porter, were long-fingered, bejeweled, and elegant. Their style of dress was different too. It was the same cut—high waisted in the Greek style—but they were nearly devoid of decoration. They wore simple white muslins with only a colored ribbon round their slim waists. Of course, when one looked as lovely as those ladies did, she supposed there was no need for decoration.

Finella felt rather like a squat mushroom popping up in a field of elegant lilies.

If there was one thing that was on the positive side of her situation, it was that she was to land at Bedford Square. Her father's estate abutted the Duchess of Ralston's land and that lady had taken pity on her father. The baron had not the first idea of what was to be done about a season. He'd not even known a season would be necessary until the duchess informed him of it. The baron had been greatly relieved to put his daughter in the duchesses' capable hands. Her father's parting words to Finella were: "Try not to wed a vicar, it's a dreary sort of existence, you won't be able to put a foot out of place." With that sentimental advice, he'd kissed her forehead and put her in a carriage in the company of Lucy Lenter, who was to act as her maid.

Now she had arrived to Bedford Square and the duchess had greeted her warmly. She'd been only a half hour ago sent above stairs to get settled. Finella was delighted to find a jar of biscuits on the bedside, as she was positively starved. As she chewed her way through them, she admired the room. It was so bright and then there was something about the decorations. It felt very restrained, which she had not thought she would like, but it was very calming. Her room at home was a riot of color —pink and grey striped chairs, a pink silk bed covering, and a wonderful wall-covering of peacocks and palm trees. Cream dominated this room and it gave her some new ideas about what would be pleasant.

Lucy, who was a housemaid at home and who'd been pressed into service as a lady's maid, hurried in. She spotted the biscuits and said, "Don't mind if I do."

Finella handed her the jar. "You've been below stairs," she said, "what are the household's servants like?"

"As to that," Lucy said, "I find 'em as I expected 'em. Noses all pointed toward the heavens and narrowed eyes all looking down upon me."

"No!" Finella said, quite distressed that Lucy would feel looked down upon. It felt particularly personal, as it was her primary fear that people would look down on her. They already physically looked down on her due to her lackluster stature, but she very much feared they would look down on her in every possible manner. Finella did not think much of her looks and her conversation could be awkward, even to her own ears. She was not a beauty, she was not a scholar, she was just...Finella. She might be good humored and goodhearted, but was that enough?

"Aye, it was something terrible down there," Lucy went on, recounting her introduction to the servants. "You know me, I don't make more of it than it was. The whole encounter was capped off when I was shown where I was to lay my head at night. I reckon a poor chimney sweep is treated better. Awful, is what it is." Lucy sighed dramatically. "I suppose I'll survive it, even if I do have to sleep in a closet on a mattress thin enough to serve as a tablecloth."

"Oh, Lucy, what are we to do?" Finella said, chewing worriedly on a biscuit. "I could not bear for you to be treated poorly. You've been so good to come with me, when you could have stayed at home."

"Aye. It was a bit of a wrench to give up my housemaid duties what with how much I like to dust things, but I'm all for sacrifice, everybody knows it. Now, there's only one thing for it," Lucy said. "We tell the duchess that you suffer from nightmares and I'll need to be very nearby. She's got rooms aplenty on this corridor."

"I see," Finella said hesitatingly. "I suppose we might try —"

"Now, let me get to these trunks. I'd like to think they'd unpack themselves, but I reckon I'd be let down."

"Goodness, yes, there is so much of it," Finella said. "And poor Lucy, you've been through it today, I will help you get it done."

"If you insist," Lucy said, graciously allowing herself to be helped.

Trunks and hatboxes were emptied and examined. Finella had taken great care with her wardrobe. Other ladies might throw on anything and look very well, but she had to attempt to flatter her particular silhouette. The baron had hired a dressmaker from the village that he'd heard recommended, and Mrs. Helwig had been coming and going from the house for weeks.

Finella had told the lady what she looked for and it turned out Mrs. Helwig was rather ingenious. She explained that Finella was not so much looking for transformation as she was looking for distraction. As she said, "One cannot make a person think they're looking at a table that's been set with Flora Danica when it's in fact earthenware."

Finella was not sure what Flora Danica was, but she

guessed it was some sort of expensive china.

Mrs. Helwig went on to explain that if one were to place interesting things on a dress, they would draw the eye to the wished-for areas. Apparently, Finella's bosom was to be highlighted with the right sort of corset, and her hips and lack of height distracted from. Stripes were to go longways to make her appear taller than she actually was. Ruffles created a river for the eye to follow, puffed sleeves made the shoulders look wider than the hips. Fascinating necklines were to draw the eye. On occasions when bonnets were worn, that was a real opportunity to draw the eye to Finella's face, which according to Mrs. Helwig was her best feature, and her hair, which was very good too.

She'd worn a simple traveling dress and her straw bonnet from her old wardrobe for the journey, but she was soon to face the *ton*. She would do so looking far different than she ever had.

"I never did see so many bows and gewgaws stuck on clothes in my life," Lucy said.

Finella nodded. "They draw the eye, you see."

"They do something to the eye," Lucy said.

Just then, there was a quick knock and the door swung open. The Duchess of Ralston entered the room. She paused, staring at the dresses laying on the bed.

"What on earth?" she whispered.

Chapter Two

Hugh had been sent flying into the Thames by the boom when Seddie had suddenly changed direction. He was fairly certain he'd swallowed some water before being roughly hauled onto a bargeman's boat. In the distance, Seddie was swinging around wildly with no seeming destination in mind.

As far as he could piece it together, Seddie had turned the boat one way, the boom had swung over his ducked head and then his friend had leaned or fallen against the tiller and turned the boat again, swinging the boom back as a surprise.

However it had unfolded, Hugh had ended up in the water. He could not say how long he'd been flailing around in the Thames, but his drenched clothes had felt like he wore lead. The cold seeped into his bones and he was beginning to lose feeling in his legs and hands. It had mercifully ended when a bargeman had got hold of his coat with a grappling hook and hauled him up.

The bargeman had looked him over as he lay on the deck and told him not to move, as there was no telling if something was broken. Hugh did not imagine any of his limbs could be broken, as he'd landed in the water. Though, they certainly were frozen and he could feel a bump emerging on the side of his head courtesy of the boom.

It had been hard to follow the bargeman's directions and lay still, as he'd never been so cold in his life. One of the sailors on the barge seemed to perceive his shaking and threw a canvas sail bag over him. And so, in that dignified manner he'd made his way back to shore. He'd begun to wonder what had happened to

Seddie, but then the bargeman had leaned over him and said, "It looks like your stupid friend is aiming for land, can't say he'll get there though. I never did see the like of it—he ought to be barred from the Thames and made to stay off every boat in England." Hugh did not argue the point as it happened to be a very good point.

Since then, the barge had docked, and he'd been again ordered by the bargeman to stay still. They sent for a barber-surgeon, which Hugh was a bit leery about. He was not sure he needed treatment at all, particularly not from a barber-surgeon. If he must be looked over, he would prefer it to be by his regular physician, Sir Henry Halford. He'd rubbed his hands to get the feeling back into them while he waited.

Willy Tankard, the barber-surgeon in question, had taken one look at him and folded his rather impressive arms. "Quindler, you've gone and fished out a swell."

"How can you tell?" the bargeman asked.

"The cut of the clothes. A pile of coin was paid for that coat."

"That coat's got a hole in it now," the bargeman said. "Grappling hook."

"They can't make you pay for it, I reckon."

"I ain't payin' for nothing."

"Who are you, anyway?" the surgeon asked Hugh.

"The Duke of Greystone," he said from his prone position, as the two men stared down at him.

As a usual thing, the people he encountered were happy to meet with a duke. To his surprise, the bargeman and the surgeon exchanged glances and started talking rapid fire.

"Worst luck," Willy Tankard said.

"Oh aye," the bargeman said. "Mind you, how was I to know he was a great muckety-muck when he was drowning?"

Willy Tankard nodded his head. "Nothin' you could'a done but fished him out. You couldn't have known."

"I swear if there is a way for bad luck to come a'crashin' into my day, bad luck will find it."

"I often think the same for meself."

"Let's get 'im off our hands quick."

"Aye. I don't have nothin' to do with them what strut around with titles."

"Same. How could we? We got actual work to do all day, unlike them that do nothin' but sleep and eat."

Hugh was beginning to think that being a duke was an unhappy notion to these fellows. His father had often spoken of the French nobility and how none of them had seen what was coming, none of them had believed it possible that the French people would turn against them. They assumed they were adored and admired until their heads rolled. Was this something like that? In which case, he hoped his person was not to be shortly rolled back into the sea.

"There's nothing for it," Willy Tankard said, "we've got to get rid of him. Carefully, mind."

The bargeman nodded sadly.

Hugh was becoming more and more wary. Get rid of him, how?

He attempted to rise, but Willy Tankard pushed him down again. Where was Seddie?

"Gentlemen," he said, "there is no need for violence."

"Violence?" Willy Tankard asked. He shook his head. "We got a regular delicate daisy here if he thinks *that* was violence."

"I reckon they're all delicate what live in luxury," the bargeman said. "Look at his hands—white as snow. He ain't never picked up a tool."

"Aye," the surgeon said, rubbing his chin. "Where do you live, fancy man?"

Fancy man? This really was beginning to be alarming. Never in his life had he been addressed with such mockery.

"He probably don't know where he lives," the bargeman said. "These rich types are carried round by their servants and don't got a need to know their own address."

"Grosvenor Square," Hugh said. He did not give the house number as he'd begun to wonder if they were planning to take him there so they could rob the place. Or dump him back in the Thames and then go rob the place. If so, he did not like Browning's chances of fighting them off.

"'Course he lives on one of them squares," the bargeman said. "You won't find a fella like that wanderin' round the Seven Dials."

"Or survivin' for long in them environs," the bargeman said with a snort.

"I know what we'll do," the surgeon said. "You'll go to his square and tell 'em what's gone on, they can call on some fancy-vest doctor what treats the rich. That way, I don't get blamed for nothing. I'll arrange a litter to get him to his stupid friend's carriage."

The gentlemen seemed to have a very poor impression of Seddie's seamanship. Hugh, himself, had developed a poor impression of Seddie's seamanship. Of course, there was not a carriage attending them, belonging to his stupid friend or otherwise.

"There is no carriage," Hugh said. "We came on horseback."

"For the love of heaven," the bargeman muttered. "I'll go tell his people. Use a litter to get him up to The Strand and get a hackney from there. Maybe his stupid friend will even help out if he can manage to aim for dry land on one his go rounds."

The surgeon nodded. "That's best. No treating 'im for anything, no jostling, no lettin' him try to walk, no way for a duke's relations to be screamin' that I done something to 'im. We return the fancy man as we found 'im."

"Except for the coat, what's got a hole in it. I ain't payin' for it."

"I'll back you if they try it," the barber-surgeon said.

Hugh felt the two gentlemen were obsessed with his coat, though he was not sure why they thought they'd be asked to pay for it. If anybody was going to pay for it, it was Seddie. "Tell my butler that the message comes from Sir Edward," Hugh said. He knew very well that if Browning got a message about an accident and Seddie's name was attached to it, his butler would spring into action.

~ ~ ~ ~ ~

As terrible news often has a habit, it arrived when nobody was expecting it. The first hint that something had gone terribly wrong was a knock on the door by a very rough-looking individual. Mr. Browning had expected his footman to send the wretch packing, with a proper scolding about the audacity of coming to the front doors to help walk him out of the neighborhood.

However, Jimmy came looking for him and said, "I've put that man in the small saloon, Mr. Browning. He says he has a particular message from Sir Forward. I'm pretty sure he meant Sir Edward. At least, I asked him if he meant Sir Edward and he shrugged and said, "Whatever his name is, he's an idiot.""

Of course it was Sir Edward. That fellow *was* an idiot. Further, no message from Sir Edward could possibly be good news.

Mr. Browning suddenly staggered under the weight of what it could mean. Sir Edward had dragged His Grace from his bed and taken him to sail on the Thames. Heavens above, there had been an accident. He could feel it in his bones.

Had they sunk the boat? Had there been a drowning? It would be very like Sir Edward to take an unseaworthy boat out and drown the duke! He'd already tried it once when they were boys and had only been stopped when the duke heard about it.

Despite feeling rather faint, Mr. Browning had hurried to the small saloon. There, he found a disheveled individual of indeterminate age. His face was weathered and his clothes were faded. He had all the hallmarks of a person working out of doors for his living.

"You the head man, then?" the man asked.

"Aside from His Grace, I am the head man," Mr. Browning said, working to keep any trembling from his voice.

"Me name's Quindler, I run a barge on the Thames and I fished your fancy man out of it this morning."

"Fancy man? Fished him out?" Mr. Browning said, horror overtaking him.

"That's what I said," Mr. Quindler said, "Saw the thing going on, sailed over there, and fished him out with a grappling hook. Got him over the gunwale as easy as you please. I ain't payin' for the coat!"

"A *grappling* hook?"

"Aye, I hooked it through his coat."

"A grappling hook? Through his *coat*?"

"Right through the coat I ain't payin' for. If you don't mind me sayin,' for the head man, you seem a little slow off the mark," Mr. Quindler said, eyeing him critically.

Mr. Browning took a deep breath, preparing himself for what he was to discover next. "I must know the worst of it. Is he dead?"

"Dead? No, he ain't dead. If he were dead, I'd a left him

floating for the scavengers to come along and go through his pockets. I ain't a scavenger or a mudlark, mind. Let *them* empty the pockets of a drowned man. I'm a bargeman."

Mr. Browning sank down into a chair, having been told far more than he ever wished to know about the disposition of dead bodies in the Thames. "What is his condition?"

Mr. Quindler shrugged. "How should I know? I left him with the barber-surgeon. I'm a bargeman."

"A barber-surgeon was called?" What could that mean? Was the duke even now being worked on in some terrible manner?

"Aye, he lives close by, so we sent a boy to fetch him. That fella knows what he's about."

"Mr. Quindler, are you telling me that a part of His Grace is, well is it, what I mean to say is—"

"Getting sawed off? I don't reckon so. At least, I didn't note nothin' that looked like it needed sawing off."

Mr. Browning pulled out a handkerchief and wiped his brow. He staggered to his feet. "I must go to him. He must be brought home."

Mr. Quindler shrugged again, which was really an insufficient reaction to the disaster unfolding. It seemed Mr. Quindler shrugged at all the world.

"Jimmy!" Mr. Browning shouted.

Jimmy had the door open in a trice and had likely been listening on the other side. "Send for Sir Henry. Track him down. I do not care what lady he is treating for nervous flutterings. Tell him His Grace has been in an accident, and we require his services this very minute. He is to meet us at the docks..." Mr. Browning paused and turned to Mr. Quindler. "What docks? Where are they?"

"I wouldn't go sendin' your fancy doctor down to the river.

Sir Idiot is to accompany the duke here. You see? You'd go there and they'd be here."

Of course he saw. This bargeman was irritating to say the least. "Jimmy, bring Sir Henry here. I will prepare a sickroom. We must be quick!" He turned to the bargeman. "Thank you for bringing me this news."

The bargeman stared at Mr. Browning's hands. Seeing nothing in them, he began to glower.

"Jimmy, pay the gentleman a pound on his way out."

"And extra coin for a hackney, mind," Mr. Quindler said. "Three shillings six, both coming and going."

"Very well, see to it Jimmy and then be off to Sir Henry in all haste!"

Mr. Browning hurried from the room. He staggered up the stairs toward His Grace's bedchamber. Once inside, he looked blindly round, hardly knowing what to do. Was this it? Had Sir Edward finally succeeded in killing the duke?

Montrose, the duke's valet, hurried into the room. "Mr. Browning?" he asked.

The butler held on to a bedpost. "The duke has been injured in some manner. Sir Edward."

Montrose cursed under his breath, as no further explanation than "Sir Edward" was needed.

Mr. Browning felt as if the world was crumbling around him. If the duke died, there was no heir! The direct family line was finished. He was finished. If he was not butler to the Finstattens, who was he? He was nobody! He would like to kill Sir Edward. He would do it too, if he was not so terrified of weapons, confrontations, jails, and being hanged.

"The duke must live!" he said to Montrose. "We must ready the chamber to receive him. Preparations must be made. Everything must be done. Leave no stone unturned!"

Mr. Browning hurried over to a side table and poured himself a brandy from the duke's stock. It was as good a first step as any.

~ ~ ~ ~ ~

When the Duchess of Ralston had whispered "What in the world," upon viewing her dresses and bonnets on the bed, it had very naturally created some concern in Finella's mind. Were there too many dresses? Too many hats? Not the right hats? Perhaps it was the hat with the little porcelain cherries on it? She really had been hesitant about that one as the cherries bounced around when she walked. Mrs. Helwig had been certain it drew attention to her eyes, so she'd left it up to the dressmaker.

Now, the duchess circled the bed and said, "My dear Miss Fernsby, these dresses, these bonnets, are exceedingly... decorated."

Finella nodded. "Indeed, they are. Mrs. Helwig, she was the dressmaker, explained that I would need the bows and frills in order to distract."

"Distract from what?" the duchess asked.

Finella found herself a bit perplexed by the question. Then it occurred to her that the duchess was an older lady. Her eyesight might be very impaired. Yes, of course that was it. Had she not seen the lady positively look through the vicar when he asked when he could rejoice in her presence at a church service? It was as if she did not even see him. Or hear him, for that matter. "Oh I see," she said in a sympathetic tone. "Your eyesight is fading and you cannot see me properly."

"I can see you quite well, my dear."

Was the lady fooling herself? Trying to be kind? Finella was not entirely certain.

"What she means, Your Grace," Lucy said, "is that she's a bit short and a bit round. That's why she wants all the distraction."

Finella nodded sadly. "That is indeed the case. I've been told that gentlemen prefer somebody taller, more statuesque."

"Some do," the duchess said, "but you require one who does not."

Finella had not considered that idea. *Were* there gentlemen who preferred someone like her? If there were, there could not be many. It would be a veritable needle in a haystack.

After all, *she* did not herself even prefer it and she was living inside of it. When she'd been younger, she'd routinely hung from a beam in the barn to make herself taller, before falling into the hay when her arms gave out. Then she'd decided if she could not be taller, she must have a slimmer silhouette. There had been an entire week of eating only potatoes, as had been recommended by Peggy Justwin, with no progress at all. No matter what she did, her person remained how it always was. She'd ginned up the temerity to mention it to her father once, but all he said about it was, "You were a sturdy baby, everybody said so."

"My dear," the duchess said, "all these decorations will do nothing beyond make you look like a walking fairy cake. No, we cannot have this. Your mode of dress must have a restrained hand. It must not speak for you. Or in this case, shout for you. I must take some blame for this. I should have overseen what was being done in regard to your wardrobe."

Finella sighed. "I've gone wrong. I really did not know how to go about composing a wardrobe and Mrs. Helwig seemed to know what she was doing."

"Oh yes, if you were a farmer's daughter looking to slay the local butcher, I dare say he'd be bowled over by ribbons upon ribbons." Seeming to notice Finella's dejection, she said, "Chin up, Miss Fernsby. What has been applied can be removed. Mistakes are rarely fatal."

Finella was not certain what the duchess had in mind, but

as the good lady did not seem defeated by the problem, it cheered her a bit.

"Lucy," the duchess said, "pack all this back in its trunks and boxes and tell Wagner we require the carriage. We depart for Madame Beaumont within the hour."

Lucy bobbed and hurried from the room.

The duchess said, "Stay in what you are wearing. Your simple traveling clothes will do very well until we arrange for what you've brought to be corrected."

Finella was rather downcast over causing the duchess so much trouble. But on the other hand, she had rather felt herself blindly stumbling through a dark wood when it came to preparing for her season. She'd turned this way and then that way, hoping she was on the right path. It was a great comfort that she was in the duchesses' hands, and they were very capable hands. She would follow that lady's advice in everything.

~ ~ ~ ~ ~

After he'd been fished out of the Thames, Hugh had really begun to wonder if he was to be the first victim of a nascent reign of terror—part two, English version. The bargeman and the barber-surgeon seemed to wish to be rid of him as fast as possible and appeared to view his title in a decidedly grim fashion. In an instant, he'd gone from Your Grace to Fancy Man.

As it turned out, the barber-surgeon was worried about being blamed for his condition and the bargeman had been fixated on the idea that he might be forced to pay for Hugh's coat. They'd agreed they were to return him as they'd found him, with no treatments from the barber-surgeon and not a farthing for the coat. The bargeman had set off to alert his household on Grosvenor Square.

Hugh told the bargeman to say the message was from Sir Edward as his butler would know it was not a hoax. He did not know if the bargeman would remember it though, as he and the barber-surgeon seemed to hold it further against him that he had a butler.

The surgeon yelled directions to some fellows on the banks including, if he was not mistaken, Seddie. A litter was brought eventually and Hugh was very glad to see it. He'd tried one more time to rise on his own but had been just as fast pushed down by Willie Tankard. Seddie had come along with the litter, looking as sheepish as he always did when things went awry.

"Bad luck, old boy," Sir Edward said by way of apology.

The barber-surgeon turned and stared until Seddie blushed up to his ears.

Hugh was moved off the barge lying on the litter. He relaxed and resigned himself to his fate. He was certain he could walk to the nearest hackney. He could probably ride his horse. But Willie Tankard was having none of it so he might as well enjoy the ride.

Though he was looking up at the grey clouds racing across the sky, he could hear very well the sounds of traffic coming nearer. They'd reached The Strand.

"There's a hackney," Willie Tankard said. "Careful boys, getting across the road.

There was a sudden tipping and jostling and a shout of "Hold up!"

For the second time in one day, Hugh was flung out of something. He hit the ground with a thud and landed in the mud.

"For the love of God," Willie Tankard said.

As he rolled on his back, a softer voice, a kinder voice reached his ears. "Heavens, what has happened to this poor man?"

Hugh looked up to see a positively lovely lady peering down at him. She had plump cheeks and he could guess they were dimpled though she was not smiling. She had bright blue eyes and her fair hair peeked out from a simple straw bonnet.

She grasped his hand and he delighted in it. It was such a small hand and he wagered it was very soft underneath her glove. "Are you in a deal of pain, Sir?"

"I hardly know at this point," Hugh said.

Another voice, still feminine but perhaps not as soft and delightful, stepped in. He'd recognize that particular voice anywhere. The Duchess of Ralston.

What was this charming little lady doing with the duchess?

"That, Miss Fernsby, is not a sir. That is the Duke of Greystone."

Miss Fernsby. That was her name. Charming Miss Fernsby.

Just then, charming Miss Fernsby dropped his hand. "Goodness gracious, I am sorry, Your Grace."

"Don't be sorry, Miss Fernsby. I am not sorry."

Her plump cheeks blushed very prettily.

The duchess said, "What have you got yourself into, Duke?" Then her eyes drifted to Sir Edward. "Or perhaps I should not bother to inquire."

Seddie had the good sense to say quiet and just whisper, "Your Grace."

"I fell off a boat, very stupid of me," Hugh said. "I can walk perfectly well, but this fellow, Mr. Willie Tankard, has insisted I stay prone."

The duchess turned to Mr. Tankard. He shrugged and said, "Didn't want to get blamed for his condition, Your Grace."

"What a situation," the duchess said. "Duke, get on your feet and get into the hackney. I'd take you home myself, but Miss Fernsby and I are on an important errand. Sir Edward, pay these men generously and then follow the hackney home with the duke's horse. Mr. Tankard, I absolve you of all responsibility in this matter and thank you for your efforts."

The duchess speedily sent everyone in their right directions and Hugh saw the last of Miss Fernsby. Who was she? Where had she come from? Would she attend Almack's? She must attend the opening ball. The Patronesses could never overlook such a charming person.

What a morning. He'd nearly drowned, wondered if he were to be actually drowned by a bargeman and barber-surgeon, been dumped on the road, and met a lady who...well she was not cold and all sharp points. No, she most definitely was not that.

He might be thinking about her little hand in his for quite some time.

Chapter Three

Finella's trunks of dresses had been tied to the back of the duchesses' carriage and the coachman had been given direction. They were to see Madame Beaumont, a lady located on The Strand. As they'd traveled along, the duchess had described the dressmaker in both glowing and alarming terms.

Madame Beaumont was said to be all elegance and the most skilled dressmaker in Town. She was also described as being painfully direct and Finella was not to take any of her insults to heart.

As the carriage turned onto The Strand, the carriage jerked and men shouted. She peered out her window and saw an injured man who was being carried on a litter roughly falling to the ground. The carriage had stopped and she'd leapt out of it to provide what assistance she could render.

Her heart still pounded over the encounter. She'd held his hand. He was the Duke of Greystone. He was simply marvelous. His hair was the shade of dark toffee, his eyes were a deep blue shade and crinkled when he smiled.

He had smiled at her. The Duke of Greystone had smiled at Finella Fernsby. He'd said he did not regret holding her hand. It was a memory she would treasure all her life.

The duchess had not given her too much more time to reflect on it, as Finella had been hurried back into the carriage and they drove on to the dressmaker.

Finella found herself grateful that the duchess had warned her about Madame Beaumont's insulting manner. They had entered a small shop, or it seemed small from the outside.

It was narrow in width but very deep. It was filled with dressmaker's forms and fabrics and ribbons and buttons of every description.

A woman of middle years wearing a spotless and starched apron and a measuring tape draped around her neck stared at Finella. It was clear enough that the lady had mastered the art of a haughty expression.

"Madame Beaumont," the duchess said.

The madame slowly looked Finella up and down and clasped her hands together in prayer. Looking toward the heavens, she whispered, "Mon Dieu, Her Grace has brought Madame Beaumont pomme de terre boueuse."

Finella's French might not be entirely fluent, but she knew when she was being called a muddy potato.

"Yes, yes," the duchess said, "The girl was just now kneeling in the mud, it cannot be helped. You will be further affronted when you have a look at the clothes she's brought. The point is, we need it all fixed."

The coachman had hauled in the trunks. The madame had opened one and pulled out a dress that was one of Finella's favorites. It was a blue silk that had been decorated round the bosom with blue sequined butterflies. It had matching, but smaller, sequined butterflies round the cap sleeves and the hem. The dark color of the blue made her seem narrower than she was and the sequined butterflies were the points of interest to draw the eye.

Madame Beaumont dramatically dropped the dress on the floor of the shop and held her arm out. This, as far as Finella could understand, was a signal for one of her seamstresses to rush forward and support her to a chair. The madame sank down into it and gently rested the back of her hand across her forehead. "Never have my senses been so assaulted. I am vertigineuse."

Finella was fairly sure vertigineuse was French for dizzy.

"Brava," the duchess said. "Worthy of Drury Lane, Madame Beaumont. Now do collect yourself and advise us on what to do."

Madame Beaumont, seeming to sense she would not get far with the duchess by way of histrionics, rose and snapped her fingers. Seamstresses of all descriptions came from every corner of the shop. She pointed one hand at the trunks and boxes and the other at the shop's door.

These seemed to be well understood instructions. Most of the seamstresses took to unpacking the trunks, making little sniffs of disapproval as they did so. One dramatically held up the bonnet with the porcelain cherries as if it was evidence of a crime. One of the seamstresses went to the door, closed the shade, and put a sign that said "closed" in the window.

Madame Beaumont, noticing Finella's eyes drift toward the door, said, "I cannot allow a passerby to view this abomination. It will damage their eyes."

The duchess patted Finella's hand.

The dresses were unpacked and hung round the shop. Madame Beaumont paced around, examining them. She sighed, she muttered, she exclaimed when it seemed she was particularly affronted. She even leapt back from a dress that had ruffles running down the middle of it as if it were a wild animal. Her seamstresses stared at the collection with frowns. The madame turned. "Your Grace, you have brought me what is almost une impossibilité. Almost."

"I suspected you'd say something like it," the duchess said.

Madame Beaumont disdainfully picked at a sequined butterfly. "These other London dressmakers, yes, they would say it is impossible. They are not France. Bien pour vous that you have come to me. Nothing is impossible for Madame Beaumont!"

"I will suppose that means you can do something with

it," the duchess said. "We will need at least one dress ready on Wednesday, suitable for an Almack's ball, and some of the day dresses fixed. Further, make up six new day dresses and four gowns, you will understand the style I prefer. The bonnets should be easily managed. Do send a message when you require us again. For now, I leave you to it."

As they took their leave, Finella distinctly heard Madame Beaumont mutter, "She leaves us with this atrocité. Beaucoup de travail."

Finella got back in the carriage rather downcast over Madame Beaumont's very total disdain for her wardrobe. But then, she remembered she'd held the hand of the Duke of Greystone, and he'd smiled and said he did not regret it.

It had been something out of a Shakespeare play. The heroine comes to the aid of the wounded hero. Of course, Finella was not so delusional as to imagine there was anything else in it but a lovely memory.

Still, who could have imagined something like that would happen to her? She would hug that memory for all her life—the day she had held the duke's hand in his desperate hour of need.

~ ~ ~ ~ ~

It was the first of *The League of Butlers* meetings of a new season and Mr. Browning used his usual excuse for leaving the house on a Thursday afternoon. He had, allegedly, six elderly aunts who had nobody else to depend on. It was the easiest thing in the world to be required at their bedside for one reason or another—an apoplexy, a fall, a nervous condition, he'd even used a sudden bout of insanity last year. There was no end of things that might happen to an elderly lady and with six of them stumbling round the town, his staff ought to be surprised he was not gone every day of the week.

What a few days it had been! Sir Edward, or Sir Idiot as the bargeman had very aptly named him, had brought back His

Grace in a very wet condition. They'd had to compensate the hackney driver for having to stop his business until the seats dried out. The duke claimed there was not a thing wrong with him except almost drowning and he would just go upstairs and change his clothes.

Sir Henry was already awaiting him in his bedchamber and Mr. Browning was determined the duke must be prevented from casually brushing off the misadventure. He must be seen by the physician!

The butler had pulled out the ironclad argument that he used very sparingly and only when he had no other option. He'd deeply sighed and said, "I promised the duchess before she traveled to the great beyond that I would make certain you were always safe. I feel I have failed Her Grace."

At the mention of his mother's last wishes, the duke had sighed. "You won't rest until I am seen by Sir Henry."

"It would be impossible. Also, Sir Henry is in your bedchamber."

The duke had trudged up the stairs to cooperate. Mr. Browning had never had a particular conversation with Her Grace about protecting the duke, but he could not think she'd be against it as she looked down from her heavenly perch.

He'd then turned to Sir Edward. In his best baritone, he simply said, "Sir Edward?" His words might mean any number of things. It might mean he was asking if Sir Edward required refreshments. Or, with the right tone applied to it, it might mean that he was denouncing Sir Edward as the most irresponsible person to ever cross the threshold of a Finstatten residence.

That fellow had hurriedly taken his leave, which indicated he had sufficiently understood Mr. Browning's meaning at that particular moment.

Sir Henry had given the duke a thorough going over and was able to relieve Mr. Browning's worry over broken bones.

There was not even a sprain. However, he had expressed concern over a lump on his head and the idea that the duke had likely swallowed water. His head should be fine as long as he did not jostle it too much. His stomach would probably be all right with the water, but Sir Henry claimed they must be watchful of the lungs. If any of the Thames sloshed around the lungs, it could lead to various difficulties, some of which might be severe.

Severe! Mr. Browning had heard it as clear as a bell. The duke was in danger.

The duke had been advised to stay abed for twenty-four hours. He was very against it, but Mr. Browning had merely looked at the ceiling as if he once more apologized to the dead duchess for failing to protect her son. That had done the trick.

The duke proved to be an irascible patient, but he always had been. The household was well-prepared for the various shouts of "I'm bored" echoing through the corridors.

Mr. Browning had sent Jimmy to the duke with the backgammon set to attempt to entertain His Grace. Somehow Jimmy had returned having drunk an excessive amount of brandy and had to be sent to his bed.

They'd managed to keep the duke contained for the requisite time, but once that expired he'd shouted for his valet and gone straight to The Devil's Den.

Now, Mr. Browning had come to *The League's* headquarters in Cheapside precisely on time. He prided himself on being precisely on time, every time. If necessary, he'd been known to stop his hackney a street away and wait for a few minutes before proceeding on to arrive precisely on time.

He was not alone in the habit. All his fellow butlers made it a point to arrive precisely punctual. Except for Mr. Rennington, who often arrived early to calm his nerves and had once run late by a few minutes to gravely shaking heads.

They could not leave the square all at the same time

without attracting notice, so they staggered their departures and then delayed or hurried to arrive on time.

They filed up the stairs, nodding to one another, and Mr. Browning unlocked the door to the headquarters.

As always, it was in good order with not a speck of dust to be seen. They all paused reverentially and took a moment to gaze at their motto, hanging above the mantel.

Cum Virtute. With Valor. Those were the words they lived by. Mr. Browning turned the gold band on his finger whose inscription on the inside said just the same. It was the constant reminder they all carried with them to remind themselves that they were not just butlers. They were at the tippy-top of the mountain. They were the butlers of *The League*. They were elevated and they acted with valor in all things.

Mrs. Belkey, the landlord's wife, bustled in with a tea tray, as she would have been expecting them. "Sirs, welcome back to London," she said, "I hope you find everything in order."

Of course they assured her that they had. Mrs. Belkey was extremely reliable about keeping the place up. Mr. Browning imagined she felt the honor of being even tangentially connected to such a vaunted institution as *The League of Butlers*. While she might not know the details of their club or what their meetings entailed, she would instantly perceive the tone of things by their motto so prominently placed.

Assuming she understood Latin. Well, if she did not, she'd probably asked somebody about it.

Mrs. Belkey shut the door behind her and Mr. Penny poured out the tea. That gentleman smiled and said, "Mr. Rennington, do you hear how Lady Thurston gets on?"

Mr. Browning kept his expression neutral, but what a season it had been last year. Lady Thurston, née Lady Eleanor, had been so obsessed with her idea of being a lady-botanist that she'd taken a boat ride alone with a gentleman in order to break into the back doors of The Royal Society, all to hear a lecture. At the time, Mr. Browning had understood their preferred suitor, the baron, had been outraged over it. Then Mr. Rennington had spun a story of mixed-up sachets and the lady ingesting something that had affected her wits. Then the baron became not so outraged, even when he discovered it was not true. Then they had wed. It had all been very strange.

Mr. Rennington, who was looking far more calm these days, said, "Lady Thurston writes the earl and countess that she does very well. Of course, they inform me of it, as I have known Lady Thurston since she was a baby. She and Lord Thurston are in the midst of planning a rather extensive apple orchard. They're quite taken up with it."

"I suppose your Mrs. McFarland has gone back to her old tricks though," Mr. Harkinson said.

Mr. Browning frowned. Ever since Mr. Harkinson had got through his own season, which had been positively hair-raising, he was intent on being amused by another member's difficulties. Mrs. McFarland, the housekeeper in Mr. Rennington's household, had been harassing him for years. There had been some notion at the end of the last season that he'd finally stood up to her, but none of them had known how long that would hold. By all reports, she was a tough old bird.

"Hah!" Mr. Rennington said, sounding delighted. "How would I know what tricks she's up to? She's gone, she married a grocer she can boss about it. In her place, Mrs. Hugson has arrived and she is exceedingly deferential. Very pleasant woman, Mrs. Hugson."

Predictably, Mr. Harkinson looked a little let down to hear it.

"Excellent news all round, it sounds to me," Mr. Penny said. "And then, Mr. Browning, it seems as if you will sail into a church with ease this season."

Mr. Browning was, naturally, pleased to accept the compliment. Though, he could not ascertain if it was a general compliment or about something specific.

"I have heard the encounter mentioned twice within my hearing," Mr. Wilburn said. "I imagine it got round as it's also said that the duke inquired of a patroness whether the lady was offered a voucher."

What encounter? What lady? How had a patroness got involved in it?

"To think," Mr. Rennington said, "there he was, near drowned on account of Sir Edward's terrible seamanship, and the lady was suddenly by his side."

What lady? Who? Nobody had mentioned a lady to him.

"She stays with the Duchess of Ralston," Mr. Penny added.

"Of course, if there was anything of concern..." Mr. Harkinson said.

"I knew it!" Mr. Feldstaffer said. "It was too good to be true. It's always too good to be true, everybody knows it."

"Do you hint at the title, Mr. Harkinson?" Mr. Wilburn said.

Mr. Harkinson nodded. "For one thing. It is very new."

Mr. Browning realized he would never get to the bottom of all these comments by nodding and pretending he knew what they were talking about. He said, "Gentlemen, I am entirely in the dark. What encounter? What lady?"

The butlers turned to him in surprise. Mr. Wilburn said, "The talk is of a Miss Fernsby leaping out of the Duchess of Ralston's carriage to render aid to the duke. Then he makes inquiries about whether she will attend Almack's."

What was this about a Miss Fernsby? The bargeman had said nothing of a Miss Fernsby. The duke had said nothing about a Miss Fernsby. He supposed the idea that the lady had been in the Duchess of Ralston's carriage was encouraging, but who was she? It did not bode well that she was a miss and not a lady.

"Her father's title is new," Mr. Harkinson said. "The ink is barely dry. Miss Fernsby's father is the first Baron Dunston, and it has been recently given. Before that, he was just another of the gentry class."

Mr. Browning did not think that ideal. No, not at all. The Finstattens were of old blood. This lady, whoever she was, could not have the proper breeding that came with a long history as a member of the *ton*. How could she possibly have the elegance and sophistication that would be required of the duke's future duchess? Would she have any experience hostessing, or even attending, sophisticated dinners? Did she have the necessary witty repartee that would be expected? Did she have that certain savoir faire that came with the best houses? Did she understand how to run an elevated household? Did she know how things were done?

This Miss Fernsby might be a climber, what some in the *ton* called a 'mushroom' for their ability to spring up where they were not wanted. They attempted to fit in but it was not authentic. It was as if they wore a mask to attempt to fool people. In Mr. Browning's considered opinion, they were the worst sort of person.

Well perhaps not the worst. There were murderers to think of. But if not the worst, then very, very bad.

"I suppose the lady must be very comely to have made such an impression on the duke," Mr. Penny said in his usual cheerful manner.

Mr. Harkinson suddenly guffawed. Mr. Wilburn bent down and stared at the collection of biscuits on the tea tray.

The rest of the butlers were silent, staring at them.

Mr. Wilburn cleared his throat. "As to that, I have seen her in the company of the Duchess of Ralston. They were making a call at the next door."

"That's when I saw her too," Mr. Harkinson said. "I had stepped out to take the air."

"There is nothing particularly wrong with the girl, is what I say," Mr. Wilburn said.

Nothing particularly wrong? Where were the descriptions of her beauty and grace? Her gentle manners? Her elegant bearing? Was a Finstatten to be mentioned in the same sentence as "there is nothing particularly wrong with the girl?"

"Nothing particularly wrong," Mr. Feldstaffer said. "That sounds a bad business. Yes, I am convinced of it. When a person says there is nothing particularly wrong, what they mean to say is there is nothing particularly right."

Mr. Harkinson was nodding in approval over Mr. Feldstaffer's assessment.

"Mr. Wilburn?" Mr. Browning asked. He would not bother inquiring of Mr. Harkinson, as that fellow was always a bit too delighted over something going wrong for somebody other than himself.

"Well," Mr. Wilburn said, looking over Mr. Browning's head as if the words he sought might be found there, "she has a pretty face, yes, that did strike me. And very fine hair, fair curls. As to anything else...perhaps the lady is just the smallest bit...on the short side of things."

"So short," Mr. Harkinson said, shoulders shaking.

Mr. Browning surmised that Miss Fernsby was rather petite. He supposed it was not the worst thing in the world. Her lack of history in the *ton* was rather more concerning.

"Some gentlemen prefer it, I understand," Mr. Penny said. "Lady Melberry is quite renowned for being short."

"So is Lord Melberry," Mr. Feldstaffer said. "He didn't have much choice. They're a regular pair of leprechauns, those two."

"Horrible little creatures," Mr. Rennington said. "Just as well England is not plagued by them."

Mr. Browning covered his surprise. This was the first he was hearing that Mr. Rennington gave any credence to leprechauns.

Mr. Wilburn put his attention on his tea. Mr. Harkinson said, "Mr. Wilburn, you'd best tell the whole of it."

"I knew it! There's more," Mr. Feldstaffer said.

"There is not a lot more to tell," Mr. Wilburn said. "Mind you, I only had a very glancing look. If one were to rely on my exceedingly glancing view—"

"She's a bit squat," Mr. Harkinson said. "She is short and too round and her father has a very new title."

Short and round. A new title. That title was only a baron. This did not at all sound propitious. Mr. Browning must find a way to put a stop to it, if in fact anything were developing. He found it rather hard to believe that there could be anything developing.

Then he had a thought. "How did this encounter with Miss Fernsby occur?" he asked. "What are the details? Where were they?"

"The duke had just been accidentally rolled off his litter on The Strand," Mr. Wilburn said. "Miss Fernsby rushed out of her carriage and knelt by his side."

Mr. Browning breathed a sigh of relief. "That is the answer, gentlemen. The duke was injured, he was prone, and Miss Fernsby was kneeling, thereby disguising her...well, her."

"Oh, I see," Mr. Rennington said. "He did not get a proper view. He works on false assumptions."

"No doubt, Mr. Rennington, if he even has any assumptions," Mr. Browning said. "If he does have assumptions, the duke might think her very tall, rather than very short. How is one to tell when a lady is kneeling? Yes, that would explain it."

"But," Mr. Penny said in a hesitating tone, "might it not be the case that the duke might prefer Miss Fernsby's sort of silhouette?"

"A Finstatten? I would not think so," Mr. Browning said with a raised brow.

Chapter Four

Hugh had reluctantly agreed to be abed for twenty-four hours on the advice of Sir Henry. Really, though, it was for Browning's sake. The fellow was forever worrying that Hugh would die, especially when he was out with Seddie, which was not an unreasonable concern. Then, when Browning had trotted out the disappointed looks and the promise to Hugh's mother to keep her boy safe...well, there was not much to be done at that point but acquiesce.

He hated to be abed. The minutes seemed like hours. There was no reason to be lying prone unless a person was asleep or dead. He'd shouted that he was bored a few times, confident that Browning would do something about it.

His butler had sent Jimmy up to play backgammon with him. When Hugh tired of that, they played cards. When he got bored with that, they played a drinking game. Hugh was certain that Browning had not been overjoyed to find his senior footman coming back downstairs foxed.

When he'd not been corrupting the footman, his mind did drift to Miss Fernsby. What a charming person she was. She'd knelt beside him and held his hand with not a care for her dress. The road was muddy, he was wet, it seemed precisely the conditions a fine lady would avoid. She'd no care for her glove when she'd placed her little hand in his wet and muddy hand. When she'd stood, he'd seen that her dress had been terribly soiled. She had not even glanced at it.

And then her look of concern! She had been concerned without having the first idea of who he was. He might have been an apothecary or a solicitor, or even a bargeman. He might have been anybody at all, but she'd not cared for that. He'd appeared injured and she'd been concerned. He must think it spoke well of her character.

Well, he supposed he would see her at Almack's. His inquiries had confirmed that she'd received a voucher. He could take that opportunity to properly thank her and find out more about her.

Just now, he was at his desk in the library, looking at a pile of papers his steward had sent him. It was a tedious business. So many gentlemen had told him how lucky he was to be the master of such a vast estate. He supposed so, but overseeing the whole pile was endless. Just now, one of the more problematic tenants had taken it into his head to run a large debt at the local tavern and the barman had made a complaint to the steward. Apparently, the fellow kept coming in and then causing trouble when he got thrown out.

Hugh suddenly sat up. Through the closed door he heard her. Blast. His sister had stormed into the house again.

Lucinda was much older than he was and walked around with a chip on her shoulder. Or maybe it was a boulder on her shoulder. Apparently, before he'd been born, she had been well aware that the entire family waited anxiously for a boy. Then when he had made his appearance, all eyes were on him as the heir. He'd been told there had been a deal of fretting that he must survive his first years.

Once, when he'd been around eight and Lucinda was eighteen, she'd said to him, "I always hoped you would never be born, to spite them."

The library doors flew open and there she was. She was a tall and pinched woman and Hugh thought her looks very well represented her temperament. "I heard Sir Edward tried to drown you," she said.

"As you know, Seddie is never malicious. If he almost drowns a person, it is quite accidental."

"I've told Browning to send in a tea tray."

"I'm sure he was in raptures to see you."

Lucinda sniffed. Hugh thought she must be very well aware that the butler was not overfond of her. Browning would never say anything to indicate it, but he had a certain tone he used that was clear as day. Seddie was the other person in Hugh's sphere who often got that tone from his butler. It was distinctly disapproving. It was if Browning sent the message, "I need not say anything to say *everything*."

"So, here you are at twenty-seven," Lucinda said. "Congratulations."

He knew very well what she meant by noting his most recent birthday. She meant to mention the family tradition and somehow insert herself into his search for a wife. Lucinda valued her judgment above all others. She also had some very high-flown ideas about being a Finstatten. She was in the habit of reminding her husband that she was a Finstatten so he might recall that he'd won a very great prize. Hugh did not think Lord Gaddington saw it exactly that way. Lucinda would want to stick her nose in with all her opinions. He would not let her do it though. The last person he'd want to assist him was his sister.

"And you did promise Papa you would follow the tradition," she said.

Browning entered and set the tea tray down. "Will there be anything else, Your Grace?" In his lower, disapproving tone, he said "Lady Gaddington?"

"That is all, Browning," Hugh said. "We probably did not even need tea. I doubt Lucinda will stay long."

"Do not be too sure," Lucinda said.

Browning raised his brows ever so slightly before making

a dignified exit, closing the doors behind him with a resounding thud to express his opinion.

"He's just as sour as ever, I see," Lucinda said of the departing butler.

Hugh did not bother to mention that while Browning was always on the grim side, he was particularly grim to see her.

"So? What is this I hear about a certain Miss Fernsby?"

How would she know anything about Miss Fernsby?

"Do not pretend you do not know what I'm talking about. Word has gone round that the lady came to your aid while you were inexplicably lying in the mud of The Strand."

"I fell off the litter the bargeman and barber-surgeon forced me to lie on after fishing me out of the Thames."

"And I heard that you inquired of the Countess of Cholmondeley if Miss Fernsby will attend Almack's."

Hugh had no idea all that would be traveling round. The town was confounded. A man could not say one sentence outside of his club without it being repeated everywhere.

"What if I did?" he asked.

"What do you know about her, Hugh?"

"I know her name is Miss Fernsby and she rides round in a carriage with the Duchess of Ralston."

Lucinda had poured her tea and emptied half the sugar bowl to sweeten it. Hugh thought it was a shame that all that sugar did not sweeten her temperament.

"She is the daughter of a baron. A new baron. A very, very new baron. Apparently, this new baron's land abuts the Duchess of Ralston's land and the lady took it into her head to have pity on Miss Fernsby and bring her to Town."

Hugh should have known Lucinda would know more than he did. She spent her life trading in gossip. There was not a drawing room she would not have passed through over the course of a week.

"And?" he asked her. He thought he understood her, knowing her as he did, but he would pretend he did not.

"She is new. That means she has been raised in a gentry household, not a peer's household. I wonder, could she really have the right air, the right manners, the right friends, to be connected to the Finstattens? She was probably raised in some sort of farmhouse. Perhaps she milks her father's cows."

"I did not examine the lady on any of those subjects, but I did find an appreciation for her concern over an injured man lying in the mud, her pretty curls, and I strongly suspect she has dimples."

"For heaven's sake, Hugh, stop dodging and weaving around what I mean. You know it yourself—she's a mushroom. A mushroom of the worst sort."

Lucinda was forever worried about mushrooms. She, and women like her, were determined on some sort of high wall around her notion of the "right people." Anybody wishing to burst forth into the green garden of the *ton* without the proper credentials was a climber, a striver, a mushroom. They must be yanked from the soil and thrown back over the wall to rejoin the hoi polloi, where Lucinda thought they belonged. Meanwhile, Hugh knew perfectly well that if *she'd* been born to a new-minted baron, she'd be fighting her way up through the soil and viciously clawing at anybody attempting to stop her.

"I do not particularly care for your ideas about social climbers, or mushrooms as you call them," he said. "I never have."

Lucinda rolled her eyes, which he considered a very unfortunate habit. "A convenient stance for a duke. However, if there is no exclusivity, who are we?" she asked. "Is the queen to throw open her doors and have tea with a tradesman? Perhaps I ought to have my coachman in to dine? If we do not respect rank, the whole country falls apart."

It was very like Lucinda to assume a patriotic duty in trying to keep those she deemed less worthy out of the *ton*.

"Miss Fernsby seemed very charming," Hugh said. "I met her for a moment and she seemed charming. Furthermore, she has a voucher to Almack's, so I presume the patronesses do not agree with your assessment."

Lucinda waved her hand as if to dismiss his words. "Miss Fernsby has a voucher because the patronesses do not dare cross the Duchess of Ralston. If she were not under Her Grace's protection she would never be offered one."

"Well she was, and that's that."

"You are the Duke of Greystone. Everybody in the wide world knows you will wed this season. You will be hunted from every direction. You cannot go round making inquiries about a lady you met for a moment and thought charming. It's bound to give Miss Fernsby ideas. Ideas, I might add, that will be well above her reach."

"Lucinda," Hugh said, taking on a more irritable tone, "this town is full of magpies carrying gossip round and you are the leader of the mischief. Furthermore, Miss Fernsby did seem charming and as I do not subscribe to your mushroom ideas, I do not see how her father's new title makes the slightest bit of difference. Now, you really should be off. Seddie will be here soon and the two of you are like oil and water."

Lucinda had taken herself off, as he thought she would. Seddie liked to tease, and his sister did not like to be teased. They'd known each other forever, as Seddie was a childhood friend, and they'd disliked each other forever too. She would never forgive Seddie for the various nicknames he'd christened her with over the years. Frowning Finstatten and The Peevish Miss, being two of them.

She'd gone, though Hugh did not imagine that it would be the last of her meddling. In the meantime, Seddie was not set to arrive. He would see his friend at Almack's this evening.

He supposed he'd see Miss Fernsby too. He did not give a toss if she was a mushroom.

~ ~ ~ ~ ~

Madame Beaumont had heeded the duchesses' direction regarding having a dress ready for Almack's. She'd sent over of a few day dresses too. Finella had no idea whatsoever what the dressmaker was to do to her clothes that would transform them in some manner that would meet with approval. She had not really understood what was wrong with them in the first place.

Now she stared at the dresses. All the decorations that Mrs. Helwig had painstakingly added were gone. The dress for Almack's was to be the dark blue silk that had been so prettily decorated with sequined butterflies. The butterflies were off the dress and piled inside a paper bag pinned to the hem. In place of the sequined butterflies, the neckline of the dress was lined with embroidered butterflies in the exact same color as the dress. They were not even noticeable unless one looked closely.

"I really do not think it draws the eye," she said to Lucy.

Lucy examined the dress with her arms folded. "Maybe that whole idea of drawing the eye this way and that way was not right from the beginning."

"It sounds right though, does it not? Draw the eye to where you want it to go?"

"Maybe the thing is to just be as you are and let other people's eyes go where they feel like going."

"Lucy, have you seen the ladies of this town? Every time I go out in the carriage with the duchess, I am further struck by it."

"Aye, I've seen 'im. One nose higher than the other."

"I'm very sure gentlemen prefer that sort of thing," Finella said dejectedly. "I know the duchess said I must find a gentleman who will prefer me, but how many gentlemen of that stripe could there be?"

"Maybe more than you think. Sometimes I think you do not see yourself as you are. Plenty of ladies would trade their height for that pile of blond curls, I reckon. In any case, I don't see that you got much choice in it. Who else could you wed but a fella who prefers you?"

"Well I do not know. I was perhaps hoping that I might change myself a bit. In the meantime, while I was getting that done, my dresses would distract and draw the eye."

"The duchess ain't gonna approve it if you're set on trying another potato diet."

"Oh no, no, that did not work. But I could just starve myself for a few weeks? I did think about it while I was at home and then...I just put it off. You know how hard it is with Cook making so many cakes. But now I really feel I can do it."

Lucy's eyes drifted to the near-empty jar of biscuits at the bedside.

"Yes, take them," Finella said. "Take them to your room."

The jar of biscuits would not be going very far, as Finella had ginned up the nerve to tell the duchess she had nightmares, and it would comfort her to have Lucy nearby. The duchess, not wanting to be woken herself from whatever that entailed, put Lucy in the next room over. Still, Finella felt that even if the biscuits did not go far, getting them out of her own room was a very good start.

Yes, it really was. It showed her will and determination. She was not even sad to see the biscuits go. Or at least, not very sad.

"You'll be thinkin' about that duke what you fell on the ground over."

"I did not fall on the ground. I knelt beside an injured man. And no, I am not thinking about the Duke of Greystone at all. Why would I think of him? What would be the point of Finella Fernsby thinking about the Duke of Greystone?"

"That's a lot to say, just to say you ain't thinkin' of him," Lucy said with a snort.

"It's not a lot to say. I just wanted to make my point. My clear point. That I am not thinking about the Duke of Greystone. I am not such a ninny as that. Clearly."

"Or maybe, you just think you *shouldn't* be thinkin' of him. Thoughts are a strange thing, in my experience. They go where they want and don't care where you want them to go."

Finella sighed. Sometimes, Lucy was very wise. She *had* been thinking about the duke, even though she knew she should not. It really was very hard not to. Even as he lay there in the mud, she could see how glorious he was. Far too glorious for the likes of her.

She supposed she'd been so struck by how friendly he'd been. Her father had warned her that they stood near the bottom of the steps when it came to lords and ladies. At the top of the steps stood the dukes. Neither of them had met a lot of dukes before, they only had the Duke of Ralston to compare to. He was long dead, but when he'd lived, he'd been a very formal sort of gentleman. They'd gone on the assumption that all dukes would be very reserved, particularly to someone whose father had just managed to get on the steps. The Duke of Greystone had not seemed at all reserved.

"Well now," Lucy said, "I reckon it's time you get into that dress the madame has sent you. Wear the dress and hold your head high, that's my advice."

"Hold my head high to show that I am confident?" Finella asked.

"Aye, if you prefer. I was more thinkin' it would make you

look taller."

~ ~ ~ ~ ~

Mr. Browning did not listen at doors. Certainly, he would never stoop to such a debased habit. On the other hand, there were many reasons why he might be going up and down a particular corridor that passed the library doors while Lady Gaddington was in there with the duke. It must also be noted that Lady Gaddington spoke rather loudly.

So it had happened that he did hear bits and pieces of the conversation behind those closed doors. He had not liked what he heard. Lady Gaddington did not know this Miss Fernsby individual, but she seemed to know plenty about her. Her family's new title was mentioned more than once.

And then she said it. Miss Fernsby was a mushroom.

Unlike the duke, and as much as it pained him to agree with Lady Gaddington, Mr. Browning did take the idea seriously. As should everybody in England. Every person had their place, and they needed to stay there. People could not just wander out of their place to pick a new place. Was he, Matthew L. Browning, to be on the same level as a grocer? Or perhaps he ought to expect a voucher to Almack's? He could swan in and ask the Duchess of Devonshire for a dance. It was absurd. People could not go round thinking they were equal to everybody else! What kind of world would that be?

That was precisely a mushroom's philosophy though. If one had the funds for a London house and the funds to entertain lavishly, one must automatically be admitted into the *ton*. These people boldly imagined that money was everything. They imagined they did not require breeding and manners and history. They all found out in time that the best houses would never allow a mushroom through their doors.

Inevitably, mushrooms settled into their own second-class society. They ran round pretending their existence was glorious and threw their parties. All along, though, they knew. They did not quite measure up. Were Mr. Browning himself to ever be invited to one of these entertainments put on by a mushroom, he would decline in the most blistering terms.

Just last year, one of the leading mushrooms, a certain Mr. James Calder, from New York, of all places, had thrown a masque. It was said that all sorts of shocking and debauched behavior occurred. Of course that was how it was—they were mushrooms! They did not know how to properly act. They did not have the instincts for it.

Miss Fernsby, as far as he knew it, did not even have the excessive funds of a usual mushroom. She was a poor mushroom. Else, why would the duchess need to sponsor her?

Who ever heard of it? A mushroom with no money.

What was perhaps even more disturbing had been the duke's defense of Miss Fernsby. It seemed the only thing that mattered to His Grace was that she was found charming and she might have dimples.

Mr. Browning was holding tight to the idea that the duke's second look at Miss Fernsby would put an end to any notions of her charm. After all, anybody might seem charming when a gentleman was lying prone in the mud of The Strand. Let him see her at Almack's and he would think differently.

The butler comforted himself in the idea that the mushroom who was Miss Fernsby was likely to turn up to that storied institution in some sort of gauche dress. She would not know any better. The duke's inherent instincts would form a revulsion to it.

Yes, that was what was needed. A natural revulsion of Miss Fernsby.

Chapter Five

Hugh had suspected what he would encounter when he entered Almack's. As he was a duke, and as everybody would know he was to wed this year, he was far too tempting a catch to be able to slip in ignored. The patronesses all took an excessive pride in having "made the match," and so descended upon him.

The Countess of Westmoreland got to him first and took him in hand. She had a long list of suitable ladies he was to be put down for. He listened agreeably, as what else could he do? Once the countess had run out of breath and ladies, he said, "I would like to be put down for Miss Fernsby's card. She comes with the Duchess of Ralston. The dance before supper, preferably."

"Miss Fernsby? Oh, I see, Miss Fernsby. Well goodness, Sir Roger has already requested that dance."

Sir Roger? He was forty if he was a day. What was he doing taking the dance before supper? Or any dance, for that matter.

"I see," Hugh said. "Then what other dances would Miss Fernsby be open for?"

"All of them, I believe," the countess said.

"Put me down for the first," he said. "I leave to you what else to do with me."

The countess nodded. "I will give you a list once I've arranged it."

Just then, he was slapped on the back. He turned to find Seddie grinning at him as if he'd not almost killed him on the Thames.

"You look better than the last time I saw you."

"I imagine I would, considering you went to great lengths to drown me," Hugh said drily.

"Nonsense. I was in far more danger than you ever were. I thought Browning would kill me before I could get out of your house."

"He is not amused," Hugh said.

"He is never amused."

"He follows me around, waiting to hear if I will cough due to an infection of the lungs."

"He needs to keep you alive until you get an heir, his livelihood depends on it. Once you have a boy on the ground, I doubt he'll care if you throw yourself into the Thames on a daily schedule."

"After that misadventure, I presume you do not mean to go forward with the regatta," Hugh said.

"Are you mad? Of course I'm going forward. I hired a man who showed me all the ins and out. We've been out twice already and I've got cracking good."

Hugh was sure he looked dubious over the idea.

"You and I will sail through the finish line, leaving everybody else behind."

"Me?" Hugh asked. He did not at all care to try out round two of Captain Seddie, Seaman of Misadventure.

"I will remind you," Seddie said, "that you are my oldest friend and I depend on you. Who else could I possibly get?"

Seddie was forever trotting out the "oldest friend" business and the truth was that the "who else" he could get was nobody. Nobody would be as daft as Hugh to do it. He sighed, which Seddie took as an enthusiastic affirmative.

They made their way into the ballroom. Hugh scanned the crowd. "Let me know if you spot Miss Fernsby," he said.

"Miss Fernsby? The lady that you encountered on The Strand?"

"Yes, the lady who came to render aid just after I was unceremoniously dumped on the road. That lady. I found her charming."

"Really? I would not have guessed she was your type."

"What is my type, exactly?"

Seddie tapped his chin. "Hmmm. Come to think of it, nobody knows. As for *my* type, Lady Genevieve is still at home. I hope she gets here in time to see us win the regatta."

"Lady Genevieve will take a dim view of what has happened so far. You know how sensible she is and how she deplores the things you do. I expect she will scold you over it."

"Only if somebody tells her. In any case, I find her scoldings rather endearing."

"Your Grace!"

After his ears were nearly assaulted by the greeting, his arm was actually assaulted with a lady's fan. Lady Violet's fan, to be specific.

He would be most unhappy if the Countess of Westmoreland had put him down on Lady Violet's card. She was the younger sister of one of his circle, the Earl of Packington. He'd had the bad luck to be introduced to the lady at Packington's house party last summer. The girl had not even been out and yet she'd swanned around as if she were the hostess. Packington had been very liberal and included her in the dinners and parties.

Hugh found her a nuisance. She had a brittle laugh, which she employed often as everything in the world was found amusing. She was coquettish. She was determined to be daring. Hugh's sister, Lucinda, thought she was marvelous, which must be a mark against her character. At the house party, it had felt as if she were following him. Any time he tucked himself away in a quiet corner, there she was. He'd taken to reading in his room to avoid her. He did not like any of it.

"Lady Westmoreland insisted on putting your name down for my second. I said, Lady Westmoreland, what could the illustrious Duke of Greystone want with little *me*?"

That was a very good question. He wondered how Lady Westmoreland had answered, as he could not think of a single thing he wanted from Lady Violet. He also did not know why she imagined she was little, as she was as tall as he was.

"Well," Lady Violet prattled on, "she could not even meet my eye, so I do not dare imagine what devilish thing you said to her."

"I said nothing to her," Hugh said.

Seddie poked him in the ribs, as he would be enjoying the exchange. At Packington's house party, Seddie had been endlessly amused by Lady Violet asking him if he'd seen the duke. Sometimes he would tell her and sometimes he would send her on a goose chase.

Lady Violet launched one of her brittle laugh-salvos. "Oh, it was as bad as that? It cannot be repeated? You are shocking, Your Grace."

Hugh forced a smile. He would very much like to have the latitude to actually be shocking at this moment. If he could, he would say, "Here's something shocking. You are annoying." He did not have that luxury, though. Nobody did. A gentleman must be courteous, even when he was pushed to his limit.

"Sir Edward," Lady Violet said, "I understand you are to take me into supper."

"Am I?" Seddie asked, looking not quite as amused as he had been.

Lady Violet nodded. "Wait and see if I don't pry from you what shocking thing His Grace said to Lady Westmoreland."

Hugh turned to smile at his friend. Seddie was in for a long supper. Seddie put a good a face on it as he could and just muttered, "Well…"

Hugh's eyes drifted round the ballroom. Then he spotted the Duchess of Ralston. And by Her Grace's side, Miss Fernsby.

She was looking terrific. When he'd seen her on The Strand, she'd worn a plain straw bonnet. He'd noted the fair curls peeking out from its brim, but now she was without a bonnet and he saw the full glory of it. Waves and ringlets framed her lovely face. She smiled at something the duchess said and there were the dimples. He'd been certain she had dimples. Those round little cheeks could not be without dimples. She really was charming.

"Lady Violet," he said with a curt bow and strode off. Seddie could manage her. Or try to. Hugh had the charming Miss Fernsby to see.

~ ~ ~ ~ ~

Finella had not been terribly confident when she'd viewed herself in the glass, after having been wrangled into her blue silk dress. There were no sequined butterflies to hide behind. There was just Finella. She wore the simply gold cross her father had given her for her twelfth birthday. She admired it but did not think to would particularly draw the eye.

Her spirits had improved a little bit upon noting the duchesses' approval of the dress. As the duchess must know best, Finella decided to be satisfied with it. She would not be the prettiest lady at the ball, but it seemed she would at least be respectable.

When they'd entered Almack's, Finella got her first look at the real power of the Duchess of Ralston. The patronesses all but tripped over themselves to make their greetings to the lady.

Finella could not say any of those ladies tripped over themselves to make her own acquaintance. They were perfectly polite, and she attributed that to the fact that the duchess escorted her there. Otherwise, she very much doubted they'd have given her a second look. Or a voucher, for that matter.

She'd been fully prepared ahead of time that a patroness would manage her dance card. She did not mind it actually. She'd attended a few assemblies at home and had found standing around with her card in hand, waiting for a gentleman to approach, a nerve-wracking operation. It brought out all her insecurities.

At home, as a matter of happenstance, there were far too many young gentlemen and far too few young ladies. She could be assured of having a full card. Even then, even knowing it would be near impossible to sit out a dance, it had made her nervous. Here, with all these fine-looking and sophisticated people, she could have been so easily overlooked.

And then, the thing she was not meant to be thinking about drifted back into her mind. The fine-looking and sophisticated Duke of Greystone. The duchess had made an offhand comment in the carriage that Finella was already introduced to a gentleman who was sure to attend, despite the unusual circumstances of their meeting. Finella had felt such a thrill to hear his name spoken aloud. She reminded herself that the very lucky thing about thoughts was that nobody else could hear them.

She was very glad she did not have her card in her hand so she did not have to acknowledge that the duke came nowhere near her. Why would he? She had surreptitiously glanced round the ballroom and seen him talking with a very elegant lady. She was tall, very tall. They looked so natural together, as if they were a set. He was glorious, the elegant lady was glorious, and all must be right with the world.

Just now, the duchess had introduced her to the Marchioness of Souderton.

"I particularly wished you to know Lady Souderton, Miss

Fernsby, as I am involved in the charity she founded. The Impoverished Pupils Fund."

Lady Souderton nodded. "It is my wish that all human potential is realized. Young boys and girls who show a particular proficiency must be helped along in their studies."

"That is such a worthy cause," Finella said. "My father has paid for the schooling of several of our tenant's children. He says that wasting a God-given intelligence is a sin."

"That is precisely it," Lady Souderton said, looking very approving.

"Miss Fernsby."

Finella slowly turned. The Duke of Greystone. She felt her heart pounding in her chest. Was it noticeable? The sequined butterflies would have covered it up!

"I must thank you for the kind aid you rendered when coming upon me on The Strand in a very awkward situation."

Ah. That was why he'd approached. He was a gentleman, and he'd come to thank her. Of course he would. A duke was bound to have meticulous manners.

"What is this I am hearing?" Lady Souderton asked. "Was there an accident?"

"Sir Edward nearly drowned the duke," the duchess said. "Which is very like Sir Edward, I suppose," she said drily.

The duke smiled. That glorious smile. "Sir Edward does on occasion imagine he can do things and then in the doing finds out he cannot," the duke said. "That particular morning, he imagined he was an expert seaman. I was knocked overboard and fished out by a bargeman."

"His Grace was very stoic when I saw him," Finella said boldly.

"Was I?"

"I did think so," she said. She paused and then hurried on, certain she'd made a blunder. "But perhaps it was too bold to make such a comment." She could feel the heat on her face, which would not be attractive. She was so fair that when she blushed...well was it even a blush? It was more of a flush that would encompass all her face and her neck. Her father called it "gone strawberry."

"Stoic or not, somehow Sir Edward has roped me into acting as his crew for the regatta," the duke said. "I hope Miss Fernsby plans to attend it. I might require aid again."

If Finella could do so without looking a complete ninny, she would whip out her fan and wave it violently to cool her face.

"We will be on our own barge, Duke," the duchess said. "I rented it ages ago before they were all taken."

This was the first Finella had heard of attending the regatta on a barge. It was rather thrilling.

"The Countess of Westmoreland has put me down for your first, Miss Fernsby," the duke said.

"Has she?"

The duke nodded. "At least, I asked her to."

He asked to be put down for her first? Did he request it because he wished to dance with her? Or had he done it out of a sense of obligation? It was very hard to know!

"Oh I see," Finella said nonsensically.

"Well I asked about the dance before supper first, but Sir Roger had already beat me to it."

"Sir *Roger*?" the duchess asked.

She did not sound very approving of the notion. Finella had no idea why, as she had no idea who Sir Roger was.

The duke nodded at the duchess. "That's what I thought about it."

They both thought the same thing about Sir Roger. What? What did they think?

"Miss Fernsby." The Countess of Westmoreland returned with Finella's card.

As she handed it over, the duchess said, "Lady Westmoreland, Sir Roger for Miss Fernsby?"

The countess looked the smallest bit embarrassed. "He can be very determined, Your Grace," she said by way of an answer before hurrying off to deliver other ladies' cards.

Finella found herself growing leery of Sir Roger, whoever he was.

Just then the orchestra, which had been tuning, suddenly quieted. The sets were forming.

The duke held out his arm. "Miss Fernsby."

Finella laid her hand gently on his arm, silently scolding it severely not to tremble. The duke had taken her first dance at Almack's. Lucy would fall over to hear of it. She could almost fall over herself.

Perhaps he only did it as a courteous thank you. Nevertheless, she was to dance with the Duke of Greystone for her first dance in London.

She could never have imagined it.

Of course, that was not entirely true. She had imagined it. But it was the sort of dreaming that one knows will never happen, like imagining one could fly. It was the sort of imagining that a person kept to themselves because of the impossibility of it. A person would be foolish to speculate on flying like a bird. Or dancing with the Duke of Greystone.

He led her to a set that was forming and introduced her to Sir Edward and his partner for the dance, Lady Margaret. Finella recalled seeing Sir Edward on The Strand when the duke had taken his unfortunate fall off the litter.

"Miss Fernsby," Sir Edward said in a jolly tone. "Our heroine of the hour."

"I am sure not," Finella said.

"When a gentleman nearly drowns in the Thames and then is flung into the mud of The Strand, what else is he to wish for than a charming lady kneeling beside him?" Sir Edward said.

"My friend is verbose and very much an incorrigible flirt," the duke said.

"I can confirm that, Miss Fernsby," Lady Margaret said. "Do not listen to a word Sir Edward says."

Sir Edward laughed over the condemnation and Finella got the idea that it was a usual one. Still, he seemed a very jolly sort of person.

Another couple joined the set, and Finella was momentarily startled to see that the couple they faced on the other side of their square included the lady she'd seen earlier, conversing with the duke. She glanced at Finella and there was the smallest wrinkle of the lady's nose. It might have passed by unnoticed, but Finella was so alert to any sort of disapproval that she was always on the lookout for a passing expression of disdain. She supposed it must be her looks that garnered it, as the lady did not know her.

As fast as the nose wrinkle came, it went. Then the lady smiled and attempted to catch the duke's eye. He seemed to be particularly avoiding it.

The Countess of Chamondeley called out the steps and the orchestra struck up. They began the grand rond and Finella placed her left hand on the duke's right and her right hand on Sir Edward's left. If there was one thing she could be confident in, it was her dancing. She could be very graceful while dancing. Lucy had speculated it was because she was closer to the ground than most so she was not prone to a wobble.

As they went round in a circle, Finella could not help

but to notice the determined staring from the lady across from them. She wished to catch the duke's eye, but Finella did not think she'd been successful at it.

"I wonder, Miss Fernsby," the duke said, "will you go to Lady Thurston's Poetical Tableau? I believe the duchess often attends it."

Finella nodded. "Indeed, yes. The duchess told me that since she obligates everyone to attend her Secrets Exposed party, it obligates her to attend whatever odd entertainments other people might dream up."

"It is always an odd evening, it is usually entertaining though."

Finella laughed. "The duchess told me that Lady Thurston reported furniture was sold off last season."

"She sold off Lord Thurston's favorite chair for spite on account of...well never mind why. He's been complaining about it, as he can't find a replacement that equals it."

"I can imagine his distress," Finella said. "My father has a favorite chair in his library. The leather is cracked, but he will not get a new one. He says a man's form takes years to make certain indentations that make it comfortable."

"Yes," the duke said, laughing, "I suppose that is right."

As the duchess was a very forthright sort of person, Finella already knew the reason for Lady Thurston to go so far as to sell her lord's furniture. The lady believed her husband to be involved with an actress. And then there had been something about her lack of pin money.

They had returned to their place in the set. Finella and the duke had their backs to the orchestra, making them the top couple. After several beats of music, they began the allemande. The duke turned her with confidence and it was marvelous.

"Perhaps our boxes will be nearby one another," the duke

said.

"Boxes?" Finella asked, entirely lost.

"At the poetical tableau. Lady Thurston sets up her ballroom like a theater and everybody is assigned a box."

"Ah, I see," Finella said. Certainly he could not wish for his box to be nearby just to continue thanking her for stopping on The Strand. Gracious, she hardly knew what to think. She could not allow her thoughts to get ahead of her, but really, her thoughts were racing forward.

Chapter Six

Hugh was delighted with Miss Fernsby. He'd long grown tired of ladies of the *ton* who liked to be bold and shock. He did not care to engage in witty parries back and forth. Miss Fernsby had thought she was very bold to name him stoic when she'd approached him on The Strand. Her entire face had gone red over her supposed daring. It really was endearing. Miss Fernsby's idea of bold was about as dangerous as a kitten.

Her looks were rather endearing too. He was much taller than she was, so he looked down upon her piles of blond curls. When she spoke to him, she peered up at him and he saw the dimples every time she smiled. Her eyes were pretty too, a dark blue set off by her fair complexion. Everything about her was fresh and pretty. She did not seem very sophisticated, which he was glad of. He did not suppose many ladies would mention their father's preference for a chair in which his backside was imprinted through long use. It made him laugh to think of it. There was something refreshingly ridiculous about it.

If there were anything to mar the dance with Miss Fernsby, it was other people. Lady Violet was in the couple across from them and that lady worked with enthusiastic determination to catch his eye, which he absolutely refused to do. He had a feeling Lady Violet had maneuvered her partner into his set and Hugh found the idea irritating. If he were being chased, he'd appreciate it if she just said so. Then he could respond in kind and they could be done with it. He was not the slightest bit interested and he hoped she'd not expressed any hopes to her brother. Packington was a friend and a fellow member of The Devil's Den. He'd prefer not to have any awkwardness between them.

Then, he could not help but notice his sister Lucinda. He'd not seen her until after the ball began, though he would have been surprised if she had not attended. Lucinda could not bear it if the ladies in her circle were to talk about an approved entertainment she had not attended. She must be in all the right places and know everything that had transpired. She gloried in mentioning Almack's to an acquaintance who might not have received a voucher. Hugh imagined that if the day ever came when she did not receive one herself, she'd climb to Gaddington's roof and throw herself off. He was not certain Gaddington would be heartbroken over it.

Now, she was standing at the edges of the room with Lord Gaddington, who was looking as put upon as ever. He did not know what Lucinda was going on about, though if he had to guess at it, the subject was Miss Fernsby. His sister was talking rapid-fire between glances in Miss Fernsby's direction. Hugh imagined Lucinda was explaining the whole mushroom idea to her beleaguered husband.

He did not know why she bothered. It seemed to him that Gaddington had long closed his ears to whatever his wife was ranting about at any given moment. He'd replaced his hearing with the occasional nod. Hugh was confident that if Gaddington had been asked to repeat one of his wife's speeches he would not have a clue what she'd been going on about.

At least Hugh would see Miss Fernsby at Lady Thurston's poetical tableau without the annoying accompaniment of his sister. Lucinda had long ago named Lady Thurston's tableau as far beneath her notice. Hugh thought the real reasons she avoided it was that she had not a drop of humor in her, and she had no wish to view anything connected to marital strife, as it might hit a bit close to home.

The dance ended and Lady Violet strode over, leaving her partner behind. "Your Grace, could this be the Miss Fernsby we've all heard about?"

Hugh was irritated beyond reason. He would not wish Miss Fernsby to be made uncomfortable that she was talked about, all because he'd made inquiries into her attendance at Almack's.

"Miss Fernsby, may I present Lady Violet Ward, sister to Lord Packington."

"Lady Violet," Miss Fernsby said.

"Gracious, Miss Fernsby, how propitious you were on hand to rescue our duke."

"I am afraid that whatever you have heard was very exaggerated, Lady Violet," Miss Fernsby said. "I only stopped to see if there was any assistance needed."

"And it was then that you discovered he is a duke!"

"Yes, that is right," Miss Fernsby said, looking a bit confused.

Hugh could see well enough that Miss Fernsby could not at all comprehend what Lady Violet hinted at. She would suggest that Miss Fernsby had all along known he was a duke and had leapt out of her carriage to throw herself at him. Lady Violet would think it because it was the type of thing Lady Violet would do. Miss Fernsby was a different type of lady.

He turned to Miss Fernsby. "I will escort you back to the duchess," he said. He had done just that, and he was very sorry to do it. He would not have minded dancing with Miss Fernsby longer.

Seddie sidled up to him. "Lady Violet is in a bit of a snit, I think."

"I do not concern myself with the many moods of that lady," Hugh said.

"You saw as well as I did, she was trying to catch your eye during the last set," Seddie said. "And then she practically raced to your side when the set concluded. Now you'll have to dance with her and she'll have your full attention."

"Only for a dance," Hugh said, "then she will lose it again."

"And Miss Fernsby? Will she keep your attention longer?"

"I imagine so," Hugh said.

"I like her," Seddie said. "She's not stiff."

Hugh nodded. "She's not all sharp points."

"No, she certainly does not have any sharp points," Seddie said with a laugh.

"I'll see her at Lady Thurston's tableau," Hugh said. "Find out where else she'll be when you dance with her."

"Battle orders understood, Captain. Least I can do after… well, you know."

Of course Hugh did know. Seddie would satisfy himself that this very simple request absolved him of trying to drown his friend in the Thames. The music began to tune once more. He sighed. "I suppose I'd best go and find Lady Violet."

"Unless she finds you first," Seddie said, strolling away.

As it happened, Seddie's words were prophetic. Hugh had not had time to look for Lady Violet before she found him first.

"Your Grace, you have been very naughty," she said. "I can tell you, now that Miss Fernsby is out of earshot, that I tried and tried to catch your eye in the last set."

"Did you?" Hugh said, pretending he'd known nothing about it.

"Gracious, my mother used to always say that gentlemen were rather oblivious."

"I suppose so," he said, having no wish to argue with Lady Violet's deceased mother.

"No matter," Lady Violet said. "I will just have to be more

direct. I am nothing if not accommodating."

Terrific.

Hugh led Lady Violet to the line for the reel, all the while keeping an eye out for Miss Fernsby.

~ ~ ~ ~ ~

Right up until the last dance, it had been a glorious evening. Finella had never imagined the evening would go so wonderfully. She had danced with the duke. She had also danced with Sir Edward and she'd been so bold as to ask about the duke.

According to Sir Edward, the Duke of Greystone, or Finstatten as his oldest friend called him, was a fine gentleman. He was very good humored and never held a grudge, as evidenced by their most recent adventure on the Thames.

As she had reflected, she could not deny that she'd found her introduction to Lady Violet a bit offputting. She could not quite understand the lady. However, she'd met several other ladies who were all very pleasant. The gentlemen she'd danced with had been all very polite and a deal more seasoned than the gentlemen she had danced with at home. But most of all, she'd danced with the duke. She did keep coming back to that.

Finella knew very well that her imagination had taken flight without her common sense when she silently began trying out Finella Finstatten. She was entirely ridiculous.

Yes, the duke had been kind to her. Yes, the duke was a very friendly sort of gentleman. Yes, he was a glorious specimen of a man. Yes, she had thrilled to be near him. Yes, he had smelled wonderfully of coriander soap. Yes, she had thrilled to lay her hand on his hand. And yes, she was being entirely absurd.

Bringing her thoughts back down to earth, she decided she must be satisfied with how she'd got on in general. She'd danced with pleasant gentlemen and aside from a nose wrinkle from one lady, who she now knew was Lady Violet Ward, sister of the Earl of Packington, she seemed to be accepted. That had been her biggest worry and it seemed it had been all for naught.

But then came the only truly awkward part of the night. Sir Roger.

She had not known what both the duke and the duchess had meant when they'd frowned over his name being on her card. She'd since danced with him though, and now she thought she had a better idea of what they'd frowned over.

For one thing, he was far too old to be taking a dance with a lady launching at Almack's opening ball. Her father was in his fortieth year and Sir Roger looked to be the same age. It was very odd that he should request a dance with her, which she knew he had done from the Countess of Westmoreland.

For that matter, why did Sir Roger wish to dance with anybody at all? He was not very good at it, and he did not seem to enjoy it.

Now he was escorting her to the supper room. He had been in a hurry to get there and had sped her ahead of other couples heading in the same direction. He steered her to a chair and snapped his fingers at the nearest footman.

"I will have tea. Lemonade for the lady. Bring us the dry cake. If you turn up with buttered bread, I'll hit you over the head."

Finella was shocked to her shoes at how he spoke to the young man. The footman himself seemed acquainted with Sir Roger, as he did not look very shocked. Nor did he look intimidated. He narrowed his eyes, turned on his heel and stalked off. She was also taken aback that Sir Roger had just decided she ought to have lemonade rather than tea without even asking her. It was very high-handed. Rude, even.

"Got to know how to manage these fellows, else you'll end with the stale bread. They say there's butter on it, but I challenge that claim."

"Oh I see," Finella said noncommittally.

"I suppose you'll want to know about my estate," Sir Roger said.

She did not wish it in the slightest. She did not care if Sir Roger lived on the moon.

"Norfolk. Two thousand acres, give or take. Roomy house. Dower house, too. My mother lives in it. It's a mile away from the main, which is still too close. Unpleasant woman. I'm a baronet so my son will inherit the title. Not like some ridiculous knight. Never saw the point in a knight."

It slowly began to dawn on Finella what this conversation was about. Sir Roger viewed himself as a suitor. It was preposterous. She might not be the belle of the ball, but she was not going to consider a man her own father's age. She'd rather be a spinster if it came to it.

"As for my philosophy on how things are meant to be done," Sir Roger said, "I hold my servants to task. There is no relaxing the rules, no days off for holidays. I provide them a livelihood and bed and board and they ought to be grateful for it. Give a servant an inch of room and they'll drag you along for a mile. I won't have it. Bad enough they'll all be lying around doing nothing while I'm in Town and they're in an empty house. Well for you to know how things are done."

Finella did not wish to know anything about it. Now that she did know it, she felt very sorry indeed for Sir Roger's staff. Her father was far more liberal. The baron's idea of holidays was for the staff to make sure he did not starve by setting up a cold sideboard and leaving bottles of hock and claret, then they could do what they liked. On the eve of Christmas, they always had a very good roast, but on Christmas Day it was a cold ham and rolls while the servants celebrated with the baron's wine below stairs.

On top of Sir Roger being far too old, she really did not like this man.

"Sir Roger," she said, "if you will excuse me for a moment."

"Retiring room? Weak stomach, have you? Inconvenient."

She nodded. She could not care less if he found it inconvenient. Anything to put him off. Finella hurried from the dining room and down the corridor to the retiring room. Going through the door, she entered another long corridor with a series of doors running along it that led to small compartments. A girl was in attendance on a small stool with a table containing all manner of pins, needles and thread, and other accoutrements a lady might require.

Finella passed her by with a friendly nod and went to the last door at the end of the corridor. She let herself in and closed the door.

It was comfortably appointed with a table and a looking glass, a hair comb and pins, an elegant little stool, and a small sofa covered in grey velvet. And of course, a chamber pot with a carved wood lid.

She sank down on the sofa and weighed whether or not the duchess would be annoyed that she'd left Sir Roger to sit alone in the dining room. Considering the lady's reaction when she'd heard that Sir Roger was on Finella's card, she thought not. It was rude to leave him sitting alone, to be sure. But then, her experience of Sir Roger so far was that he was rude too. She very much hoped his servants were enjoying themselves during his absence.

She heard the outer door open and the chattering of two ladies as they came in. Perhaps she was not the only one to have made an escape to the ladies' retiring room from an unpleasant gentleman.

"Pins, girl, I need pins," lady said.

"Quick, now," the other lady said.

"Yes, your ladyships," the girl said.

Finella did not know who the ladies were, but they seemed rather bossy. They must have got the pins and let themselves into one of the compartments as she heard a second door close.

"Sit at the glass and do your pins while I lounge on the sofa. I am off my feet from dancing," the second lady said.

"I hardly know how my hair is mussed, I did not even dance this evening."

The other lady laughed. "Gaddington did not care to take you for a spin, Lucinda?"

"You know *him*," the lady Finella now knew was Lucinda said. "He just stands around like a block of wood. I knew how it would be, but dancing is not why I came this evening."

"I suspect you have something to tell me. And I suspect I know what it's about."

"Have you seen her, Meg? Have you seen Miss Fernsby?"

Finella froze. Who were these ladies? Why should they be talking about her? Who were Meg and Lucinda?

"I saw her, and I noticed that your brother took her first."

Her brother? This lady, this Lucinda, or Lady Gaddington as she would be known, was the duke's sister?

"He is so outrageous," Lucinda said. "I told him, he cannot just go about doing whatever strikes his fancy. He is a Finstatten, for heaven's sake."

"I suppose he's not inclined to follow that advice," Meg said.

"He is maddening, he really is. She is a mushroom. I cannot even believe the patronesses have let her in."

"The Duchess of Ralston sponsors her, that's why."

"But a mushroom!"

"A short mushroom," Meg said laughing.

"Come, let's go back. Gaddington will be toe-tapping by now and I've got to get him home. If he does not have a brandy in hand within the hour he will get especially cross. When he gets especially cross, he starts looking at the bills. There are several bills I would prefer he does not examine too closely just now. Harding and Howell, you know."

Finella heard the ladies make their departure. She felt she could not move. She was frozen in place. She had never in her life heard a conversation about herself. Is this what everybody thought? Had she been delusional to have been pleased by how things had gone? It seemed so.

The events of the evening had almost made her forget herself. She'd almost forgotten how she would measure up to the tall and elegant ladies she was surrounded by. Now she was reminded. She was a mushroom among lilies.

She had thought herself a mushroom when she'd arrived to Town and now she had heard it said.

Tears sprung up and she brushed at them. Crying was unacceptable. She would not do it.

She must put things in perspective. All that had happened was the duke had been kind in asking for one of her dances. She had helped him in his hour of need and he had thanked her for it. His sister did not think she measured up and the lady was entitled to her opinion. Lady Gaddington had not known she was being overheard. She was having a confidential conversation with a friend. Anything at all might be said in such conversations. Finella was not meant to hear it.

In any case, nothing that was said was not true. She had deluded herself over the duke's kindness.

Finella heard the outer door open once more and she prayed she was not to hear anything more about herself.

"Miss Fernsby?"

It was the duchess. Finella grabbed at a stack of small

cotton squares and dried her eyes. "Your Grace," she said in as cheerful a manner as possible.

She opened the door and came out to the corridor. Finella put on a sanguine expression. At least, she hoped so.

"I have taken a guess that you hide here to be away from Sir Roger," the duchess said.

Finella nodded. "I am sorry," she said. "I do not like him and he began to talk about things that were, well they were uncomfortable."

"Do not be sorry, I do not care for the man myself. He's been a confirmed bachelor all these years and I think that's what he should stay. However, I suspect it's just occurred to him that he needs an heir."

Finella physically recoiled. "Your Grace, I would never consider it. Not under any circumstances. I'd rather die alone."

"Yes, yes, well I do not think it will come to dying alone. Let us go. Sir Roger can wonder about where you disappeared to all he likes. He will not dare say anything to me."

Finella nodded. She kept her thoughts on the present minute and away from the past minutes. That was the only thing she could do—walk forward, minute by minute. She wished the duchess never knew what had been said. She did not wish to let the lady down. She would swallow this and there would be time later to cry on Lucy's shoulder.

~ ~ ~ ~ ~

Mr. Browning refilled the brandy decanter and brought two glasses into the drawing room. His Grace had just returned from Almack's and, as was his habit, he'd brought Sir Edward with him. Both gentlemen would have had a dry night, as Almack's refrained from serving wine. They would be in a hurry to remedy the deficiency.

"You ought to go to bed, Browning," the duke said.

Mr. Browning nodded. "Thank you, Your Grace. I will just take care of a few things before I retire."

There were no "few things." Mr. Browning would hardly leave a task undone until two o'clock in the morning. No self-respecting butler would be so careless. He'd left several items in the hall that he could put away so that he might dally and overhear whatever news there was about Almack's.

"Make it a large one," Sir Edward said to His Grace. "Almack's tea does nothing for me and drinking it in the company of Lady Violet does even less."

"Here you go. She was tedious, I imagine."

"She was as determined a minx as I've ever encountered. She's galloping on the hunt and you are the fox she's after."

"I presume she did not come out and say so."

"Oh no, you know how a lady goes about such things. She smacked me with her fan a hundred times and demanded to know what shocking thing you said about her to the Countess of Westmoreland. Then she accused me of being shocking for not being able to repeat what was said."

"A complete fiction she managed to invent for herself. If I had anything shocking to say, I would hardly say it to the Countess of Westmoreland."

"Yes, well, I got tired of the endless nagging and innuendo, so I said if I recollected it correctly you told Lady Westmoreland that you despised Lady Violet with the heat of a thousand suns."

Raucous laughter took over the drawing room.

"I am sure you should not have done that," His Grace said. "I would not like any problem to develop with Packington. Did she storm off?"

"She did not. She laughed and said I was very naughty and sooner or later she would discover what was really said."

Mr. Browning did not know too much about Lady Violet.

He'd seen her once, passing by in a carriage, and he knew she was the Earl of Packington's sister who was just out this season. She was an earl's daughter and she looked elegant. He really did not think Sir Edward had the right to be rude. Nor should the duke laugh about it. She was, as far as he could see it, an eminently suitable lady.

At this rate, His Grace would never find anybody to wed, and he must wed. He must wed this year.

"I noticed Sir Roger took Miss Fernsby into supper," Sir Edward said.

"What is that old fellow thinking?" the duke asked.

"I imagine he is thinking he'd best get an heir and a spare on the ground lest his title travel elsewhere. It is a thing he should have been thinking about twenty years ago. But then, I suppose he was as much of a curmudgeon then as he is now. Perhaps he tried and could not find anyone to agree to putting up with his sour face forevermore."

"No doubt," the duke said. "But to think he could measure up to Miss Fernsby? It's entirely absurd. By the by, did you find out where she is going regarding entertainments?"

"She doesn't know much. The duchess has a tight rein on the calendar. She knows she is going to the poetical tableau at least. However, she only knows about that because Lady Thurston happened to come up in conversation and the duchess mentioned it. That's how she found out about the regatta too, it was just mentioned in conversation."

Mr. Browning had heard enough. The duke was becoming fixated on Miss Fernsby. Why? She had nothing particular to recommend her.

What was he to do about it? He was meant to be leading this matchmaking adventure. His fellow butlers were depending upon him to steer the duke in the right direction, and they considered Miss Fernsby the decidedly wrong direction. From what he'd heard, *he* considered Miss Fernsby the decidedly wrong direction too. The duke's whole future was at stake. The name of Finstatten was at stake. The glorious history of the family was at stake. If the old duke were here, he'd put a stop to it.

The old duke was gone though. That left Mr. Browning with the problem on his hands alone.

There was only one thing to be done at this moment. He would retire to his rooms, pour himself a generous glass of sherry, pick up his book, and try to forget all about it. Tomorrow was a new day and, with any luck, something would occur to him to get this ship sailing toward the right port.

Chapter Seven

Finella had put a brave face on things in the carriage with the duchess. They'd left Almack's and left Sir Roger with no explanation for why Finella had disappeared.

The duchess deemed this perfectly acceptable. She said when a gentleman does something affronting, it was fine to be quietly rude. A woman must have her weapons.

Finella *was* affronted by Sir Roger. She realized that her feelings of insult were not so much what his behavior said about him, but what it said about her. Sir Roger seemed to think she would be a willing lady, else he would not have launched into a description of his assets so quickly. Not just willing, even. He viewed her as a lady whose acquiescence was assumed, as if she could not have any other option. She was taken for a lady who did not need to be wooed. That said something about her worth, or lack of it. She did not suppose Sir Roger would have the effrontery to approach a lady like Lady Violet in the same manner.

After all, Lady Violet was not a mushroom. As had been so recently pointed out to her.

Finally, blessedly, Finella bid the duchess good night and retired to her room. Lucy took one look at her, went into her own room, and brought back the jar of biscuits.

She handed it over and said, "What's happened? I can see it all over your face. Did the duke fail to turn up?"

"No, no, he was there," Finella said, chewing on a biscuit. "The duke was very kind."

"What then?"

Finella poured out the story of escaping into the ladies' retiring room to escape Sir Roger, only to hear the duke's sister name her a mushroom.

"A mushroom? What is wrong with that lady?" Lucy asked.

"It is not what is wrong with her, Lucy. It is what is wrong with me. Now, you are not to feel sorry for me. Not everybody in the world can be a beauty. Or as they say in Town, a diamond of the first water. I am not a diamond of any water. The important thing is that I accept myself for myself. That is all. I'm not the least bit upset over it."

Finella took that moment to sob and entirely discount the idea that she was not the least bit upset.

Lucy patted her hand until she could somewhat recover herself. "I would have hit that lady over the head with my parasol. That would have taught her a lesson."

"I did not have a parasol, and if I did, I would not hit anybody with it."

"You could have used your reticule. Not as effective but it might have left a mark. Now, I know just what is needed." She slipped out of the room. Finella heard her go down the stairs and hoped she was not raiding the kitchens for more biscuits. It was the sort of thing the cook would notice.

After some minutes had passed, Lucy returned with a glass of water. She did not imagine there was anything soothing in a glass of water, but she appreciated the thought. Especially since the duchess had their good neighborhood well water from home brought in via cartloads of bottles.

Finella sipped it and then choked on it. "Lucy, what is this?"

"Gin, I've seen where the cook hides his supply."

"It's terrible."

"It will settle you, though."

As Finella was far more used to settling herself with a biscuit rather than gin, she managed another sip and that was it. Lucy got her undressed and tucked the blankets round her, cursed the head of Lady Gaddington, and then took the glass of gin to bed with her. Finella supposed the gin would settle Lucy instead.

She'd lain awake long into the night. She came to the conclusion that it would have been preferable to never have encountered the duke on The Strand. She'd come to London with modest ideas. Appropriately modest. Then she'd met the duke, the friendly duke, and all her common sense had flown out the window. She'd lost her modest ideas and had begun to take on ideas far above what they should have been. She blushed to recall that she'd even thought the idea of Finella Finstatten. She was embarrassed for herself!

Perhaps she should be grateful that Lady Gaddington had popped the bubble of her irrational imaginings.

She would wed, hopefully. And it would not be to the likes of Sir Roger, either. She need not lower herself that far. However, she must think more realistically. When she'd been at home, she'd imagined a middling sort of gentleman, he might even be as highly placed as a viscount, though she'd be satisfied with less. There was nothing at all wrong with a mister, as long as he was a gentleman. She'd lost her wits to think she might have attracted a dashing duke. It was entirely absurd.

Her feelings had been hurt, but nobody in the world but Lucy knew it. She would keep it that way. She would hold her head high and stop wishing or pretending to be anything other than what she was. Just Finella Fernsby, the short and Rubenesque daughter of a newly-titled baron. She was not for everybody, but she must have faith that she'd be for somebody. She did not need an army of admirers, just one. After all, did not

Mrs. Pumpernick like to say there was a proper cup for every pot of tea? She must just find her pot of tea and all would be well. She and her pot of tea would live quietly, they would not be leading society or even much in it. Finella would be very satisfied with her lot in life.

For now, until her pot of tea turned up, she was determined to conduct herself well and be a credit to her father. He was made a baron, and she was his sole representative in Town. She would not let him down with any foolish notions.

The days that followed were quiet. They had no plans to go out in the evenings and they had no plans to receive visitors. Their sole activity outside the house was a carriage ride. The duchess liked to be driven round the park in the afternoons. She had a finely made brougham with blue velvet seats and all manner of conveniences. There was even a small, folded table attached to the back that could be used for a picnic though they never did any such thing, as the duchess thought eating out of doors was barbaric.

As they drove through the park, the duchess would inevitably spot a barouche and then explain what a nonsensical notion it was to have a carriage with the top down in a country where rain might strike at any moment. While the duchess was talking of the mistake of purchasing a barouche, Finella would gaze out the window, hoping to see the duke.

She reasoned with herself that it was perfectly fine to wish to see him on horseback. After all, she only hoped to *see* him. Anybody might see anybody else with there being nothing in it. She was certain the duke was admired wherever he went. She was just one more admirer. A very many people wished to see him with nothing in it. Just a simple admiration, as happened every day.

She never did see him, though.

As they were living so quiet for a few days, Finella became much more acquainted with the duchess. She had of course known her while she'd lived at home. But she had not really known her. The duchess had always been their very grand neighbor and they were occasionally invited to a dinner at the house, along with a select group of the other neighbors.

It was not until her father had been made a baron that the duchess had paid more attention to Finella.

She found the lady very to the point and full of good sense. The duchess did not fan herself over something gone wrong, nor did she blame the staff when a thing was not quite right. Just two days ago a plate of fairy cakes had come up for tea and they were discovered to be inedible. It was finally figured out that a new kitchen maid had accidentally put salt in the sugar bin, then realized her mistake, panicked, told nobody, and just tried to get the salt out. With limited success, apparently.

When the fairy cakes came back down to the kitchens, the poor girl did not even wait to be found out. She screamed it was all her fault and then sprinted to the servants' quarters to pack her bags. Wagner had stopped her from leaving by explaining that it was careless, but not the crime of the century. The duchess had laughed so hard she had tears in her eyes when Wagner told her the tale.

Now they were biding their time in the drawing room in the quiet of the late afternoon. Finella had picked up a book, as it was the sort of thing one could look absorbed in without really being absorbed.

Somewhere near four o'clock there was a knocking on the front door. A minute later, Wagner entered the room and said, "Your Grace, a certain Sir Roger Brimley has arrived and inquired if Miss Fernsby is at home." Wagner's tone hinted that he could hardly believe that events had forced him to say such a thing.

Finella felt rather frozen. She had not expected to have to fend off Sir Roger while she was inside the duchesses' house.

"Miss Fernsby is certainly not at home," the duchess said

briskly.

Wagner had nodded and not looked very surprised. He shut the drawing room doors behind him and went to give the heave-ho to Sir Roger.

"He's a persistent old fool," the duchess said.

"Perhaps he meant to press me on where I disappeared to when I left him at the table at Almack's," Finella said.

"You owe him no explanation," the duchess said. "If he persists in making himself a pest, I will have a direct word with him." The lady suddenly laughed. "Gracious, does Sir Roger imagine he measures up to the Duke of Greystone?"

Finella did not answer, as there was not a thing to say. If the duchess meant to hint something about the duke, well, it was ridiculous. She would see that in time. She was very kind to imagine it, though.

Wagner came in holding a bouquet of pink primroses. "Your Grace, Sir Roger has insisted, and I mean *insisted*, on leaving these behind."

The duchess sighed. "Give me the note and put the flowers in the servants' hall."

Wagner nodded, handed her the folded paper tucked between the stems, and carried the flowers out with a look he might have saved for a collection of weeds.

The duchess unfolded the note. "Good grief. He writes 'Miss Fernsby, I pray you have recovered from whatever took you to the ladies' retiring room. Stomach complaints, bad business. I look forward to encountering you again. Sir Roger Brimley.'"

"Oh dear," Finella said softly.

"And he sends pink primroses! Really, I think Sir Roger has lost his wits. Never mind it, Miss Fernsby, he will get the message eventually. Let us hope I do not have to deliver it directly. I will count on his good sense to alert him to the foolhardiness of this venture."

Finella certainly hoped Sir Roger would go away with little trouble. He ought to be pursuing a lady his own age, though she realized why he could not. He was after an heir, and so would look for someone very much younger than he was. Whatever his reasoning, he was most certainly not her pot of tea.

"Well goodness, Lady Thurston's poetical tableau is on the morrow. It is probably a good thing we will be well rested. I've no idea what she's got in mind this year, but it is certain to be dreadful."

"I understand she sets up theater boxes in her ballroom?" Finella said.

The duchess laughed. "It is one of the things that tickles me the most. Lady Thurston is forever ranting about her lack of pin money, but if she saved the money she spends on that whole set-up for her tableau, she'd be swimming in money."

Finella had not a clue what the morrow's evening would entail. She did know one thing, though. The duke had said he would be there. She would be able to look at him. Just look at him, obviously, like any other person might do in a perfectly regular manner. Lucy had counseled her to *not* look at him. Finella was to pretend she did not even know the duke was alive. His sister had insulted Finella in the worst possible way and that meant the entire family must be shunned. She'd heartily agreed with the advice, though she knew perfectly well she would not take it.

And then, there was every chance she might meet someone who would be more suited to her. Certainly, that was a possibility. Lady Thurston might have invited her pot of tea. Finella really felt like she had straightened herself out. Her reckless imagination had been put in its proper place and her mind was now driven by facts and reality.

Just as it should be.

~ ~ ~ ~ ~

Hugh had no idea what Lady Thurston was planning to assault the *ton* with this year. He imagined it would be worse than last year, as that seemed to be the general trend. Last season, she'd presented herself as Oizys, the Greek Goddess of misery and woe, and she recounted how she'd sold off Lord Thurston's favored chair. He was not certain what could be worse than that, but as the lady seemed to have a boundless imagination, and as he suspected she'd spent a year thinking about it, he supposed she'd thought of something.

The main reason he'd attended year after year was because his club, The Devil's Den, did an annual and very raucous recreation the very next night. Seddie usually played the part of Lady Thurston, donning a ridiculous wig with enthusiasm, while Lord Germaine took on the outraged Lord Thurston and Sir Jeremy played the elusive actress that had been mentioned. It was a tradition, and they were all sworn to secrecy about it. If it were to get out, Lady Thurston and her friends would go mad. They took the tableau very seriously, even though it was absurd.

He had another reason for coming this time, though. The charming Miss Fernsby would attend with the Duchess of Ralston.

She was so pretty. She was so soft-looking. She was rounded rather than sharp points. Oh, and the dimples in her round little cheeks. He hadn't known that was what he was looking for, but he'd known it when he saw her. And then, her character and temperament had already proved themselves to be superior. He had not mentioned it to Seddie, but at Almack's he'd noted that Miss Fernsby had excused herself away from Sir Roger and she'd not come back. That told Hugh she had a backbone too. She might be all gentle smiles and sweetness, but when it was necessary she could take action on her own behalf. It was just what a lady should be. There was something of the noble in it. And her hair—he wanted to bend down and kiss the top of her pretty head.

He made his greetings to Lady Thurston, who was dressed in what appeared to be widow's weeds. He hoped she had not decided to knock off Lord Thurston to put an end to their battles.

Hugh entered the ballroom, which was already crowded. The sides had the usual theater boxes set up, with brass plaques indicating which box belonged to which party. Sideboards lined the bottom of the room, and Lady Thurston's stage was at the top. Some of Lady Thurston's friends, the usual group who accompanied her on the stage, drifted round the room. They were dressed in weeds too. Whatever Lady Thurston was to present this evening, her choice of wardrobe indicated all was still not well with Lord Thurston.

He did not see Miss Fernsby, but he did see Seddie. His friend was just now cornered by Lady Violet. He turned the other direction and hoped he'd not been noticed.

The other direction turned out to be even worse. There was his sister, she'd spotted him and was making her way over to him. What was she doing here? She never came to Lady Thurston's tableau.

"Lucinda," he said dully. He never made any effort to seem delighted to see her, but she did not seem to pick up on it. Or maybe she did and just did not care. She must be well-used to Gaddington not being delighted to see her.

"I cannot believe it," Lucinda said.

"Already fanning yourself in faux delicacy? The tableau has not even started yet. What are you doing here, anyway? I thought this evening was beneath your notice."

"It is beneath my notice," Lucinda said. "I came because I have been to your house twice, and twice Browning has claimed you were not at home. I know you were though, and probably still abed, as that butler actually had the audacity to stand in front of the stairs to stop me from passing."

Lucinda was right, he had been at home, and in bed. She was in the habit of arriving before noon and they were not a household of early risers. Cook was used to sending up breakfast between twelve and one. According to his butler, the staff were well satisfied with the schedule. Very few people ever left the duke's employ, lest they find themselves in a situation where they were expected to commence working when the sun came up. "Browning has been instructed that you are not to have access to the private parts of the house anymore. You might swan in whenever you like, though I wish you'd stop that too, but the furthest you'll get are the public rooms. It is my house, not your own."

Lucinda waved off that idea as if he'd not said anything at all. The fact was, he'd directed Browning to keep her from going up the stairs and if he was not mistaken his butler had been delighted to do it. He imagined if he'd said to Browning, "And if she gives you any trouble, feel free to hit her over the head with a paperweight," he'd be delighted with that too.

"I've seen her, Hugh. Miss Fernsby, I've seen her."

Hugh swiveled his head, looking around. "Where? Where is she?"

"Here? I am not talking about here," Lucinda said. "I saw her at Almack's."

"So did I."

"Do be serious," Lucinda said. "She's not at all the thing. She cannot be a Finstatten. Even if she was not so new, which she is, and even if her father was higher than a baron, which he is not, and even if she had a credible dowry, which she does not, she is not suited to it. Her looks are pedestrian. She is not elegant."

"Pedestrian? Have you seen her hair? Her dimples?"

"She's short. If she wore a different dress, she could be a

milkmaid."

"A *charming* milkmaid."

"She is most definitely not the thing and you know it."

"I know no such thing. Why don't you track down your husband? I'm sure he enjoys your company. He must be desperate to be reunited with you."

"At least Gaddington is not a mushroom."

Hugh turned on his heel and left Lucinda standing there.

He attempted to dodge Seddie and Lady Violet but he was not successful. He should have been, but Lady Violet did not have any compunction against practically shouting a greeting. "Your Grace! We're over here."

We're over here. She said it like he must have been seeking her out, as if it were a set thing that he must be looking for her.

Hugh sighed. "Seddie, Lady Violet," he said.

Seddie was looking like a cornered animal, which was understandable. However, Hugh would kill him if he attempted to ditch him with Lady Violet.

"Guess what?" Seddie said, staring at him. "Lady Violet insists she must sit in our box. Apparently, Packington has sanctioned it."

"My brother says I will be quite safe," Lady Violet said, giving her fan a snap to open it and fluttering it in front of her face.

Hugh was really annoyed. Yes, she would be quite safe. Neither he nor Seddie would compromise her in any way. Not if she were the last lady in England. Now he wanted to kill Packington. How did one tell a friend that his sister was annoying?

He did not know. He could guess it was never done, else plenty of people would have mentioned the same about his own sister.

As he was pondering how to get away from Lady Violet, he saw her. Miss Fernsby. At first, he saw the duchess. But then there she was, her head of fair curls emerging from behind the duchess. Miss Fernsby looked divine. She was dressed in a very dark green velvet gown that really set off her hair. Her only decoration was a small gold cross round her neck.

"Excuse me," he said, "I must greet Miss Fernsby."

"Miss *who*?" Lady Violet said, as if she did not know who he talked about.

Hugh did not stay longer to hear what she would say next. He was certain Seddie did not appreciate getting stuck with the lady again, but there was nothing for it. In any case, he supposed Seddie owed him a thousand favors for dragging him into participating in the regatta after nearly drowning him. Seddie might have forgotten it, but he had not.

He approached and caught Miss Fernsby's eye. She flushed, he'd seen that before. She went pink all the way down to her lovely neck. That must be a good sign, he thought.

"Duchess, Miss Fernsby," he said.

"Your Grace," she answered prettily.

"There you are, Duke," the duchess said. "Are we ready to hold on to our chairs? I cannot imagine what Lady Thurston has planned this time, but I suppose that is part of the appeal of it. It is the anticipation of seeing something surprising and she never does disappoint."

"She seems to be dressed in widow's weeds," Hugh said.

"Indeed, though by all reports Lord Thurston is still very much alive. The weeds seem to be a hope, rather than a reality."

"Hugh? Your Grace?"

Hugh pressed his lips together. Lucinda.

"Do introduce me to your new friend, Hugh."

"Lady Gaddington," the duchess said, "I have never known you to be here in the past."

"Gracious, yes, I suppose I have missed it until now," Lady Gaddington said.

"I see," the duchess said. "This is my young protégé, Miss Fernsby. I squire her around Town this season. Miss Fernsby, this is Lady Gaddington, she is sister to the duke."

"Miss Fernsby," Lucinda said, looking down her nose.

"Lady Gaddington," Miss Fernsby said, in a voice just above a whisper.

Chapter Eight

Hugh could not ignore that Miss Fernsby's flush had faded upon being introduced to his sister. She was positively pale. He got the feeling that she was intimidated by his sister. He supposed he could see why. His sister was older and married, she was a titled lady, and she had a certain stern and austere air about her. She made a sport of intimidating those she thought she could intimidate and Hugh already knew Lucinda's opinion of Miss Fernsby. Gentle Miss Fernsby did not seem to have the hard shell that might repel such an affront.

He could not say anything about it in the moment, as that would be awkward and would embarrass Miss Fernsby. He did not give a toss if he embarrassed Lucinda. If he could, he would tell Miss Fernsby to never be intimidated by Lucinda. His sister was a miserable and bitter gossip and was only admired by her equally miserable and bitter circle of friends. Not even her husband was an admirer. Miss Fernsby was worth a thousand Lucindas, even if his sister was a countess and she was a miss.

His sister's very presence and the way she looked down her nose in condescension made Hugh feel protective of Miss Fernsby. He had the urge to knock Lucinda out of the way, as he'd once done when he was ten and she was twenty. He'd come upon her scolding a footman for some alleged crime and threatening that she would get him dismissed. The poor fellow was fairly new and just then white as snow. Hugh was so enraged that he'd meant to knock her out of the way but knocked her so hard she hit the floor. He hadn't been sorry. Then he'd informed the footman that his father would not heed any of Lucinda's complaints against him as he was well sick and tired of hearing her complaints on every subject in the world.

Lucinda had been shocked that he'd thrown her to the ground, attempted a tantrum to no avail, and then stomped up the stairs. Hugh poured the footman a thumb's worth of brandy and informed Browning of what had occurred. His father never heard anything about it.

As much as he would like to, he could not knock her to the floor now. But he would get rid of her.

"Lucinda," Hugh said, "Gaddington was looking for you, very insistent about it, he cannot bear to be parted from his sweet-tempered bride. Duchess, Miss Fernsby, might I escort you to the sideboards? We'll all probably need fortification for what's to come."

~ ~ ~ ~ ~

When Finella had entered the ballroom, she'd seen the duke immediately. Perhaps that was because she was looking for him, but if she had been looking for him it was only to look *at* him. In the very usual and casual manner that everybody did. As a usual thing.

She'd spotted him standing with Sir Edward and Lady Violet. Just as he should be. Lady Violet was very tall and elegant. He was very tall and devastatingly handsome. Finella had swallowed a small sigh. Just looking at Lady Violet made her feel shorter and shorter and shorter.

But then the duke had met her eye and walked over to her and the duchess. Finella had not expected that. He'd done his duty at Almack's. He'd taken a dance to thank her for her aid on The Strand. There was no need for him to do anything further.

As she was contemplating those ideas, *she* had barged into the conversation. *Her*. The author of Finella's current insecurities and worries. Lady Lucinda Gaddington.

At Almack's, Finella had not been able to see Lady Gaddington when she'd overheard herself being described as a mushroom. She been holed up in her own compartment in the retiring room. Now she did see her. She was tall and a bit pinched in the face. She looked like the sort of person who would say hateful things. Or perhaps it seemed so to Finella because she'd heard the lady say hateful things.

In that first moment of being faced with Lady Gaddington, it felt as if she went toe to toe with her arch enemy. It felt as if they must do battle. It felt as if Finella must say something to defend herself. She must hit back over being named a mushroom. It briefly drifted across her mind that she might say, "Well if I am a mushroom, you are an asparagus. Not everybody likes asparagus."

Then she reminded herself that Lady Gaddington had not the first idea that she'd been overheard when she'd gossiped in Almack's retiring room. She did not know she'd been overheard by the very person she was saying insulting things about. Only Finella and Lucy knew it. It was lucky she did remember that, as it would have been entirely absurd to call a lady an asparagus. She was never very good at composing an insult. She'd not tried it often and she had not the quick wit to parry with any speed or sense.

Fortunately, the duke had mentioned to Lady Gaddington that her lord was looking for her and then he'd escorted her and the duchess to the sideboard. At least the encounter with Lady Gaddington did not go on longer. Finella could see from the lady's expression that she disliked her. On account of being a mushroom, she imagined.

The duke had suggested the white wine from Burgundy and Finella had nodded. She would prefer something sweeter, but she did not have the wherewithal to do more than nod at this moment. She really was very shaken, but she must do everything to hide it. She did not wish to appear foolish, and she especially did not wish that the duchess might suspect anything was wrong.

How disturbing it was that Lady Gaddington had approached and asked to be introduced to her when Finella knew what she actually thought. Had she done it just so she could privately laugh at Finella and tell her friend about it?

It occurred to her that if she'd never overheard Lady Gaddington in the Almack's retiring room, she might be positively thrilled that the lady wished to make her acquaintance. What a blissfully ignorant situation that would have been. As it was, she was all too familiar with the truth.

It brought to mind the old proverb of hearkeners never hearing good of themselves. She supposed it was a proverb because it was true. But why did people go out of their way to dislike and disdain other people? What was the point of it? Mrs. Francis, one of their neighbors at home, had something terrible to say about everybody. Finella could never see why she went on with it. It could not make her happy. Why didn't Mrs. Francis just wish to be happy? Now it occurred to her that Mrs. Francis had probably said plenty of insults about Finella. She'd just not overheard them. It gave her a chill, wondering if she'd just been blindly staggering through life without knowing what people thought about her.

The duke had asked her how she'd spent her days since the ball at Almack's but fortunately she was not forced to answer. *Very* fortunately, as she was sure she would have spouted some utter nonsense, so discombobulated were her thoughts at this moment. She'd probably have said something about the duke's sister being an asparagus, to the confusion of everyone within earshot. As it was, she was saved from embarrassing herself. Lady Burberry had just called out that everyone was to find their boxes.

The duchess led Finella to their box and, as it *was* the duchesses' box, they were near the front. Whatever they were to view would be done up close. Finella had not the first idea how Lady Thurston went about insulting her husband, but she was grateful that she would have time to sit quietly and gather herself together after the shock of Lady Gaddington approaching her.

"I suspect it is well that we have supplied ourselves with wine for this adventure," the duchess said, settling herself in her chair.

Finella sat down next to her and watched as the crowds found their own boxes. The duke and Sir Edward were just across the ballroom. She watched as Lady Violet let herself into their box. The lady laughed as if it were a great joke and settled herself between the two gentlemen.

What must it be like to have the height and the confidence of a Lady Violet? Finella could hardly imagine it. She did not suppose Lady Violet would ever be in danger of overhearing herself described as a mushroom.

Finella averted her eyes from the duke's box and in doing so, spotted Sir Roger. She had not seen him until this moment. It was clear enough he had seen her though. He waved enthusiastically. She averted her eyes from him too. Finella stared at the glass of wine in her hand, as that seemed the safest direction at the moment.

"Come now, everyone," Lady Burberry said. "That's right, everybody get settled."

The crowd did settle themselves and the room grew quiet. Though it was quiet, there seemed a tension in the air, as if everyone leaned just the littlest bit forward in anticipation.

"Welcome, ladies and gentlemen," Lady Burberry said. "Gracious, we are together again, where does the time go? It seems only a minute ago, we were gathered here for last year's tableau and here we are once more. As you know, Lady Thurston's creations are masterpieces of drama and pathos. I have no doubt if Mr. William Shakespeare were alive today, he'd be here with us, eagerly anticipating what we are to hear and see.

Ladies and gentlemen, I give you—a poetical tableau."

Next to Finella, the duchess snorted and sipped her wine. A butler and three footmen struggled to pull the curtains back from the stage, while two more footmen snuffed the candles of the candelabras set up round the room. One lone chandelier stayed lit, and the ballroom took on a dim and ghostly mien. Finella shivered despite herself and took a gulp of wine. She worked to keep a grimace from her expression—it was so tart.

The curtains were pulled back to reveal Lady Thurston and four ladies who were also dressed in black bombazine. They stood round a coffin.

An actual coffin.

Finella almost dropped her glass at the sight of it. Lady Thurston stepped forward. "Behold, a funeral for a marriage."

"Funeral for a marriage," the four ladies whispered.

"Good grief," the duchess muttered beside her.

"The union between two people is meant to be a genial thing," Lady Thurston intoned. "It has every chance of being happy when two people deal fairly with one another."

"Fairly," the four ladies whispered.

"But when insults of the pin money and actress variety are forever hurled upon a fair lady's head, it can only result in one ending. A funeral for a marriage."

"Funeral. For a marriage," the four ladies whispered.

Finella was horrified, though the duchesses' shoulders were shaking with laughter.

Lady Thurston turned dramatically and pointed at the coffin. "The last rites have been read!" she shouted. "The vigil has ended! The black-bordered cards have been sent to alert all and sundry that the marriage is dead!"

"Mailed. Dead!" the four ladies said, sadly shaking their

heads.

Finella found herself a bit frightened by this display. It might not be a real funeral, but it felt real. It also felt like tempting fate in some way.

"All that is left is the burial and a headstone that reads, "A dead marriage lies here—1786 to 1806."

"1806," the ladies whispered.

Finella gulped more of her wine. She did not care so much now that it was tart. She would have nightmares about this. She'd told the duchess she was prone to them in order to secure the room next door for Lucy. Now she would really have them.

And then, to increase the horror, the lid of the coffin was suddenly flung open of its own accord. Finella bit back a scream and dropped her glass. As her wine glass smashed on the floor, a man emerged from the depths of the coffin.

Finella was not the only one shocked. The audience gasped. Lady Thurston, herself, staggered back as if she'd seen a specter.

"Heaven help me," the duchess said quietly. "It's Lord Thurston."

Lady Thurston's husband had been hiding in the coffin the whole time? Certainly, Lady Thurston had not known it. Not by the look of utter shock in her expression. Neither had her lady friends known it, as they were slowly backing up with eyes wide.

Lord Thurston climbed out of the coffin. Loudly he said, "I have a poetical tableau of my own this year since it is, after all, my own house. Despite my wife's ramblings, there is no actress, the lady I am tied to for life has sufficient pin money, and I want my favorite chair back." He turned and pointed at Lady Thurston. "You, madame, are deranged. Everyone, enjoy your evening!"

Lord Thurston leapt down from the stage, waved and

smiled, and strode out of the room to stunned silence.

Lady Burberry, being a master of ceremonies of sorts, stepped forward. "Well goodness," she said. Then she applauded so that everyone might know this spectacle had concluded. Lady Thurston was helped off the stage and out the ballroom doors by her ladies.

"That outdid anything my poor imagination could ever conjure," the duchess said, laughing. "Lord Thurston has reached his limit, I suppose. What a night." She turned to Finella. "Gracious, Miss Fernsby, you are white as a new snow. Do not be shocked over it, it was just nonsense between two people who do not know how to negotiate with one another and do not have the good sense to keep it private."

"Yes, yes, of course," Finella said. "It just took me by surprise."

"That display took *everyone* by surprise."

The duke suddenly appeared. "Miss Fernsby, I did notice you dropped your glass. Do not move. You must not stand among the shards wearing only delicate ballroom slippers."

Finella had almost forgotten that her glass had smashed on the ground over the startling emergence of Lord Thurston from the coffin.

The duchess peered down. "Yes, I see what you say, Duke. Miss Fernsby is surrounded by shards. We'll need a footman with a broom."

"I would not deem a broom sufficient," the duke said. "We all know that glass tends to leave slivers behind that are impossible to see. It must be swept *and* mopped. At least, I have reason to know it. Sir Edward has probably broken a dozen of my glasses and I have heard about it rather endlessly from my butler. Do not fear, Duchess, I will get the lady out."

Before Finella could guess how the duke planned on getting her out, she was swept into his arms and gently set down on the ballroom floor, away from the glass.

"Duchess, I will give you a hand to get out the other direction, away from the glass," the duke said.

Finella felt a bit woozy on her feet. Had she just seen a man leap from a coffin and then ended in the duke's arms?

The duchess was got out of the box on the other side and she took Finella by the arm. "You seem a bit dazed, Miss Fernsby. Perhaps we will not stay to congratulate Lady Thurston. She usually takes a half hour with her ladies to recover herself, but I think it might be a deal longer this time."

Finella nodded.

"I will see to it that your carriage is called," the duke said, striding ahead.

"Miss Fernsby!"

The call came from behind her. Finella knew it was Sir Roger and she really did not wish to turn around. Perhaps she might pretend she did not hear him. She and the duchess were nearly at the doors.

"Miss Fernsby!" Sir Roger called, catching up to them. "Have you been hurt?"

"No, not at all," Finella said.

"Well I did see the duke pick you up—"

"We are just going, Sir Roger," the duchess said briskly.

"Indeed, as you should! That coffin was a shocking display. I would not permit a lady in my sphere to witness anything like it."

The idea of living in Sir Roger's sphere gave Finella a rather sick feeling. The idea of Sir Roger holding dominion over her was awful. It would never happen. She'd go home and become a spinster if this was her only choice. She could live in her father's house, and eventually her brother's when he assumed the mantle of baron. She'd take up work as a seamstress to pay her way. Assuming she could learn to sew more proficiently than she currently could. Still, to hear it said, to know he imagined it possible…

"We are not in your sphere, as far as I know it, Sir Roger," the duchess said.

A footman opened the outer doors for them and Finella breathed in the cold air. The duke was holding the duchesses' horses and her coachman was on the box, ready to go.

The groom got the door open and put down the step. The duchess pushed Finella ahead of her and she climbed in. Outside, she heard her say, "Duke, thank you for your assistance. Sir Roger."

With that, the door was closed and the carriage set off. What a night. She'd been confronted by Lady Gaddington, except Lady Gaddington had not known Finella knew what had been said at Almack's. She'd seen a positively hair-raising performance that had culminated in Lord Thurston jumping out of a coffin. She'd been carried to safety, away from broken glass, in the duke's arms. The evening was not at all what she'd imagined it would be. She'd thought she was to see a tableau while admiring the duke from afar and hoping to meet someone more suitable to someone like herself.

Lucy was going to fall off her chair when she heard what had gone on.

~ ~ ~ ~ ~

Mr. Browning would know far less about the duke's thoughts than he did if it were not for Sir Edward forever hanging round the duke's drawing room. The duke told Sir Edward quite a lot and Browning made it a point to be nearby.

He did not think of it as spying. It was rather more a collecting of information to best protect the duke. He'd been keeping his ears wide open since the duke was a boy and it had served them both well. Once, when the duke was but eight years old, Mr. Browning had put a stop to a foolhardy plan he and Sir Edward had cooked up together. The two of them had kept disappearing into an old outbuilding. Then he'd overheard them discussing "the boat." Browning was determined to investigate.

What he found was a lot of discarded wood nailed together in the vague shape of a crate and a sheet of paper inside it, detailing what it was about. It had some ridiculous scrawl on it, like "figure out what to do about all the holes." The rest of it was mostly a map. They'd planned to launch this collection of old boards, with themselves in it, on the River Orwell to see if they could make it all the way to the English Channel!

A quiet word with the old duke had put a stop to it and the young marquess had not died in a tragic drowning incident thanks to Mr. Browning's interference.

Just as he always did, he'd listened in on the conversation that was had after Lady Thurston's poetical tableau. Most of what he'd heard was raucous laughter over Lord Thurston popping out of a coffin. Mr. Browning could not imagine what had gone on, but the unhappy union between Lord and Lady Thurston was not his problem. What seemed to be his problem was that the duke had not developed the revulsion to Miss Fernsby that he'd been counting on.

Then he heard a bit of the conversation that chilled his heart.

"You caused no end of talk with your little maneuver," Sir Edward said to the duke. "I imagine some of the gentlemen took note of it for future use, should they ever encounter a similar situation."

"If you refer to ensuring Miss Fernsby did not cut her foot, then I would not call it a maneuver. The lady was in grave danger from broken glass and she has a rather lovely little foot."

Sir Edward laughed raucously. "Grave danger, indeed.

Well, in any case, it was a rare opportunity to sweep a lady into your arms without censure."

"She is very soft all over," the duke said, "though as a gentleman I suppose I should pretend not to have noticed."

Into his arms? What in the world was Miss Fernsby doing in the duke's arms? Why should that lady have a lovely foot? Why should she be soft?

"Sir Roger practically had steam coming from his ears," Sir Edward said. "I believe he is on the hunt in that direction."

"Old fool."

The conversation had moved on to the re-creation of the poetical tableau that would proceed at The Devil's Den, which Mr. Browning could not care less about. If the duke and his friends wished to mock Lady Thurston's idea of what was poetical, it was all the same to him.

He had bigger problems. Somehow, there was no revulsion to Miss Fernsby developing.

Chapter Nine

Mr. Browning settled himself in a meeting with his fellow butlers in Cheapside as Mr. Penny took on pouring out the tea. He found himself wishing he did not know as much as he did. Something had happened at the poetical tableau that had caused the duke to save Miss Fernsby from broken glass by way of picking her up.

He did not know what the other *League* members knew. He suspected they knew quite a lot, considering all the head shaking that Mr. Feldstaffer was just now engaged in.

Mr. Penny handed him his cup and said, "Well gracious, I suppose we've all heard."

"Of course we've all heard," Mr. Harkinson said. "People living in the wilds of America have probably heard. They're probably talking about it around a campfire in the west as we speak."

Mr. Browning stared at Mr. Harkinson. He did not know why pioneers of the American west were to be brought into it.

"It is my understanding that Miss Fernsby had dropped her glass and shattered it on account of the shock of Lord Thurston rising out of the coffin nobody knew he was in," Mr. Wilburn said.

"Broken glass, bad business," Mr. Feldstaffer said. "If there's a shard of glass anywhere, I'll step on it."

"It does show a delicacy of feeling, to my mind," Mr. Penny said. "What I say is, a delicacy of feeling to be so shocked at the appearance of a man coming out of a coffin."

"I'd wonder at anybody who wasn't shocked," Mr. Wilburn said.

It did not show a delicacy of feeling to Mr. Browning. She had not fainted, which is what a delicate lady would do. She'd dropped her glass. It showed clumsiness if it showed anything at all. Sir Edward had smashed glasses all over the duke's house and nobody accused him of a delicacy of feeling. Furthermore, there had been no need for the duke to rescue her from her own clumsy mistake. Why could not Sir Roger have done it?

"Well, after all," Mr. Rennington said, "I suppose Miss Fernsby is not so bad."

Not so bad? Is that what they had come to?

"Perhaps not the brilliant match you were hoping for, Mr. Browning," Mr. Rennington went on, "but it won't cause talk beyond some jealous matrons who did not land the duke for their own daughter. Miss Fernsby is perfectly acceptable."

"Perfectly acceptable?" Mr. Browning said. "Perfectly acceptable is in no way acceptable for the Duke of Greystone. Gentlemen, he is a Finstatten."

Mr. Browning really thought that one simple sentence should say it all. The Duke of Greystone was a Finstatten. They were speaking of one of the oldest families in England. Only the highest standards would do.

"Nothing to be done about it, though," Mr. Feldstaffer said.

"You're stuck lowering your standards, Mr. Browning," Mr. Harkinson said, not appearing at all sad about it.

The very idea of a lowering of standards was anathema to Mr. Matthew L. Browning. He served in one of the most elevated households in England. He could go no higher unless he served the palace. He had known, even as a young man, that he was meant for such a refined environment. He had been lucky enough to be sponsored by his parish and had gone away to school. Mr. Browning had turned up with rather rough manners, as he'd not seen anything different.

Then he did see something different. The headmaster, Mr. Russell Manchin, was a stickler for manners and protocol. Mr. Browning learned about proper dress and table settings, he refined his accent and his manner of eating. He developed a discerning taste. When he'd returned home between terms, his father had accused him of acting like a prince. He'd not answered his father aloud, but he'd thought, "Thank you, sir, that is the goal."

He had come so far. He would not allow Miss Fernsby to drag him down!

"I really feel," Mr. Penny said, "that there is no lowering of standards here. After all, Miss Fernsby is the daughter of a baron, new as the title may be. Now, while she might not be the image you had in mind, you know, being on the short side—"

"And the round side," Mr. Harkinson said rather gleefully.

"Rubenesque, is how I would describe it," Mr. Penny said. "If that is what the duke prefers..."

"I agree with Mr. Penny," Mr. Rennington said. "As well, if this were the Renaissance, Miss Fernsby would be very much the style."

If this were the Renaissance? Mr. Browning could hardly understand what had happened to his fellow butlers. There was a time when they would go to any lengths to secure the right match for the lords and ladies in their purview. Now they were to approve Miss Fernsby because she might have been the style two hundred years ago?

"The important thing is that the duke seems satisfied with the direction things are going," Mr. Penny said, sipping his tea.

The important thing was the duke was satisfied? The duke's satisfaction had nothing to do with it! He might be satisfied today, but what about tomorrow or next year or in ten years? This was just like the rickety boat he'd built with Sir

Edward to launch on the River Orwell. The duke must be saved from his own ideas.

"It seems things are settled, then," Mr. Wilburn said. "Perhaps not how we all saw things unfolding, but settled well enough."

Mr. Browning felt as if his spine had turned to iron. Nothing was settled. His fellow butlers might be willing to give up easily, but they were not the butler to the Duke of Greystone. This butler did not roll over at the first difficulty. This butler did not lower standards. This butler did not settle.

There was nothing for it. He would have to go it alone. Mr. Browning was going to have to go rogue.

As soon as he thought up a roguish idea, he would act on it. He would save the name of Finstatten at any cost. The old duke and duchess would be depending on him from their perches in heaven. He would not let them down!

~ ~ ~ ~ ~

Finella had arrived home from the poetical tableau to find Lucy sprawled in one of the chairs of her bedchamber looking very sleepy. As there was a glass by her side that seemed to have a little bit of water in it, Finella was very afraid that her maid had stolen more of the cook's gin.

Whether she had or had not, she became far less sleepy as Finella told her of all the events of the night. The very first thing that she'd relayed was having to face Lady Gaddington. Lucy was the only person in the wide world who would understand why that had been such a trial.

Lucy finished the glass of water, or gin, and said, "So you thought about callin' her an asparagus. In the end, though, you didn't call her an asparagus. A'course, I would've called her a twice-pinched harpy. Shame, that."

Finella was not quite in agreement there, though she was gratified by Lucy's support. She moved on to tell of the tableau,

Lord Thurston leaping out of the coffin, the broken glass, the duke sweeping her up, and Sir Roger following her out to the carriage.

"So you been in the duke's arms now," Lucy said. "How was it?"

"How was it? Lucy, I am not to think of how it was. It's not very ladylike. I don't imagine."

Lucy waved her hands as if to dismiss her comments. "If a woman ends up in a man's arms, she's dotty if she don't reflect on it."

"Well I suppose it was very nice," Finella said. "Though it was just to save my feet from stepping on glass."

That was, of course, a complete fib. It was far more than very nice. She would dream of that brief moment for the rest of her life. Though it all happened so quickly, she had already examined every second of it. If she had been told beforehand that it was to happen, she would have been dubious over the idea that the duke could sweep her up as he had, as if she were not at all heavy. He must be very strong! And then, when he *did* sweep her up, she'd breathed in the scent of him, the coriander soap, both the citrus and warmth. She had felt the rough wool of his coat against her bare arm. It had been positively thrilling.

"Lolling around in the duke's arms was just very nice, was it?" Lucy said, with a snort. She rose and began to help Finella out of her dress and into her nightclothes. "Well now, I reckon you'll have sweet dreams about that very nice embrace."

Though Finella demurred, that was exactly what she did.

The day following the poetical tableau, the duchess was determined that they go out in a carriage so that Finella might take in the air as a restorative. They set off at five o'clock, which was far later than they usually went out. As a habit, the duchess usually liked to set off around two o'clock. The park would not be too crowded at that hour and that was how the duchess preferred it. She had no need to go flouncing around the park to be noticed. She was the Duchess of Ralston, she was already sufficiently noticed.

The change in time came about when the duchess decided that she was not doing enough for Finella. While the duchess had no need to be noticed, Finella did. The duchess had set out to sponsor her, she'd promised the baron that Finella was in expert hands, and she must do the job creditably.

Though the duchess had repeatedly insulted anyone foolish enough to own a barouche, she began to see that it might be advantageous to ride in a carriage with the top down in order to show off a young lady. She'd rented one, decided it smelled like other people, and sent it back. Then she'd borrowed one from their neighbor, the Earl of Westford. Apparently, whatever the earl smelled like, which seemed to be a lot of leather, was deemed acceptable.

As the horses walked the barouche down the carriage road, the duchess clasped her bonnet. "Gracious, I do not like all this blowing about."

"Perhaps we ought to have come in your carriage," Finella said. "You would be more comfortable."

"Nonsense," the duchess said. "I am determined to show you off."

Finella swallowed a sigh. She really did not feel like any prize to be shown off.

"Miss Fernsby," the duchess said, "I feel you do not have a lot of confidence in yourself."

Was it so obvious? She supposed it was. "It's true," Finella said. "I don't think I've ever been very bowled over by my looks, though especially since I came to Town. I did not have a lot to compare myself to at home, but here..."

"It's all nonsense. It's nonsense existing in your mind.

You've got the prettiest face going this season, your dimples are inestimably charming. The wind has caused some of your pretty curls to escape your bonnet and it appears lovely. You must just have confidence in yourself. Furthermore, I believe I now understand your temperament. You are rather a soft touch, which is very engaging."

Finella nodded because she felt she ought to. She thought the praise rather highflying, though she did like her hair and she did think she was a soft touch.

"Do not compare yourself to a lady who is tall when you are short. Do not compare yourself to a lady who is all cool wit when you are a soft touch. Be yourself and proud of it. Do you know what some people called me before I wed the duke? I was Lady Margaret at the time. I overheard a gentleman name me "Middling Margaret." He'd heard it at his club apparently. But guess who did not find me middling? The two gentlemen who offered for me, one of which I accepted."

Finella could not conceive of the idea that anybody had ever named the duchess "Middling Margaret." How dare that gentleman!

"One of the things that was very satisfying to me in those early years was that the gentleman who had applied that moniker to me very suddenly found himself having to address me as Your Grace. It probably choked him to do it. He's long dead now, which is the other thing I can be satisfied about."

Finella laughed despite herself. She very much wished she could take on the duchesses' attitude about things. The lady had heard something terrible, just as Finella had. Rather than wilting like a dying flower, she'd gone forth with confidence. She laughed in the face of her detractor and then as a final blow, outlived him.

She tapped her chin as she watched carriages pass their rather slow-going barouche. Why could not she take on the duchesses' attitude? It seemed very foreign, of course. It would be rather an about-face. Finella was not accustomed to putting herself forward or being confident. But on the other hand, it was not against the law, was it? Nobody could do anything about it. She'd already heard something said about her that was terrible. What else could they say?

Perhaps she would consult Lucy about it, as her maid was full of good sense.

In the meantime, Finella sat up straighter, determined to try it out. She imagined herself a very powerful and admired person. She thought of Lady Gaddington being sorry for what she said. Then she thought of Lady Gaddington wishing to be friends with her, as Finella Fernsby had become very renowned and sought after. For some reason or other. Finella would hold her at arm's length and display a certain coolness that would be understood. Lady Gaddington would be entirely cast down over it.

"Miss Fernsby."

Finella was pulled out of her daydream by Lady Violet. The lady was on a very fine chestnut mare and dressed in a blue wool riding coat, accompanied by two grooms. She looked exceedingly elegant. Finella felt as if she was a balloon of rising confidence that had just been pricked with a pin and slowly deflated.

"Lady Violet," she said. She did her very best to be friendly, though it was irritating that the lady looked divine on horseback.

"Miss Fernsby," Lady Violet said. "Do you ride?"

"Indeed, yes, quite a bit at home. I did not bring my horse to Town though." Finella wondered at the question, which had seemed a bit condescending. What lady from the countryside did not ride her own horse and drive her own curricle? Perhaps Lady Violet meant to point out how glorious she was looking, astride her own horse.

"I recommended to Miss Fernsby to leave her horse at home," the duchess said. "A lady on a horse in the country is all well and good, but here..." The duchess waved her hand vaguely round.

Finella tried not to laugh. Somehow, the duchess had managed to condemn a lady riding her horse in the park without saying it directly or even why.

It had certainly hit its mark, as Lady Violet looked rather startled.

Recovering herself, she said, "Your Grace, I understand you host one of the events of the season. Secrets Exposed."

Finella wondered if the duchess would recognize that as the fishing expedition that it probably was. She understood that the identity of the twenty ladies selected to participate each year was always eagerly anticipated and that ladies could be very let down if they were not chosen. Finella herself was a bit terrified of the prospect. She assumed she would be one of the twenty ladies included, as the duchess sponsored her. It felt a little fraudulent. If the duchess knew nothing about her, she doubted she would be chosen.

"Indeed," the duchess said to Lady Violet. It was said enigmatically and gave the lady no information.

"I see," Lady Violet said.

Finella was not so certain she did see. One would be very foolish to attempt to manage the duchess.

"Goodness, there is the duke and Sir Edward ahead," Lady Violet said. "Your Grace, Miss Fernsby." She spurred her horse off in their direction.

Finella squinted her eyes. Yes, there he was and looking very handsome astride his horse. He was mounted on a very fine grey and Finella could see how spirited the horse was. A horse of that caliber did not like to stand still and so danced back and forth in protest. She almost wished she was on her own horse now, as she rode a grey too. They were a very particular type of horse, she'd always thought.

What unfolded next was very strange. She was almost sure that the duke had spotted Lady Violet. He leaned toward Sir Edward to say something. Then they spurred their horses into a gallop across the green of the park. Lady Violet made an attempt to follow them and then gave up and reined in.

"Poor Lady Violet," the duchess said.

Finella supposed the duchess thought what she thought about it. However, naming that elegant lady "poor" seemed a stretch.

"She looks very well on a horse," Finella said.

"She's at least got that going for her."

Finella looked quizzically at the duchess.

Her Grace smiled. "She is too young, you see. Not in years, but in mind. She'll be much better suited next year. For now, though, she will chase what she will never catch and she will drop hints about being included in Secrets Exposed which I would never do. Lord Packington would be well advised to rein her in a bit."

"Goodness, I hadn't thought."

The duchess nodded sagely. "I hold nothing against her, it is just the childishness in her that must be got over. She is not the first lady arriving to Town too soon. No doubt she harassed Packington over it, against his better judgment. Now she is playing at being a seasoned lady when she is no such thing."

That put quite a different spin on Lady Violet. On the other hand, Finella could not feel too sorry for the lady. She'd return next season looking just as elegant as she did today.

For now, Lady Violet continued on down the carriage road with her grooms trailing behind until she was out of sight.

"Duchess, Miss Fernsby!"

Finella turned round in her seat. There he was. The duke. Gracious, he and Sir Edward must have circled round.

"Your Grace, Miss Fernsby," Sir Edward said.

Both gentlemen, and certainly their horses, were out of breath.

"We noted you up ahead and now here you are behind us," the duchess said, looking very amused, "how extraordinary."

"Ah yes," the duke said. "Our horses suddenly demanded a gallop."

"Yes, it did seem it was required at a lucky moment," the duchess said.

Despite the duchesses' broad hint that she'd understood they'd galloped away from Lady Violet, neither of the gentlemen answered. If they had done so to escape Lady Violet's company, they were too gentlemanly to say so.

"The regatta is on the morrow," the duchess said, "how do your preparations for it get on, Sir Edward?"

"Rather terrifically, Your Grace," Sir Edward said. "I've been out several times with a seasoned sailor and have really picked up the hang of the thing."

The duchess looked skeptical. "See that you do not drown the duke."

Sir Edward had the good grace to blush.

"Miss Fernsby," the duke said, "have you ever attended a regatta before?"

"Never," Finella said. "I've actually never set foot on a boat. I'm looking forward to it."

"I do not like the bouncing around myself," the duchess said, "but it is only for a short period of time so I will put up with it. I have no idea how people sail all the way to America without losing their minds over it."

"You should be all right on a barge," the duke said, "they don't seem to take the waves as harshly as a sloop. Miss Fernsby, what is your favorite color?"

Finella thought that question came out of nowhere. "Goodness, I have a fondness for yellow. I suppose it is not a particularly sophisticated preference, but it is such a happy color. It seems to me."

"It is tradition," Sir Edward, "that each boat must tie a colored scarf or shawl round the bottom of their mast. It makes it easier for the people standing on the banks of the river to see who is who."

Finella was certain she'd gone purple. What did it mean, asking for her favorite color? Would there be a yellow shawl tied round Sir Edward's mast? If there was, what did *that* mean? Did the duke just ask her what her favorite color was as a casual question or was there something in it?

"I do wish you gentlemen luck," the duchess said. "Though you are up against the Duke of Barstow. He's won it three years running."

"Miss Fernsby, you will know that duke by his mast decorated with a red silk shawl in honor of his red-haired duchess," Sir Edward said. "I hope when you catch sight of him, he is trailing far behind us."

Finella thought the Duke of Barstow was quite romantic to tie on a red shawl for his red-haired duchess. After witnessing the poetical tableau, her ideas of marital happiness had been somewhat shaken. She must remember that Lord and Lady Thurston must be the exception to how things usually were. Not every wife was putting on a funeral for a marriage to denigrate her husband and not every husband was jumping out of a coffin in answer to it.

But then, if the Duke of Barstow used a color to signal a lady, did they all do that? She did not know!

"Well now," the duchess said, "I believe I've been exposed to the wind sufficiently for one day. I will take Miss Fernsby home."

"We will escort you to the gates, Duchess," the duke said. "If you are not opposed to it."

"Far be it for me to refuse an escort," the duchess said, looking very pleased.

Finella could not work out the duke. He seemed to like her. She would imagine it was just grateful friendliness over their encounter on The Strand, but this seemed a bit much for that.

Did he like her? It seemed extraordinary, but it also seemed as if it might be true. She did her best to stop her thoughts about it, as she would rather her cheeks not resemble two aubergines. High color was a family curse of sorts. Her father had darker hair, a light brown shade, but he had the same skin. He could go purple in the face when he was pleased, displeased, or just out in a strong wind. As much as he'd teased her over "going strawberry," he was just the same.

The duke walked his horse alongside Finella as their barouche made its slow way forward. They fell to talking about the duke's horse and her own grey. They were both in agreement that greys were more energetic than other horses and could be surprisingly clever and headstrong when they felt like it. The duke's horse was dammed by Bab, which was a very fine family lineage. Her own horse's history was not so elevated, but Finella had fallen in love with Kestrel the moment her father had brought the mare home. Kestrel was terribly stubborn, but on the other hand she did like to gallop and she would do absolutely anything for an apple and a good rubdown.

At the gates, the duke tipped his hat and the barouche rode on.

"Miss Fernsby, you had a very pleasant conversation with the duke while I was left to parry Sir Edward's nonsense."

Finella had not even thought of that. “I am sorry, I should have noticed.”

The duchess patted her hand. “Have all the pleasant conversations with the duke that you like. As for Sir Edward, well, all I’ll say about it is I hope he and the duke survive the regatta. As has long been known about him, Sir Edward is not brimming with sense.”

Chapter Ten

Hugh was in the main room of The Devil's Den drinking a glass of good claret. Though he was a member of White's for tradition's sake, he rarely went there. The Devil's Den had been founded by him and his friends in the first year they'd been set loose in London. They wished for a place that suited them and was entirely devoid of stern old fellows frowning at them, arguing about politics, and complaining about their gout. When the time eventually came when Hugh was frowning, arguing about politics, and shifting his foot on account of his gout, he'd go to White's then.

When they'd looked round for a space for their club, it was discovered that Lord Winters had a low one-story building owned by his family that they did not use for anything. His father had come close to selling it, but the sale had not gone through. Now it was leased to The Devil's Den for one pound a quarter. Since they did not have much rent to pay, they spent most of their membership fees on a well-stocked cellar, an excellent cook, and their intrepid steward who kept the whole thing going, Mr. Albert.

The rooms were furnished in a deliberate mishmash of whatever could be found and brought in. A baroque piece here, a Queen Ann there, there was even a massive bird cage, large enough to walk into, that currently housed the bet book. They did not want the place to appear carefully composed; it was not the nature of the club.

This evening, the night before the regatta, was a gathering for war plans. At least, that was what Seddie called it. Really, it was for the members to discuss the various strategies of those who would participate in the regatta.

"You see what I say," Lord Rareton said. "If we all set out to block Barstow's wind, he has to be beaten this year. He cannot walk away with it for the fourth year in a row. The Devil's Den has a reputation to uphold. It does not matter as much which one of us wins, it matters that *one* of us wins."

The lord had tacked sheets of paper on the wood wall to create a big map of the Thames with the starting point and the location of the turnaround buoy marked out.

Hugh noticed Seddie's eyes glazing over as Rareton rambled about what the tide would be doing and made guesses on the wind direction and speed. He did not think Seddie took much of it in, which was probably not a good sign. They were likely to be a shambles on the morrow. As he had already come to that conclusion before now, he'd demanded two life rings be brought aboard. Hugh planned on tying a rope around one of them and then tying the other end of the rope around his ankle. If he was thrown into the Thames a second time, he would bring a life ring with him. A person could not depend upon a bargeman being nearby on a regular schedule.

"All right now, I think our plan is set," Lord Rareton said.

Hugh turned to Seddie. "Do you understand the plan at all?"

"No," Seddie said with a laugh. "You know Rareton, he always complicates things. We'll just set off and see how we go. A to B, start to finish. Nothing easier."

Hugh had suspected as much.

"Duke," Lord Packington said, approaching them, "my sister asked me specially to inform you that her favorite color is French verte. Whatever shade that might be."

"I see," Hugh said. A heavy hint from Lady Violet on what color shawl should be around their mast. "Regarding the color we will carry, unfortunately, we are already committed. The

Duchess of Ralston has made her wishes known."

Of course, the duchess had not said anything about it. However, he did not wish to have anything uncomfortable with Packington on account of Lady Violet.

"Ah, the duchess," Packington said, sounding satisfied with the answer, "she cannot be crossed, eh?"

"Definitely not," Hugh said. He was rather glad he thought of laying it at the duchesses' feet. He'd already purchased a pretty yellow shawl for the mast and had Browning pack it in a canvas bag to be ready to go. He'd had the tradesman describe the shade to him and was told it was sunshine yellow, which he thought was very apt to describe Miss Fernsby. If he'd been forced into showing the color for Lady Violet he would have first had to discover what French verte was. At least he'd heard of yellow even if he could not see what others saw on account of his blindness to that shade. He suspected French verte went by its other more common name of green, which he also could not see very well.

Since he could not see either one of the shades, he very much preferred the simpler idea of Miss Fernsby's lively yellow.

He laughed to himself as he recalled how flushed her face and neck had gone when he'd asked about her favorite color. She was so charming. She did not pretend to prefer French verte, she made no attempt at elegance and sophistication.

Miss Fernsby was sunny yellow and he very much preferred it.

~ ~ ~ ~ ~

Browning had seen the duke off to his wretched club, The Devil's Den. Sir Edward had come for him in his carriage, as was their habit. They tended to drink to excess at that club and both gentlemen were convinced their horses could not abide a drunken rider. As far as Browning was concerned, the duke was better off in a carriage so he did not get attacked by footpads in his befuddled state.

He expected a quiet night, as it always was when the duke was out. However, no sooner had the duke left than Lady Gaddington had swanned in. It was his pleasure to inform her that the duke was not at home while he blocked the stairs.

She stared at him and said, "I know he is not here, I watched him leave. I'm not here to see the duke. I'm here to see *you*."

Browning had staggered back just a little, but avoided planting himself on the stairs, which would have been undignified in the extreme.

"Yes, yes, I can see you're shocked. Do come into the drawing room. I have something that must be urgently discussed."

Browning was in a bit of a tizzy over it. Lady Gaddington never had anything to discuss with him and, furthermore, virtually all of her discussions were unpleasant. She did not wait for him to answer her but charged ahead in her usual high-handed fashion. She carried a cloth sack and he desperately hoped he was not to hear that she'd left Lord Gaddington and was moving back into the house.

He took heart that it was not a very large sack and followed her into the drawing room.

Lady Gaddington threw the sack on a sofa and poured herself a small glass of the duke's brandy from the sideboard. "I suppose you know about Miss Fernsby."

Browning nodded. "I have heard that person's name mentioned."

"It's not on, Browning. The duke has lost his sense. That girl is a mushroom of the worst sort."

While Browning quite agreed with her, which did not happen often, he remained expressionless.

"If this is allowed to go forward, Hugh will regret it. He will wake up one day, with a squat mushroom of a duchess, and wonder why nobody stopped him. His father-in-law will be recently of the gentry. I'm quite sure he is crass. Out of anyone, Browning, I would think you would make some effort to stop this madness in honor of my mother and father."

Mr. Browning stood straighter at the mention of the old duke and duchess. He had no doubt Lady Gaddington was right in her assessment, but he did not know what he could do about it.

"Steps must be taken, Browning. Steps, for the duke's own good. This infatuation will pass and he will wonder what he ever saw in Miss Mushroom."

"Rest assured, Lady Gaddington, if there were any steps to be taken, I would take them."

"Excellent," she said. "As there is a step that can be taken. I understand that each boat is to display a color by way of a shawl tied round the mast. Lady Violet, a lovely earl's daughter, has chosen French verte."

"French verte?" he asked.

"Yes, yes, stupid to call it that when green will do." She pulled out a green shawl. "Hugh will know nothing about the tradition of shawls. Sir Edward is in charge of his boat and that means nobody is in charge. You may say you heard of the tradition and give him this shawl. Say something like it's the queen's color. He'll have no idea that he's signaling Lady Violet. It will give her encouragement though, to redouble her efforts. He just needs to spend more time with the lady."

"He *does* know about the tradition of the shawls, though," Browning put in. "He has a yellow shawl packed and ready to go. Miss Fernsby said yellow was her color."

As usual when Lady Gaddington was crossed, her features grew even more pinched than they usually were. When she'd been a child, it had been the signal that an explosion was imminent. But then, she suddenly smiled.

"Yellow." she said. "Where is it?"

Browning's eyes must have drifted to the table near the drawing room doors that the duke called the coming and going table. It held mail going in or out or anything that needed to be taken or left for somebody. Just now it held the small canvas bag with the yellow shawl.

She marched over and ripped the yellow shawl from its bag. She replaced it with the green shawl and closed the drawstrings of the bag. "This is better than I could have possibly planned. God is on our side to arrange it," she said. "Now you need not say anything at all. If you are asked about it later, say I was here and insisted on waiting in the drawing room and then once I was convinced the duke was not here, I left."

Browning stared at Lady Gaddington, trying to understand what she was talking about.

She sighed. "Don't you see? He will proudly display that shawl, believing it is the yellow one. Hello, Browning? He is a Finstatten."

It finally penetrated Browning's mind. "Oh, I see. Because he is blind to those colors." It was a well-known Finstatten quality. Browning had never thought of it as a deficiency, the Finstattens did not have deficiencies. It was just something that set them apart. A distinction, as it were. The old duke's valet used to sew descriptions on the inside of his clothes so he knew what he was wearing. They were very descriptive too. A vest might be "a very dark green brocade with a subtle yellow edging of the pattern."

Lady Gaddington nodded. "He's especially colorblind with yellow and green, just like my father. You see what I say about God being on our side? Not only will he signal Lady Violet, he will signal Miss Fernsby too. Her yellow will be nowhere to be seen. He'll have no idea. We will guide him in the right direction without an all-out war over it."

"But he will discover it eventually. Sir Edward is likely to say something about it before they even set off."

"Possibly. But then the worst that could happen is Hugh sails with no shawl visible. That is still a message to Miss Fernsby. In any case, you know how disorganized Sir Edward is. I think he'll be running round like a blind chicken just trying to keep them afloat and won't pay any mind to it."

"I am not certain this is a wise idea," Browning said.

"Really. What is *your* brilliant idea? Tell me at once so we can enact it in all haste."

"Well as to that, I have not precisely landed on anything as of yet."

"That's what I thought. It's time to be bold, Browning. In defense of the name Finstatten."

Lady Gaddington finished her glass of brandy, took the yellow shawl, and exited the house.

Browning stared at the canvas bag, now containing a green shawl. What should he do? Should he tell the duke? If he did, His Grace would certainly want to know how he'd allowed Lady Gaddington to take the yellow shawl.

He'd say, "Why did you not tackle her, Browning? How did you allow her to take the yellow shawl?"

He had no answer for that.

And then, had he not committed to doing something roguish to stop this infatuation with Miss Fernsby? Had he not felt a disdain for his fellow butlers and their inaction? Had he not vowed to himself that he would take bold action once he thought of something? Had he not imagined meeting with *The League* to triumphantly relate how he steered the duke away from Miss Fernsby after they had given up on it?

Had he not just had to admit that he did not have any idea of how to do it?

It felt very wrong to collude with Lady Gaddington. That lady had been a thorn in his side for over twenty years. He could never have imagined siding with her on anything.

And yet, he did feel compelled to do something to save the duke from himself.

Perhaps the thing to do was nothing. The duke did not require him to wait up when he went to The Devil's Den. Once the bells of St. Margarets had rung this evening, the signal from Lord Bestwick that the weather cooperated and the regatta would commence in the morning, the duke had laid out his directions to the household.

His Grace arranged for a cold plate to be waiting for him in the morning so that Cook did not need to get out of bed so early. His valet had even laid out his clothes so that he would match, as the duke had told him he need not rise either. The coachman and grooms were not needed, as Sir Edward was to fetch him in his carriage.

The duke would come in late tonight and leave early in the morning for the regatta. Browning would not even see him. There would not be time to even mention that Lady Gaddington had been to the house. He might just leave the whole thing in the hands of fate. If he was asked about it, he could say he had been struck down with a violent fever and when he'd woken, he thought the encounter with Lady Gaddington had only been a dream.

Browning had a great urge to hide under his blankets, so that was what he did.

~ ~ ~ ~ ~

Finella had gone downstairs before the sun was up. Or maybe it was already up and just could not be seen. A heavy fog had rolled along the streets coating everything in a grey mist.

She was certain it would not last, London seemed very fond of a heavy fog to start the day, but there was no sign of rain.

They were to set off early. The bargeman had come to the house yesterday and requested to see Wagner to make the arrangements. The duchess had insisted he be brought into the drawing room to communicate the plan directly to her.

The poor fellow had looked as if he'd taken a wrong turn somewhere to have ended in a duchesses' drawing room. He'd gathered himself together though and mapped out how it would be. They must set off early, or else they would not find a good spot to anchor. They could not anchor any place that took their fancy, as they could not get in the way of the race. The bargeman knew just where he wanted to be. It would be just south of the bridge that would mark both the start and finish and would have a fine view of the entirety of the race.

He and the duchess worked out all the plans. Finella and the duchess would come in her carriage and a second carriage had been hired to carry Wagner with all their supplies. There were to be folding tables, while the bargeman would supply chairs. A full breakfast would be packed, though the bargeman warned against hot eggs. He'd seen it tried and it always failed. They set the time and the location of the pier where the barge would be waiting for them. She was named *The Betsy*.

Finella heard it all, though her mind was elsewhere. All she could think of was that the duke had asked her what color she favored. She still was not certain what it meant, but Lucy was sure it meant that the duke would fly her color, just like the knights of old who jousted. It was a very romantic notion, though Finella did not know if it were true. But it might be true. What was she to think if she saw her color?

Finella had got herself into such a state about it that she thought she might die if the duke did have something yellow tied to the mast of his boat, and she might die if he did not.

The carriage rolled through the foggy streets, little

droplets of mist rolling down the windows. If she were at home, she would be snuggled into her velvet settee in the drawing room, a blanket on her knees, a book in her hand, and tea by her side. It was extraordinary that she was just now in a carriage, rattling through the street, a duchess by her side, on her way to a regatta, and wondering if the duke would show yellow on his boat. Whose life was this? It certainly did not seem like Finella Fernsby's life.

They'd come to the wharf as the mist was rapidly burning off and the sun was ordering it to go away. It was a hive of activity, as the duchess was not the only person who had rented a barge. Finella suspected every barge available would be out on the river to see the regatta. Or as Lucy had described it, "A bunch of lords pretendin' to be admirals."

The bargeman brought his crew to the carriage and the young men began to unload the second carriage of its supplies with Wagner supervising. The bargeman himself led them down the stone steps to the wharf.

Behind them, Finella heard a man call. "Your Grace! Your Grace!"

They stopped to find a finely dressed gentleman hurrying toward them.

"Lord Packington, how do you do this morning?"

Lord Packington. He was the older brother to Lady Violet, the nose wrinkler and lady who sat finely on a horse. The lady the duchess thought had come to Town a year too soon.

"I am afraid my morning has gone very awry, Your Grace," Lord Packington said, out of breath from chasing them down. "My bargeman is refusing to take us out. He says the wood of his wheel has developed a crack. I suggested glue, but he is convinced the whole thing needs to be replaced and he will not take his chances on losing steering on the Thames."

"I should say not," the duchess said.

Lord Packington shook his head sadly. "My sister is devastated over it. She was quite looking forward to viewing the regatta. I suppose it cannot be helped."

"That's quite enough hinting around, Lord Packington," the duchess said. "You'd best come with us."

"Thank you, Your Grace, thank you! I will just go and fetch Lady Violet."

The duchess nodded. "We are on *The Betsy*. We will see you aboard."

They proceeded to follow the bargeman to his boat. Finella could not say she was eager to encounter Lady Violet. Aside from her general air of beauty and elegance, Finella had not forgotten the nose wrinkle.

There was nothing to be done about it, though. The duchess had invited them aboard and so they would come.

The aboard in question was a wide flat boat with ample room for twenty or so people. The bargeman's crew were already setting up the duchesses' tables and had retrieved chairs from somewhere while Wagner rearranged the various crates he had packed for the occasion.

Once the tables were up, two were pushed together and ringed with chairs. One table stood to the side, set apart. The duchess had told her the separate table was to be refreshments for the crew. Finella thought that was a fine example of the duchesses' consideration for other people. Her father would have done just the same. He always said, "Feed people, it is the bare minimum."

Wagner laid a cloth over the longer table and began setting it up. Finella was not at all surprised that he'd brought silver platters and fine porcelain. Wagner would hardly do anything else. The duchess was to be treated as a duchess whether she was at home or floating around on a boat.

Finella had never been on a boat before. It was a very odd

sort of feeling to have the floor under one's feet rocking gently as if the world were no longer solid and steady.

It was not long before she saw Lord Packington and Lady Violet hurrying down the pier to *The Betsy*.

"Gracious, the name of the boat is *The Betsy*, how positively droll," Lady Violet said as she was being helped onboard.

The bargeman folded his arms. "Betsy is the name of my dead wife."

"Oh, I see," Lady Violet said. She quickly turned away from the disapproving bargeman to the duchess. "Your Grace, you have saved the day. My brother and I are both full of thanks. Ah, Miss Fernsby."

Finella really felt as if she said "Ah, Miss Fernsby" as if she was an aside, hardly to be noticed.

Lord Packington held a picnic basket. "Our meager contribution, Your Grace."

Wagner took the picnic basket with two fingers as if it might hold a live snake. Finella was relatively certain he would not approve of anything in it, as he had not selected it himself.

She tried not to laugh when Wagner opened it, frowned, and put it on the crewman's table.

"We'll shove off now," the bargeman said. "All these other boats are waiting for stragglers and it's our opportunity to get the spot we want."

The duchess nodded. "I defer to the captain," she said. "Everyone, hang on. We're not sailing to America but we're going far enough. I cannot be responsible for anyone going overboard."

Finella did not think there was the least chance of it, though Lady Violet appeared alarmed. Considering the duchesses' pursed lips just now, she suspected that was why the duchess had mentioned it and was trying not to laugh.

The sails were raised and the ropes thrown off. The crew used oars to push off the pier and they gently drifted away from it as the sails gently waved back and forth. Then the bargeman swung the wheel. The sails suddenly snapped stiff and they gained speed. Finella clutched her bonnet. It was thrilling.

Chapter Eleven

The Betsy sailed out into the Thames as Finella held the rail. The bargeman turned to head toward the bridge and let the sails far out. Before he turned the boat, the bargeman pointed out the buoy that would signal the turn-around for the boats. The racers would start at the Westminster bridge, turn around at the buoy, and then to the finish back at the bridge.

Halfway between the bridge and the buoy, the bargeman turned the boat such that the sails went limp again. One of the crew threw an anchor over the side of the bow. All the crew were silent, staring at the bow, until the man turned and shouted, "She's holding!" Then another of the crew threw a second anchor off the back of the boat.

It was rougher here than it had been at the pier and the boat gently rocked. Finella quite enjoyed the sensation now that she was growing used to it. It was similar to cantering on a horse. She found it was easier to stay steady when one allowed oneself to gently rock with the waves, rather than fight against them.

Finella stood at the rail, the breeze blowing the curls out from under her bonnet. She supposed she'd look a wreck by the end of it. She did not really mind, as it felt glorious. There would be a reception in the evening at Carlton House for the winner of the regatta, but she and the duchess would have plenty of time to go home and change, and straighten out whatever had happened to her hair, ahead of it.

She had not, up until now, given much thought to the prince's reception. Her thoughts had been too taken up with wondering if she would see something yellow on the duke's boat. It seemed very far-fetched that Finella Fernsby was to go to Carlton House. She had not, as of yet, set eyes on the prince, nor had she imagined she ever would. The Duchess of Ralston, on the other hand, knew everybody and was even known at the palace.

Other barges were moving into their anchor spots. The banks of the river were filled with people wishing to view the race. The duchess claimed that a decent person was foolish to do it, as there would be more pickpockets than spectators and one would be lucky not to lose a watch or a reticule.

In the distance, on the far side of the bridge, she could see that some of the racers had already taken to the water. It was too far to see anything identifying though. For instance, anything yellow.

"Breakfast is laid, Miss Fernsby," the duchess said, calling her to the table. "Wagner has done an admirable job as our ship's steward."

Finella noticed that Wagner was looking exceedingly pleased with the compliment. She had paid close attention to how the duchess conducted herself in the house and had noticed that she handed out compliments quite often. She very much thought it was something to emulate when the time came to manage her own household. It seemed to her that the staff was always very eager to see that the duchess was pleased on account of it.

Finella took her place next to the duchess. Lord Packington and Lady Violet sat across from them. She was positively starved and did like a hearty breakfast, though she always wished it was not served quite as early as it was.

She had quite given up on starving herself to attempt to be less Rubenesque. She'd tried it one day and stuck with it the entire day and night, but she spent most of the time feeling a bit woozy. She could barely get out of bed the next morning until Lucy gave her a biscuit. After all that suffering, she'd had nothing to show for it—she looked exactly the same. She had realized that Finella Fernsby was as she was and there was nothing to be done about it. She might as well go through life well fed as opposed to feeling like she was about to tip over.

As there was no sideboard, the breakfast was laid service à la Française. Wagner really had done a very fine job, though nobody would have expected anything less from him. There were no hot eggs, but rather sliced cold eggs topped with dill. Finella helped herself to bacon, kidneys, sausages, a slice of ham, hardboiled eggs, and a buttered roll while Wagner poured her a chocolate from a tin with a towel wrapped round it.

"Goodness," Lady Violet said softly.

Finella looked up and found Lady Violet staring at her plate. The lady herself had a single piece of dry toast on her own.

"What's happened, Lady Violet?" the duchess asked. "Have you never seen breakfast before? Packington, are you starving your sister?"

"No, Your Grace," Lord Packington said, blushing for his sister.

Lady Violet obviously realized she ought not have made the comment. She hurriedly said, "I cannot manage eating anything sensible on this rocking boat, is what I meant to say. Miss Fernsby is admirably immune to the movement and waves. I quite admire it."

Finella thought there was absolutely nothing Lady Violet admired about her. She was, though, very touched by the duchesses' spirited defense and she took heart from it. The lady might feel herself superior to Finella, but she had been notified that the duchess did not agree.

Finella smiled at Lady Violet and bit into a piece of bacon by way of response.

Wagner had set up the table for the crewman, which they

seemed both surprised and pleased over. Finella bit her lip when the butler told the first fellow who approached, "Anything on this table and in that basket." Wagner pointed to the basket Lord Packington had brought.

It was not lost on Lord Packington. Between his sister managing to annoy the duchess and Wagner's utter disdain for his basket, Finella imagined he might have begun to wish he'd petitioned to get on somebody else's barge.

~ ~ ~ ~ ~

Hugh should not have been at all surprised that Seddie arrived to the house over an hour late. He overslept, his valet overslept, a neckcloth could not be found, and on and on. It was the usual shambles of Seddie-planning. His butler might have roused him, knowing full well that he was running behind time. However, that fellow had one too many experiences attempting to get Seddie out of bed, only to be met with his employer throwing everything within reach at the door.

They'd made their way to the boat as fast as was possible, though Seddie's coachman refused to push the horses to do anything dangerous on account of his employer's lack of organization. Rufus had told Seddie years ago that his first loyalty was to the horses, his second was to the grooms, his third was to the equipage, and his fourth was to whatever sir or lord he served. Seddie had not argued the point, as his coachman was rather terrifying.

By the time they got to the pier, the rest of the boats were already launched and tacking back and forth just north of the bridge that marked the start. Lord Bestwick was visible at the top of the bridge, overseeing the operation. Hugh saw him look in their direction and cross his arms, so he presumed Bestwick was annoyed at their late arrival. Hugh did not blame him, he was annoyed by their late arrival too.

Hugh and Seddie threw everything they'd brought with them into the boat, including the life rings Hugh had insisted on. They struggled to get the sails up, untied the ropes, and pushed off. They would tack the first half of the race and sail downwind on the return. The sails snapped to attention and the boat picked up speed as they made their way to the other boats.

He did not know precisely how much Seddie had learned about sailing since their last adventure, though his friend claimed it was an enormous amount. At least they seemed to be sailing in a relatively straight line this time.

As Hugh was not at this moment in danger of Seddie coming about, He untied the canvas bag with the yellow shawl and tied it round the bottom of the mast. He supposed that asking Miss Fernsby what her favorite color was, and then showing that same color, would say something direct about his intentions. Those intentions were more clear than ever. After having that lovely and soft lady in his arms to remove her from the danger of broken glass, well, he did not see what gentleman would not have firm intentions.

As he would need to stay alive to follow through on those intentions, he tied a rope through one of the life rings and the other end of it around his ankle.

Seddie looked down at his ankle. "What are you doing?"

"You know what I'm doing," Hugh said.

His friend shrugged. Hugh looked ahead. There were five boats tacking back and forth, one containing the Duke of Barstow and the valet who always crewed for him. Both of them were looking rather relaxed and confident. Hugh did not know how he, himself, appeared, but he doubted it was relaxed *or* confident. He did not imagine he and Seddie had even a remote chance of winning. As far as he was concerned, the point was to survive.

Lord Bestwick was shouting out his usual speech that nobody could ever hear. In other years he'd been in a boat. This year he was high up on the bridge. It did not signify one way or another. The race would start when Bestwick stopped talking and fired his gun.

"Keep an eye on him," Seddie said. "Tell me when he raises his gun in the air."

Hugh craned his head. Bestwick was still talking. Then he could not see him as they'd sailed too close to the bridge.

The gunshot reverberated through the air.

"He raised his gun," Hugh said over his shoulder.

"Coming about!" Seddie cried in his usually dramatic manner.

Hugh ducked and moved to the other side, dragging his life ring with him. The race was on.

It came as no surprise to anybody that Barstow had ensured he was well situated for the start. He was already on the other side of the bridge and tacking to the north side of the Thames.

"We follow Barstow," Seddie said.

"Why?"

"Because he knows what he's doing."

Hugh thought that was as good a reason as any. He scanned the barges looking for Miss Fernsby. At first, he did not see her. They followed Barstow's lead and came about when Barstow did, heading toward the south side of the Thames.

Barstow's valet attempted to stare them down, clearly figuring out what Seddie was doing. Hugh presumed he meant it as some sort of condemnation, but Seddie only waved, to the valet's evident disgust.

"Coming about!" Seddie shouted.

Hugh ducked and dragged his life ring to the other side of the boat. As they got closer to the north side of the river, there she was. Miss Fernsby. The duchesses' bargeman had secured one of the prime spots. He should have known that was where they would be—the Duchess of Ralston would not settle for anything less. He could see well enough that the wind had pulled a few curls from under Miss Fernsby's bonnet. She looked lovely. He hoped she'd noticed the yellow shawl.

"There is Packington," Seddie said. "And Miss Fernsby and Lady Violet too. I wonder why they're on a barge together."

Hugh had been so taken up with the view of Miss Fernsby that he had not noticed who she was anchored with. It was very odd for Packington and his sister to be on the duchesses' barge. He did not think there was any particular connection there.

"I doubt Lady Violet will be pleased to see that we display Miss Fernsby's green," Seddie said.

Green?

"But wait, was not Lady Violet's color green too? French verte? Maybe that's another shade of green."

Hugh stared at the shawl. "That shawl is yellow. Miss Fernsby's shawl is yellow."

"No it isn't, it's green. Coming about!"

Hugh ducked and dragged his life ring to the other side. "The shopkeeper assured me it was yellow. Is it really green?"

"Green as grass," Seddie said.

Hugh launched himself to the front of the boat, wrestled the shawl off the mast and threw it overboard.

"Hold on, Finstatten! We're making our move!"

What move?

~ ~ ~ ~ ~

Finella had left her breakfast when she'd heard Lord Bestwick fire his gun for the start. She'd raced to the gunwale of the barge and squinted her eyes. The racers were still very far away so she could not see much.

The boats tacked back and forth, growing ever closer. She noted the Duke of Barstow in the lead as she'd already been informed that particular duke would show a red silk for his red-haired duchess.

And then following him, Sir Edward and the Duke of Greystone. Yes, there they were, and they carried a shawl wrapped around the mast. Finella blinked back a sudden burst of water that had made its way to her eyes. There was no yellow shawl. It was green. Very clearly green. As green as green ever was.

"Goodness," Lady Violet said, "Your Grace, it seems we chose the same color as our favorite."

"Lady Violet?" the duchess said.

Lord Packington answered for his sister. "I mentioned to the duke that my sister's color was French verte, but he apprised me that you had asked him to fly your own color, Your Grace. Of course, green is a rather common color even when you call it French verte."

Finella felt frozen. First the duke would fly a color for the duchess though she'd not heard the duchess even mention a color, and then he showed Lady Violet's color. What he had not shown was yellow.

She felt humiliated over what she'd thought, embarrassed by what she'd hoped. Why was she always allowing her imagination to run wild? She'd reined herself in and forced herself to be realistic and practical. Then she'd seen the duke in the park and she'd allowed her imagination to go off on a gallop again. She really must be full of herself to have done it.

It was an odd thought, as she'd always thought she had a lack of confidence. Even the duchess had thought so. But deep inside, she must be very impressed with herself to have imagined the duke had asked her about her favorite color for any particular reason. The poor gentleman had just been making conversation and she'd made so much of it, mooning over it with Lucy. It had really been very conceited.

"Miss Fernsby," the duchess said, "come with me to the bow. I believe we will have a better view there."

Despite not being addressed, Lady Violet had nodded at the suggestion. Lord Packington grabbed his sister's arm and held her back. Finella was grateful for it, as the last person whose company she would seek out just now was Lady Violet's.

They proceeded to the bow and looked over the Thames. Finella gripped the gunwale until her fingers turned white. It was rather painful, which was a welcome distraction. She attempted to look interested in the regatta. The sailors had passed them by and were heading toward the turnaround buoy.

"Miss Fernsby," the duchess said, "I cannot quite imagine what has happened here. I have never indicated a particular color to the duke and I do not know why he should tell Lord Packington that I did. Further, I was certain he was set on showing a yellow shawl."

Finella found herself in better control of her feelings than she would have imagined. She supposed that having been both insulted several times and recognizing her own foolishness several times since she'd come to Town had in some way toughened her up.

"It is no matter, Your Grace. The duke is free to display whatever color he chooses. Perhaps it is not for us to wonder why."

"Well I do wonder why," the duchess said, sounding unconvinced.

"I believe I know what's happened. The duke asked about my favorite color just to make conversation. Yes, I really do think that is all that happened. After all, it was Sir Edward who talked about showing colors on the boats, not the duke. Perhaps it is Sir Edward who shows the green for a lady. Or perhaps the duke shows the French verte. Whatever the case, it matters not."

The duchess was shaking her head throughout. She suddenly stopped her headshaking and pointed. "What in the world?"

Finella followed the duchesses' pointing. It was, at first, hard to make out what was happening. The Duke of Bartow's boat had rounded the buoy and let out its sails to head downwind for the finish. The other five boats trailed behind, all aiming for that buoy, though she did not see how anybody would catch up to the leader at this point. Nor did she care who won this stupid regatta.

Then she saw what had captured the duchesses' attention. The second boat had rounded the buoy. It was Sir Edward and he was standing up in his boat. The Duke of Greystone was nowhere to be seen.

Until she saw him.

He was in the water. For some reason, Sir Edward was continuing to sail and was towing the duke behind him. The duke was on his back and it appeared as if there were a rope around his ankle, attaching him to the boat. All evidence of the green scarf was gone and Finella presumed it had gone over the side with him.

"I wonder why they are doing that," Finella said.

"I *would* wonder, but with Sir Edward at the helm, any ridiculous thing is possible," the duchess said. "Look there, the duke was nearly run over by one of the other boats."

Finella knew she should feel very concerned at what she was viewing. But somehow, she felt a quiet satisfaction.

"Serves him right," the duchess said.

That was her thought exactly.

Chapter Twelve

The last thing Hugh had heard before he was flung off the boat was Seddie shouting, "Hold on, Finstatten. We're making our move."

He had not the first idea of what the move was. No move had ever been discussed. Furthermore, Seddie had not said 'coming about,' which would have alerted him to the fact that the boom was about to swing his way.

Once again, he'd been flung off the boat. As he'd tied the life ring around his ankle, it was supposed to come with him. He might have congratulated himself on his foresight, had not the life ring caught on a cleat attached to the gunwale. As it had, he found himself dragged along by the rope round his ankle.

Seddie had looked behind him and yelled, "Just let me get round the buoy and then I'll get you back onboard."

Hugh used his arms in some sort of backward paddle to keep his head above water. He was going to kill Seddie. As soon as he got out of this mess and got the feeling back in his arms, the man was as good as dead.

They reached the buoy and Seddie shouted "coming about" to no purpose whatsoever, as he was only signaling himself to duck at this point. Hugh was swung through the water as other boats were heading toward him fast. He paddled furiously as the bow of another of the sloops managed to miss his head by inches. They rounded the buoy and the sails were let out for the downwind leg. Seddie reached behind him while keeping one hand on the tiller and starting to haul him in by the rope.

Hugh reached the gunwale and clutched at it. He hung on and used the last of his strength to pull himself over the side, rolling to the bottom of the boat. The operation had slowed them down and now two other boats passed by them.

Seddie let out a long sigh. "We'll never win now."

Hugh sat up, coughing to clear his lungs. "You know what else is a never? I will never, and I mean never, set foot on a boat with you again."

Seddie seemed surprised to hear it. "I told you we were making our move."

"You did not say what the move was or that you were coming about," Hugh said.

"I thought that was obvious."

"Not obvious," Hugh said, untying the rope from around his ankle.

"I meant to go over the whole plan before the race started," Seddie said. "But then we were running late."

We were running late. That was rather rich.

"I attempted to make a quick turn to cut in front of Barstow." Seddie shrugged. "It might have worked, but with the drag behind the boat..."

It was extraordinary. Somehow, Hugh was responsible for failing to get ahead of Barstow.

This whole day had been one disaster after the next. That shopkeeper where he'd bought the shawl had sworn it was yellow. Sunny yellow, he'd said. Hugh presumed the fellow did not have a yellow shawl to sell but when he realized Hugh could not differentiate the colors, he'd been happy to pawn off a green one.

If that was not bad enough, Seddie had once more managed to dump him in the Thames and then had the unmitigated gall to blame him for slowing down the boat. As for whose fault it was that he was dragged by his ankle, well that was probably Seddie's fault too, as Hugh would never have tied himself to a life ring if he'd not been knocked off the boat the first time.

"I can see you are aggravated," Seddie said as they drifted downwind.

"That does not begin to describe it," Hugh said wringing out his coat. The day was not as cold as the first time he'd gone swimming, but the water of the Thames was. He was freezing.

"Now, I will just remind you that I did not hold a grudge that time you burnt my eyebrow off and it took months to look right again."

Hugh felt like he might have to pay for that particular crime forever. Seddie mentioned it for any and all occasions. They'd been ten years old and chasing each other with lit candles, what else could have been the result of it? At first, they had not even realized what happened, but when Seddie took a cloth to wash off the soot, his brow came with it. Seddie had looked highly ridiculous for months and had been teased mercilessly over it. Some of the village boys had begun calling him "One Brow Bromley." Seddie's mother had been distraught and examined the area of the missing brow every day for evidence of growth, as she'd been worried the hair would not grow back. On the other hand, Hugh still remembered Browning's silent look of amusement over it, as he had not liked Seddie even back then.

Barstow had pulled far ahead. He would win the regatta once more. They were set to come in fourth out of six. Hugh supposed he ought to be just grateful that he was still alive.

"Here," Seddie said, handing him his dry coat and a flask. "I brought the good brandy for just such a situation."

Just such a situation. Hugh could not help but laugh. If he did not wish for a friend who would dump him in the Thames on occasion he should never have connected himself to Seddie. He had nobody to blame but himself.

He put on the coat and took a long swig of the brandy. "I may have to kill the shopkeeper who sold me a green shawl, claiming it was yellow."

"It was supposed to be yellow?"

"Yes, Miss Fernsby said it was her favorite color."

"Ah, I hadn't really paid attention. Are you set on a pursuit, then?"

Hugh nodded. "I did not expect to meet a lady I wished to wed. I've been looking and looking. And then, there she was."

"I am of the same mind regarding Lady Genevieve. There she was."

"We've known Lady Genevieve since we were children."

"Yes, but she was a girl. Then all of the sudden she turned into a lady and there she was." Seddie suddenly got a faraway look, as he often did when he was trying to remember something. "Wait a minute, this green shawl might be a bigger problem than it looks."

"Why?"

"French verte. Remember? Packington said Lady Violet's color was French verte before you made up that story about the duchess telling you what color to fly. Verte is green. Lady Violet is going to think you flew her color."

Hugh took another swig of brandy in honor of another problem. At least he'd thrown the French verte over the side and into the Thames.

In the meantime, his ankle was beginning to throb and swell.

~ ~ ~ ~ ~

Mr. Browning had woken far too early that morning. That,

combined with having a terrible time getting to sleep the night before, made him exhausted. Of course, he knew the cause. It was a guilty conscience! He had betrayed the duke! The yellow shawl had been switched to green. Lady Gaddington had done it, but he'd stood by and allowed it. He was complicit in the crime. He was a criminal. A rogue butler-criminal.

He reasoned with himself that he'd had no choice in the matter. He had always acted in the duke's interests, and he did so now. Even when the going got difficult, he would act in the interests of the Finstattens. He had explained the whole thing to God when he'd said his prayers, those prayers primarily consisting of a request not to get caught.

Though the idea that he acted in the interests of the Finstattens somewhat soothed him, he spent the day pacing the front hall. The plot of the switched shawls was going forward. What was happening at the regatta? If there was one downside to being a butler, it was that one could rarely be on the scene, unless the scene was in the house and the butler pretended to be doing something nearby.

Anything could be happening. Sir Edward might take another run at killing the duke. The duke might somehow realize that Mr. Browning had been involved in switching the shawls. The regatta would be over by now. Whatever was to happen had happened. What had gone on? He did not like a mystery, he did not like to be in the dark.

He glanced at the other mystery, which was a letter lying on the hall table. A letter from Carlton House had arrived only a few minutes ago. A letter from the prince, himself. The prince was not in the habit of writing the duke. They traveled in very different spheres. The duke did not mind the prince so much, but he did find most of his inner circle irritating, especially Mr. Brummel. The duke and Mr. Browning were in firm agreement over Mr. Brummel, though Browning had never alerted the duke to this meeting of the minds. That fellow thought too highly of himself and who was he? Just a fellow who tortured his valet by taking half the day to get dressed.

But why had the prince sent a letter unexpectedly, on the very day of the regatta? A letter sent the very day the prince was to host a party for the regatta? Could it be a coincidence? There was no such thing as coincidence. Something had happened.

Perhaps the duke and Sir Edward had won the regatta? No, that was absurd. Sir Edward had been at the helm. They had a better chance of sailing off the edge of the world.

Did the prince send letters of condolence? Was the duke dead? Was he drowned at the hands of the incompetent and careless Sir Edward?

Mr. Browning knew he needed to calm himself, as his thoughts were taking a dark and not very sensible turn. He lived in terror that the duke would die before producing an heir and it influenced his thoughts terribly. He knew he should stop pacing. The footmen were becoming alarmed. They were used to calm Mr. Browning who faced every situation with equanimity. Now they were faced with pacing and mopping his brow Mr. Browning. It would not do.

Then he heard it. A carriage. Browning flung open the doors, determined to understand what he was up against. If the duke was dead, he must know. If his participation in the shawl switching was known, he must own it. Or at least plausibly deny it. That which could not be avoided must be faced.

He paused in the doorframe. Sir Edward was helping the duke walk. The duke hopped on one leg *and* he was soaked through. Again! He was at least alive, and no thanks to Sir Edward he was sure.

"Your Grace," Mr. Browning said, hurrying forward. "What has happened?"

"Just the usual, Browning," the duke said. "Seddie knocked me into the Thames again, except *this* time, I had a rope tied round my ankle and was dragged behind the boat."

"He tied the rope on his ankle, not me," Sir Edward said.

Mr. Browning stared at Sir Edward with a look that he dearly hoped said, "You are a menace, Sir."

He took the duke's other arm and shouted for his footmen. "Jimmy, set off for Sir Henry this instant and inform him that the duke has been injured in the company of Sir Edward. Again."

"I'm not certain my name needs to be mentioned," Sir Edward said.

"I would argue against calling on Sir Henry," the duke said, "but I would like to know if there are any broken bones."

"I should say so, Your Grace," Mr. Browning said. "One cannot be dragged through the Thames and imagine there has been no damage." He leaned back to look around the duke at Sir Edward. "Damage," he said grimly, "to the duke's person."

Sir Edward determinedly avoided his eye, which said all Mr. Browning needed to know about this latest disaster.

They got the duke into the house and up the stairs, all the while Sir Edward claiming six ways to Sunday that there couldn't be any broken bones, and he did say they were going to make their move, and no sailor ties a rope around their ankle, and he did get the duke back onboard as soon as they had rounded the buoy.

Mr. Browning could not imagine the shocking scene that had transpired. For all of London to see, too.

The duke's valet arrived and between him and Mr. Browning, they got the duke out of his wet clothes, into dry nightclothes, and onto the bed. The coat the duke wore was relatively dry, unlike the rest of his clothes. Once he was informed that the coat was in fact Sir Edward's, he threw it on the floor as a statement. It was done as if he did not pay much attention to it, as if he was all eyes on the duke. But Sir Edward would perceive the message. Then he accidentally stepped on it for good measure. A butler must have his methods of expressing his feelings.

Mr. Browning directed the valet to gently lift the duke's leg, and he slid a pillow underneath his ankle. He was no physician, but he did at least know that if an extremity was injured, that extremity ought to be propped up. It looked terribly swollen and Mr. Browning prayed the duke was not to be left with a permanent limp.

He would very much like to push Sir Edward out the nearest open window. He could not do that, he did not think, as it would be hard to say it was an accident. He turned to Sir Edward and said coldly, "Sir Edward?"

"Ah yes, well I'll be off then," Sir Edward said. "Finstatten, shall I come by at seven to pick you up?"

"Pick him up?" Mr. Browning said, incredulous.

"For the prince's party, Browning," the duke said. "I think I'd better skip it, considering."

At the mention of the prince's party, Mr. Browning recalled that there was a letter from the prince waiting downstairs. With any luck, the letter was to cancel the party. Perhaps there had been a flood or fire at Carlston House and the party would not go forward.

"Your Grace, that reminds me," he said. "A letter from Carlton House arrived here not too long ago. Benjamin, do go down and fetch it for His Grace. I imagine something has happened and the party is called off."

"What could happen?" Sir Edward said.

"Unexpected things do happen," Mr. Browning said. "I certainly had not expected His Grace to be thrown off a boat. Twice. Or dragged behind a boat. As examples of the unexpected."

The duke snorted. Sir Edward said nothing, but Mr. Browning was satisfied that he'd made his point in a particularly pointed manner.

The footman, meanwhile, had set off to fetch the letter. While he was gone, Sir Edward went to great lengths to claim the duke's ankle did not look "that bad" and the chance of anything broken was "very remote" and the swelling looked like it was "going down."

Browning counted on his expression to communicate his utter disdain for every single one of Sir Edward's opinions.

Benjamin carried in a silver salver with the prince's letter and presented it to the duke. His Grace opened it and read through it. "Blast," he said.

"Blast, Your Grace?" Mr. Browning asked.

"Here you go, Browning. Read it aloud for Seddie, so he can really take in the royal impressions of his seamanship," the duke said.

Browning took the letter, with high hopes that Sir Edward was moments away from being pulverized by royal disapproval.

Duke—

We had the pleasure of attending Lord Bestwick's regatta today. Never have we viewed such original seamanship. We certainly had never imagined an interesting swim being included in the display. We were, at first, rather affronted. But then we realized we ought to be of good cheer, remembering that you and Sir Edward have nothing whatsoever to do with our fine English navy. Had that not been the case, I am confident we'd all be speaking French by now. The captain and crew of The Contessa *will be in receipt of a special award this evening. Be in attendance to collect it. That is a command.*

George R.

Jimmy burst into the room breathless. "Sir Henry is on his

way, Mr. Browning."

~ ~ ~ ~ ~

After she'd noted the green scarf on the duke's boat, the rest of the time spent on the barge had been deeply uncomfortable for Finella. She'd watched Sir Edward haul the duke back on the boat, still with no idea how he'd got into the water in the first place. Though she had at first felt a quiet satisfaction over the duke in the water, that had faded and worry had taken its place. What if he had breathed in water? She understood that could be very dangerous.

She and the duchess eventually rejoined Lord Packington and Lady Violet. That lady had her own theory about what happened. She posited that the shawl around the mast had come loose in the wind and the duke had made a valiant effort to retrieve it, thereby flinging himself into the Thames. Lady Violet found it very gallant.

Finella supposed that might have been the case, though it did not explain how the duke ended up being dragged through the water, courtesy of a rope around his foot.

By her tone, Finella guessed that Lady Violet was supremely confident that the shawl the duke had displayed had been French verte in her honor. She was enormously flattered that he'd jumped in after it, though she could not know for certain that was the case.

Finella did not know if the lady was right to be flattered, but she did think French verte was a stupid name for a color.

They had disembarked the barge and began to make their way back to the waiting carriages. It was crowded on the pier. People may have straggled early in the morning but now that the regatta was over, everybody seemed in a hurry to leave.

She did not know where he'd come from, but suddenly Sir Roger was by her side. The duchess was ahead of her as Lord Packington had leant his arm to go up the stone steps. "Miss

Fernsby. Did you enjoy the regatta?" he asked, holding out his arm when they reached the bottom step.

She did not really require his arm, but it would be rude to ignore it. She laid her gloved hand as lightly as she could on the sleeve of his coat. She had no wish to feel his arm.

"Yes, it was very nice," she said vaguely.

"I suppose for the ladies the interest is in noting what colors the gentlemen carried."

She did not answer that, as what was there to say? She'd said yellow and he'd flown green.

In a lower voice, Sir Roger said, "I understand Lady Violet advertised far and wide that she favored some kind of French green. Seems like the duke took her up on it."

Finella did not answer that either.

"Well I suppose as an earl's daughter she can shoot that high. The rest of us, though…"

Was that a hint to her? That she ought not shoot too high? Perhaps she ought not shoot too high, but she would not shoot too low either. The too low was most definitely Sir Roger.

Fortunately, they'd reached the top of the stone steps. The duchess had sent Lord Packington and Lady Violet on their way. She turned around and frowned. "Sir Roger," she said.

And with that simple statement, she sent Sir Roger on his way too. It seemed to be the power of a duchess that she could send a gentleman on his way just by saying his name in a certain tone. Sir Roger had whispered, "Your Grace," and then scurried off like a mouse in view of a cat.

During the carriage ride home, the duchess had said, "I do not know why the duke had a green shawl on his boat, but I do know one thing—it was not in honor of Lady Violet. The man positively fled from the girl in the park. She deludes herself to think otherwise, poor soul."

Finella supposed that could be true, but what did it matter? It was not a yellow shawl. There might have been a dozen ladies who told the duke they preferred green. She'd very stupidly allowed herself to imagine she might see a yellow shawl and she had not. Perhaps she should be grateful. If he had flown a yellow shawl she would have leapt to the conclusion that it had been in her honor, but there might be a dozen other ladies who'd claimed yellow as their favorite. She was all but certain she would have embarrassed herself in some manner.

When they'd arrived home, Lucy took the news of the green shawl rather hard. Far harder than Finella had thought she would. She'd imagined Lucy would think her silly for thinking she might see a yellow shawl. She had not thought Lucy would view herself as personally injured.

"He's ruined everything," Lucy said, throwing Finella's gloves on the bed.

Chapter Thirteen

Lucy was stomping round the room after having declared that the duke had ruined everything.

"I'm not sure there was anything to ruin," Finella said.

"Nothing to ruin? I had it all planned out! You were to wed the duke and then very naturally you would need the services of a lady's maid forevermore and here I am already doin' the job. I was to go swanning around as the lady's maid to a duchess, lookin' down on all the other lady's maids. I was gonna set myself apart from the housemaids, as I was above them. I was gonna take on a refined air and only the butler and the housekeeper would command my notice. I was gonna return home to collect my things and watch everybody marvel at my step up in life. I was even gonna ask for an increase in wages, as you were a duchess. He's ruined it all."

Gracious, that was quite the plan. "Lucy, I am sorry you are to be disappointed, but I will wed somebody at some point. I'm fairly sure I will. If he is well off enough to support the wages of a proper lady's maid, rest assured the position is yours."

"If he is well off enough to afford it?" Lucy asked sounding very incredulous over the idea. "How low were you planning to look?"

"Lucy, there are many fine gentlemen who find themselves in straits for one reason or another. It has nothing to do with low."

"Oh aye. Let's just stroll down the street and capture a local vicar, he'll be in straits. Or how about an army man? He'll be in straits *and* we'll be dragged from place to place. Or any younger son will probably do—he'll be in straits and cursing his birth order for good measure."

"My father already warned me off wedding a vicar and I do not know any gentlemen in the army."

Lucy had shrugged. "That leaves the second son, then. Or even the third son, as long as we're going low. Just seems a shame to go from a duke down to a third son with no prospects whatsoever who will be faced with becoming a vicar or joining the army so you ended up with one of those fellows anyway."

Finella could not argue with that. However, it was the real world she lived in. She was beginning to think that Lucy could be just as fanciful as she had been. The two of them together had gone along with their heads in the clouds. They had been two naïve young ladies who were becoming acquainted with the realities of life very fast.

Hours later, after many complaints and dire warnings about third sons, Lucy helped her into her dress for the party at Carlton House. She had originally thought she would wear a soft yellow satin with a netting overlay in the same shade. It was one of the dresses Madame Beaumont had composed for her and it fit to perfection. She had at first wondered about the color, as her dressmaker at home had advised darker colors for her silhouette, but the duchess said the yellow announced confidence. Finella decided yellow was firmly out for now. There was no reason to remind herself of her foolishness over wishing to see a yellow shawl on the duke's boat.

Instead, she chose a dress that better suited her mood, it was a lightweight velvet in a soft grey. It had once been highly decorated with blue paste jewels around the neckline, but Madame Beaumont had ensured that it had all been removed and replaced with a subtle braided edging. Finella missed the sparkle, as it really had been pretty, but she had begun to appreciate elegant simplicity more than she had done. In any case, this subdued iteration suited her mood.

All the while that Lucy composed her hair and helped her into her dress, her maid complained about the low gentleman with no money because he was in straits they were going to be forced to put up with.

Before she'd gone downstairs, the duchess had knocked on her door and come in. "Ah, that is just the dress that will match with this little bauble." The duchess handed her a white velvet box.

Finella opened it. It was a divine very delicate platinum necklace with a large topaz surrounded by chip diamonds. "Your Grace?"

"I never wear it and I've noticed that all you seem to have with you is that gold cross. A cross is all well and good, but a lady does require some stones of her own."

"But it is too expensive. I'm not sure my father—"

"Your father is a very agreeable gentleman, in my experience," the duchess said. "Now really, put it on and say no more about it. It suits your coloring, and in any case, I have boxes and boxes of jewelry and not enough years left to wear it all."

Lucy had put it round Finella's neck and did the clasp. She examined it in the looking glass, its pale blue almost translucent and sparkling in the candlelight. It was glorious. She'd never owned a real piece of jewelry of such quality. It had the effect of making her feel very grown. The duchess really was exceedingly kind. The lady clearly made an attempt to cheer her up after what they had viewed, or had *not* viewed as it was, at the regatta. She was determined to repay the lady by keeping her head high and a smile on her face.

As Finella and the duchess entered Carlton House, she took a deep breath to steady herself. No more fantasies or imaginings. She would not do anything like it again no matter how polite the duke was. For that was really it, was it not? He was nice to her, as she was sure he was nice to everyone, and she'd lost her wits over it.

She was a grown lady with middling looks who wore a subdued grey velvet dress and a spectacular topaz necklace. Those were the facts, and facts were to be her constant companion from now on.

Finella had known what she was when she'd come to Town and it was high time she remembered it. She was just Finella Fernsby and she would not be walking into Carlton House were it not for a kind neighbor who happened to be a duchess.

~ ~ ~ ~ ~

Hugh stared at the wheeled chair. It was preposterous.

He'd been carried down the stairs and now he waited for Seddie to pull up with his carriage. He was to be carried to the carriage and this monstrosity was to be tied to the back of it.

That afternoon, Sir Henry had been to the house and had thoroughly examined his ankle. It was his opinion that there were no broken bones. Yet. There was a severe sprain and the physician was afraid there had been a small fracture. If Hugh were to put weight on it, that fracture might worsen.

Sir Henry was stern in his directions and told him in no uncertain terms that he was not to put any weight on it for at least a month. Then he'd wrapped it securely and ordered more pillows to raise it.

That was when Hugh had broken the bad news about being commanded to Carlton House that evening. Sir Henry had waved it off. He was certain the matter could not be pressed if the prince was informed of the duke's condition.

Hugh knew otherwise, though. The prince planned some jest or entertainment at his expense and would be livid if he did not turn up. Knowing the prince's temperament, and some of the friends he currently surrounded himself with, if Hugh were dead and buried it would not be considered a good enough excuse. One way or another, he had to appear. The prince must have his amusements.

Once Sir Henry was convinced of it, he said the only way Hugh could attend was in a wheeled chair. Attempting to put weight on his ankle could lead to far bigger and possibly permanent problems.

Hugh had argued for a cane.

Sir Henry shook his head dolefully.

Then he'd argued for crutches.

Sir Henry was adamant that neither would do. There was too much risk of accidentally putting weight on that foot, especially in the early days before the bone even had a chance to knit. It must be a wheeled chair. He then assured Hugh that he would arrange it, which he had.

Unfortunately, what the physician had sent to the house was the only wheeled chair he had on hand. The note said it had been donated by the family of an old dowager. It might appear a bit on the feminine side, Sir Henry wrote, but it would hold his weight just fine.

A *bit* on the feminine side? The back was carved into flowers and vines and painted pink and green. The seat was covered in tufted pink satin cushioning.

"It is not so bad, Your Grace," Browning said.

Hugh stared at him.

"All right it is so bad but just think of the alternative. Sir Henry was very clear about the danger. Your mother, the dear departed duchess, could not bear to see you with a permanent limp."

Hugh was not sure that souls that had passed to the great beyond concerned themselves with who was limping around on earth.

"In any case," Browning said, "when you sit on it, most of the pink satin will be covered."

Hugh nodded, resigned to looking ridiculous. "By the by, Browning, while I think of it, I want you to write a letter of stern complaint to the proprietor of Handel's on Oxford Street. The fellow they employ there sold me a green shawl while claiming it was a yellow shawl. It seems as soon as the fellow realized I could not tell the difference, he felt free to do it."

Browning staggered back, stumbled, and fell over a bench.

Hugh stared down at his sprawled butler. "It's not that shocking, Browning. It would not be the first time a tradesman attempted to get over on a person. They have no compunction over lying when it comes to selling their wares."

There was a sharp rap on the door, and the footman opened it to Seddie. His friend looked around. "Browning, what do you do on the floor?"

Mr. Browning got up and dusted himself off, apparently not deigning to be interrogated by Seddie.

"Jimmy," Browning said, "help Sir Edward carry the duke to the carriage. I will supervise the grooms in attaching the chair to the back."

This seemed to be the moment that Seddie noticed the chair, as he laughed hysterically.

"Just get on with it," Hugh said. "This is, all of it, your fault."

Seddie tapped his right eyebrow to remind Hugh of the time he burnt it off.

It had been quite the operation to get Hugh into the carriage and the chair securely roped to the back of it. A groom was to ride on the running board alongside the chair to ensure it did not fall off. Or stop the carriage if it did.

The ride to Carlton House was filled with Seddie's

attempts to jolly him along. It was as it always was between them. Hugh was eventually talked round into forgiving him. After all, two men who had been friends since childhood were bound to have almost killed one another dozens of times. It was just the nature of the thing. It also occurred to Hugh that he'd placed himself in that situation when he should have known better about getting on that boat.

Arriving at Carlton House demanded another convoluted operation in getting the chair untied from the back of the carriage and him into it. It was irritating in the extreme, but Hugh put up with it. He had no wish to end up lame for life because he failed to follow Sir Henry's instructions.

In any case, he had more important things to think about. As ridiculous as he would appear at this moment, he must seek out Miss Fernsby. He must say something to Miss Fernsby about the green shawl. He had not thought up precisely what that would be, but he wished to communicate the message that he'd intended to display yellow.

He supposed he'd have to tell her about the peculiarity of his vision. Daltonism, as it was formally called. He wondered if she would hold it against him. She might not care that he was blind to certain colors, but might she not worry about her children inheriting it? It was a deficiency. Browning liked to claim it was some mark of a true Finstatten as if it were a hallmark of perfection, but then Browning thought everything about the Finstattens was perfection, excepting only his sister Lucinda.

Hugh paused. He might be getting ahead of himself. He had not reason to think that Miss Fernsby might be imagining children with him. He had not imagined it himself until this moment. Though now it seemed as if the idea had been there all along and he'd just got round to noticing it.

"There we go, all tucked in," Seddie said once he was settled in the chair. "Should we take one of the blankets from the carriage and drape it across your lap to protect you from a chill, Grandmama?"

"You ought to remember I will not always be incapacitated," Hugh said.

"Too soon for a jest, I see that now," Seddie said, wheeling him in.

The prince was in the receiving line, flanked by Lord Alvanley and Mr. Brummel. Hugh could already see Brummel's raised brow, that irritating idiot. He really did not understand what the prince saw in the fellow. Hugh did not mind that he was a relative nobody, what he minded was that Brummel viewed himself as a very special somebody who was far above everybody else. He suspected that Brummel even thought himself above the prince. He also thought the prince was bound to notice it at some point, and that would be the end of Brummel.

"Your Royal Highness," Hugh said, executing a ridiculous half bow from his chair.

"Duke, what's happened to you? Have you broken something from your adventure in the water today?"

"Just a suspected fracture, Sir Henry says," Hugh answered.

The prince's eyes drifted to Sir Edward.

Seddie bowed, "Your Royal Highness."

"You are a dangerous sort of fellow, Sir Edward. Duke, I give you credit for coming in such a condition."

Hugh nodded, and resisted mentioning that he'd been commanded to appear.

Lord Alvanley, one of the few of the prince's inner circle that Hugh liked, nodded approvingly and said, "Very stoic, Your Grace."

Mr. Brummel peered down his nose and said, "Interesting

conveyance."

Hugh lifted his chin and replied, "I'd like to repay the compliment and note something interesting about *you*, but I am at a loss. I cannot quite recall your name, old fellow, though I believe it is a mister?"

This caused a snort from the prince and raucous laughter from Alvanley. Brummel was positively red in the face. Hugh did not much care. If Brummel wanted to cross verbal swords with him, he was happy to parry back. He suspected that would be the last time Brummel tried it. The fellow depended on people being intimidated by his judgments and when they were not, he had no real weapons.

Seddie wheeled him through the crowd to the refreshments room. He handed him a glass of claret.

"Ah," Seddie said, "she has finally arrived to Town."

Hugh looked about and spotted Lady Genevieve. As she was from their own neighborhood, they'd known her forever. First, she'd been horrible because she was a girl, then she'd been frightening because she was a girl, then she'd been deeply admired by Seddie because she was a woman. Hugh presumed Seddie would win her over at some point, though for now she kept him at arm's length. She was the only person Hugh knew of who called his friend Edward, and usually in a condemning, scolding, or disgusted tone. Lady Genevieve did not approve of what she referred to as "hijinks," and she had told Seddie in no uncertain terms to alert her immediately when he decided to act like a grown man. Hugh did not really blame her for it.

As for Seddie, Hugh got the idea that his friend did not at all mind being scolded by Lady Genevieve. He also claimed he did not know what would be involved in satisfying the lady's demands, but she was bound to give them up as hopeless at some point and just take him as he was.

"She looks annoyed to see me," Seddie said. "I'd best go to

her."

Before he knew it, Hugh was left alone as Seddie made a beeline toward the lady.

He had not really worked out how he was to move through Carlton House. He'd not really thought through the idea that he'd require a pusher for his chair. Perhaps he'd just assumed Seddie would do the duty, which had probably been a foolish assumption. If Hugh had known Lady Genevieve would make an appearance, he'd have known for certain it was a foolish assumption. It was unlikely Seddie would give him another thought and he'd be lucky to be remembered when it was time to depart.

It was bloody awkward. He did not have such a close friendship with anybody else here that would allow him to demand they push his chair. He should have brought a footman. At least he'd been handed a glass of claret before he'd been abandoned.

Hugh tried using his good foot to move the chair forward. It worked. A little. He'd managed to move himself forward a few inches. It was entirely awkward. He would have a chair that he could wheel himself as soon as it was ready, but for now he was stuck in the old dowager's chair. That lady had apparently had no interest in producing her own propulsion. The wheels were situated too far back to try it.

As he was considering what other strategy he might employ, he heard her. Lady Violet. If he'd been on his feet, he might have sped out of the room, pretending he did not hear her. He was trapped in his chair.

"Your Grace! You are injured," she cried, fluttering into the refreshments room.

"Lady Violet," he said, recalling that he did not just have to convince Miss Fernsby that the green shawl had been a mistake, but Lady Violet too. He would not like that lady to get ideas and she seemed to be an expert at getting ideas.

"And look here, nobody attends the injured man," Lady Violet said. "Never fear, Your Grace, you did not dive into the river for nothing! It was very gallant, though."

At first, Hugh could not imagine what had seemed gallant about ending up in the River Thames. Then it dawned on him that Lady Violet might imagine he'd jumped into the sea chasing after the shawl he'd thrown over the side.

Before he could say anything about it, Lady Violet got behind his chair and pushed him forward. "I must show you the prince's music room, it is most interesting."

"I have seen that room, Lady Violet."

"Excellent."

He was wheeled round people at speed, as if he were an express mail coach. How in the world had he fallen into the hands of Lady Violet? How was he to extricate himself without offending Packington? Where was Packington and why did he not keep a closer eye on his younger sister?

~ ~ ~ ~ ~

Finella had got through it. She'd met the prince. She thought she'd acquitted herself well enough, at least with His Royal Highness. The prince seemed fond of the duchess and as often happened, he seemed inclined to think well of any lady a friend of his chose to dispense favor upon. Lord Alvanley was very cordial too and seemed a rather genial sort of person.

Mr. Brummel was another thing entirely. Finella was very attuned to looks of disapproval or distaste. That particular skill was not needed in this case. The look of disdain on Mr. Brummel's expression was clear enough.

Had she been a bold sort of person, which she most certainly was not, she might have said…well she did not know what she would have said. She would probably have blurted out that he was an asparagus, to no purpose whatsoever.

The duchess, on the other hand, was rather falcon-eyed and had not missed the moment. She said, "Brummel, I can see well enough that your valet has tied your neckcloth too tight again. It gives you an off-putting expression. I do not know why you put up with it."

Both the prince and Lord Alvanley laughed at the salvo. As Finella and the duchess walked away, she heard Lord Alvanley say, "You are catching it from all sides this evening. Perhaps we ought to call you Pummeled Brummel."

"I do not like that man," the duchess said in a low tone. "He thinks too much of himself and too little of everybody else."

"I believe you frightened him," Finella said.

The duchess laughed. "The privilege of an old duchess. Ah, there is Lady Souderton, do go and talk to her about The Impoverished Pupils Fund. It is right, as a newcomer to the *ton*, that you begin to involve yourself in such things. I must speak to the Marchioness of Newgarden, I have an amusing anecdote to communicate that would not be suitable for your rather innocent young ears."

Having been given her marching orders, Finella crossed the room to Lady Souderton, who was just then in conversation with another fine-looking lady.

"Ah, Miss Fernsby. Your Grace, this is Miss Fernsby, she is sponsored by the Duchess of Ralston this year. Miss Fernsby, this is the Duchess of Barstow."

Finella should have guessed it, since she had already been told that her duke flew a red silk in honor of his wife's red hair. She curtsied. "Your Grace. The duke had a rather resounding victory today."

"Yes, indeed he did and he is delighted," the Duchess of Barstow said. "When I first met him, it did not go as well and he was rather glowering at this party. It was the beginning of a rather fraught courtship between us."

Lady Souderton laughed. "You cannot claim it was more fraught than mine, though. Nobody will soon forget my determined naivete in setting up my charity."

As the Duchess of Barstow laughed and recounted the story of Lady Souderton advertising for impoverished pupils and putting her own address into the newspapers, Finella saw an extraordinary sight over the lady's shoulder. Lady Violet was wheeling the duke down a corridor.

Her heart clutched in her chest for several reasons. One, he had been injured! He was confined to a chair. And two, he was with Lady Violet. The lady had been right, he'd shown the green shawl for her.

Of course, she was not at all surprised. No, of course not. It was exactly as she'd known it would be.

"My poor father," Lady Souderton said. "He was most discomfited to understand there had been a line of men outside our door on account of the advertisement."

"Gracious," Finella said, though she'd hardly been listening. Lady Violet had just wheeled the duke into a room further down the corridor.

"How do you get on, Miss Fernsby?" the Duchess of Barstow asked. "Has anyone caught your eye?"

Someone had indeed, though she would not admit it under torture. She would not look an idiot who did not understand her own place in the world. Nobody but Lucy would ever know the first thing about her foolishness regarding the duke.

"Me? No, Your Grace. I'm afraid the duchess has put out so much effort for naught."

"I am surprised," Lady Souderton said. "Those fair curls of yours must be the envy of the season."

"I second that notion," the Duchess of Barstow said. "I must have spent most of my youth longing for fair curls. Though, my duke does prefer my more fiery shade so I must be satisfied with it."

Lady Souderton said, "What do you think, Duchess? Ought we give Miss Fernsby some hard-earned advice?"

They both laughed at the idea. The duchess said, "Let's do. Miss Fernsby, do not get in your own way, that is my advice."

Lady Souderton nodded in approval. "And avoid hardheadedness if you can."

Finella nodded as if she were taking in this advice, though she really did not think she suffered from hardheadedness. At least, it had never been mentioned to her. As for getting in her own way, it might be rather too late for that particular piece of wisdom. She had managed to cause herself no end of problems by failing to keep her wild imagination in check.

Just then, there was a dinging glass and Lord Alvanley called, "Gather round, everybody. We have a trophy to hand out. And perhaps we have another prize this year too."

Chapter Fourteen

Lord Alvanley had just announced that the prince was soon to hand out the trophy for the regatta.

"Ah, I'd best go find Barstow," his duchess said to her and Lady Souderton. "I must be on hand to cheer him on for his glorious win. I am his most fervent admirer."

The crowd all turned to the prince and Lord Alvanley. Mr. Brummel stood to the side looking discomfited. Finella wondered if he was always unhappy. She supposed one might be, if one were to dislike people all the time. Especially if one were to be taken down a peg by a duchess on account of it.

The prince said a few words in honor of the regatta and in congratulations to the Duke of Barstow, who had won several years in a row. Though the prince noted that it was beginning to seem routine that the duke would win, the duke himself seemed happy enough about it. His duchess looked delighted. What a handsome pair they were.

"Now," the prince said, "we cannot allow this moment to pass without noting a rather original occurrence at the regatta. It is not every day that one views a duke of the realm being dragged behind his boat. At least, we hope it is not every day. Where is Greystone? I see Sir Edward, where is your friend?"

"I'm not entirely sure, Your Royal Highness," Sir Edward said, standing on his toes and looking around.

Someone in the back of the crowd called out, "He was last seen being rolled down the corridor by Lady Violet."

Finella saw Lord Packington mutter something under his

breath. "I'll find them, Your Royal Highness."

"Do," the prince said. "I do not like to be kept waiting."

Lord Packington hurried down the corridor. The duchess returned to Finella's side. "What in the world," she said quietly.

"I am not certain. I only saw Lady Violet wheeling the duke down the corridor."

"That brazen little vixen," the duchess said. "She is going to get herself in a lot of trouble if her brother does not do something."

Finella was rather shocked by the duchesses' assessment. She was not sure what the lady meant by it.

Just then, she spotted Lord Packington pushing the duke back down the corridor at speed. Finella hoped the duke was not flung out of his chair. She really did think he'd taken enough falls recently.

Lord Packington came to an abrupt stop and the duke held on to the sides of the chair to keep himself in it. The prince said, "There you are, Duke."

"I apologize, Your Royal Highness, I am not presently in control of where I go. Or at what speed," the duke said, glancing up at Lord Packington.

"Very well," the prince said, nodding graciously. "I was commenting on the idea that we've witnessed some entertaining moments at Bestwick's regattas, but this is the first time we've seen a duke dragged by one foot behind his boat. For that reason, we are happy to confer on the Duke and Sir Edward the Order of the Golden Foot.

As the crowd laughed, Lord Alvanley pulled a cloth to unveil a plaster foot covered in gold leaf sitting atop a pedestal.

"I would ask that Sir Edward display this golden foot in a prominent place in his drawing room so that every person who steps into it will ask him to explain the circumstances of it."

"Yes, Your Royal Highness," a very abashed Sir Edward said.

Finella noted the lady standing by Sir Edward fold her arms and look exceedingly exasperated. On the other hand, the duke had a look of vindication, so she imagined whatever had occurred on the boat was being laid at Sir Edward's door.

"Greystone, Alvanley, Barstow and his duchess, Mrs. Fitzherbert, Brummel… and I suppose Sir Edward, we will have a small dinner in the blue velvet room. The rest of you, tables have been set up in the ballroom. Enjoy."

"This is new," the duchess said. "He has not offered a dinner in other years. I think we will not stay. The prince's food is generally high-flown, but my cook suits me better and I have seen all I wish to see this evening. We will just wait for the prince's exit and then make our escape."

Finella had nodded as she was worn out from what she had viewed. The evening was as she had expected, but thinking about something and actually seeing something were two different matters. It had been like watching a lovely dream float away, even though she knew it was a dream to begin.

Sir Edward was wheeling the duke behind the prince and Lord Alvanley. Finella could not help but to take a look at him, as he really was so glorious. He was her dream, floating ever further away.

He caught her staring and smiled and waved. She hardly knew what to do so she waved back. She was sure she looked foolish doing it.

Finella sighed. There he was, being friendly again. There she was, fanning herself over it again. She would very much like to go home and chew on a biscuit to soothe herself.

The prince's party walked by, the rest of the crowd began to head to the ballroom, and Finella and duchess took their leave.

When they got home, the duchess ordered a dinner of

sorts. Cold ham, a generous block of cheddar, rolls, the good butter brought in from her estate, and a bottle of hock.

"I am very disturbed by Lady Violet," the duchess said.

"Because she might have been alone in a room with the duke?" Finella asked. "But then, other people might have been there as well."

"She is too forward by half."

"Well, I suppose if the duke encouraged her..."

"Encouraged her? That was a kidnapping, if I'm not mistaken."

Finella chewed on a piece of ham. She was grateful beyond measure that the duchess would think so. However, she was certain the duchesses' views were being warped by her fondness for Finella. She simply could not see things for how they really were. She sympathized, as it had taken her some time to see things how they were.

When Finella retired to her bedchamber, Lucy was no better. She deemed Lady Violet a wrecker of plans, as the lady was wrecking her plans. Along with the duke, of course, who was the chief wrecker of plans.

Finella fell asleep wishing the season would end and she could just go home. Her sensible, happy self was at home.

~ ~ ~ ~ ~

Hugh had finally got back to the house after being hauled in and out of a carriage and up the stairs. He lay in bed with a glass of brandy, staring out at the moon through his windows. The day had been a disaster from start to finish. First, Seddie had managed to throw him overboard again and this time he'd come away with a fractured ankle. Second, he'd been given a ludicrous wheeled chair and had no choice but to use it. Third, try as he might, he had not had the opportunity to speak to Miss Fernsby about the green shawl. And fourth, the terrible fourth, he *did* have the opportunity to speak to Lady Violet. He was sure he was going to have trouble from Packington over it.

Lady Violet had wheeled him away against his will. At first, he'd tried to be polite about his resistance to it. It was the plague of a gentleman that he must always be polite to a lady, even when he would like to throw something at that lady's head.

Then he'd out and out asked to be wheeled back to the drawing room, but she'd just laughed it off as if he were joking. And then came the part of their exchange that was likely to cause problems with Packington.

She'd wheeled him into the music room and thank the stars there were other people already in it. Lord and Lady Hankin were cozy on a sofa. They were recently wed and Hugh had the idea they could not care less where they were, and even less about the prince's prize for the regatta.

"I think, at this point," Lady Violet said as she parked him next to a harp, "I ought to call you duke. Using 'Your Grace' is too formal."

"I do not think it is," Hugh had said. He was not going to allow her to claim an intimacy that was not there. She did not have the right to call him duke and he would not be run over about it.

She'd reacted to that statement with a...was it a giggle? He did not know. It sounded childish, whatever it was.

"Very well," she said. "Your Grace. By the by, everyone is talking about the green shawl. French verte, if I am not mistaken."

Hugh sighed. Here it was. He would have to be blunt, as no amount of hints would put off Lady Violet. He said, "Lady Violet, I am blind to certain colors. I went to the shops and purchased a yellow shawl, or so I was told. I did not know it was green until Sir Edward informed me of it. I then threw it overboard."

"Yellow?"

"Yellow."

"Why?"

Why? Was she really going to press him on this? The lady knew no bounds. "Miss Fernsby indicated her preferred color is yellow."

"Miss Fernsby!" Lady Violet all but spat out the name, as if she'd never heard anything so outrageous in her life. "The Miss Fernsby that stays with the Duchess of Ralston. *That* Miss Fernsby?"

Hugh thought it rather a ridiculous question. How many Miss Fernsbys could there be?

"Your Grace, Miss Fernsby? What about my brother's house party?" Lady Violet asked. "You were very attentive to me."

This seemed to arrest the attention of Lord and Lady Hankin. They leaned forward from their position on the sofa.

Good God, was Lady Violet attempting to accuse him of leading her on? Did Packington think it? He could not think so. Hugh had done everything possible to keep Lady Violet at arm's length. There was nothing for it, politeness would have to go out the window and the truth be told. He would not be trapped into anything by this girl.

"No, I was not attentive. You followed me all over the house and I was forced to take up reading in my room."

Lady Violet went white as snow. Packington chose that moment to hurry into the room.

"Duke, the prince is asking for you," Lord Packington said. "Let us hurry."

Hugh was once more wheeled away with no say in where he was going. And not slowly, either. He held on to the arms of the chair as they flew down the corridor.

It was lucky he was holding on, too. If he had not been,

he most certainly would have been thrown to the floor when Packington made a hard stop in the main reception room.

The prince had gone on to award he and Seddie the Order of the Golden Foot. It was all highly ridiculous, but the prince did like to have his jokes. If there were one pleasing aspect to it, it was that Seddie had been ordered to display it in his drawing room.

After that nonsense was got over, it really should have been the moment when he could speak to Miss Fernsby. But no, then he'd been wheeled away to have dinner with the prince, which he would really rather not do.

It had been tedious and long. If he'd been able to walk, he might have slipped out in the middle of it to find Miss Fernsby with the excuse that he was going to relieve himself. The prince was inordinately proud of his water closets and never minded a person visiting them so they might wonder at the modernity of his designs.

As it was, he had been stuck. It had been an odd party. Seddie was much abashed and did not say much, the prince and Mrs. Fitzherbert did not seem overfond of one another at the moment, Brummel was sullen, Hugh's ankle was throbbing, and the Duke and Duchess of Barstow were more interested in each other than anybody else. If it weren't for jolly Lord Alvanley, they would have been entirely sunk.

When he could finally make his escape, the duchess and Miss Fernsby were gone from the house. So were Packington and Lady Violet, he'd noticed. He assumed it was only a matter of time before he heard from Packington about Hugh's conversation with his sister.

What a stupid, stupid day. He did not know what tomorrow would bring, but he did know that he'd be facing it in a dowager's wheeled chair. Browning claimed he would do something with it until the new one was ready, but Hugh did not know what he could possibly do.

Hugh suddenly had an idea. He'd not carried a yellow shawl on the boat as he had planned. Perhaps he ought to send yellow flowers to Miss Fernsby. He could include a note that somehow hinted at what his intentions had been. Indeed, he could do that. Yellow daffodils would communicate a new beginning.

If anybody in the world needed a new beginning it was him.

~ ~ ~ ~ ~

When the duke had left for the prince's party and the house grew quiet, Browning had marveled at his luck. He was tasked with writing a stern letter to Handel's to rebuke them for selling the duke a green shawl while telling him it was yellow.

The duke blamed the shop! He would not be caught! The relief was palpable. He'd celebrated with a glass of sherry and then set off for the attics. He was determined to find some sort of material to re-cover the duke's chair. His Grace was to be in it for a month and a Finstatten could not be seen going round in a chair covered in pink satin.

He found an old leather wing chair pushed in a corner. That would do very well. All he need do was get a knife and cut off the leather. It would be much more suitable. He was certain he could get some paint somewhere. He thought the coachman might have some for touching up the outside of the carriage. He would paint over the ghastly green and pink paint on the back of the chair.

He'd returned after explaining to one of the footmen why he was climbing into the attic with a sharp knife and assuring the lad he did not mean to do a harm to himself. Which reminded him that he had perhaps appeared unsettled to his staff over the past weeks. He cut the leather into the approximate right-sized pieces. Then he'd had another glass of sherry to celebrate that he would not be caught!

When the duke returned to the house he was in a dark mood. Sir Edward had wheeled him into the drawing room, and they'd had their usual brandy.

From their conversation, he understood that the duke had never had a chance to speak to Miss Fernsby. More good news!

Also apparently, he *did* have the chance to speak to Lady Violet and, as he termed it, "set her straight." That was not as good news.

Both the duke and Sir Edward agreed that Lord Packington would be steamed over it. Browning was rather steamed over it too. Lady Violet had everything recommending her. Why did not the duke gravitate toward suitable ladies? It was mystifying. He might be blind to color but how was he also blind to elegant looks? That had never been a Finstatten distinction, the old duchess was elegant from head to toe.

Nevertheless, Mr. Browning had not been caught over the shawl switch and the duke had not spoken to Miss Fernsby! That was the thing to remember.

Now he settled himself into his *League* meeting, prepared to astonish his fellow butlers. They had given up, but he had persevered.

Mr. Penny, as was his habit, poured the tea and passed round the cups. Mr. Browning sipped his tea and set down his cup.

"Gentlemen," he said gravely, "prepare to be astounded."

"Astounded?" Mr. Feldstaffer said. "No, I do not like the sound of that. The last time I was astounded was the time I caught sight of my countess wearing a bright green silk turban. It was a new style she very suddenly adopted. I was not the only one astounded—the earl was positively flabbergasted. It turned out all right though. She saw his expression, cried, and took it off. Her lady's maid has it now, and she looks just as ridiculous when she puts it on."

“Aside from Lady Copperstone’s dalliance with a turban, I believe we have been astounded by more recent events,” Mr. Harkinson said with a snort. “There is not a person in this town who has not heard the story of the duke being dragged behind Sir Edward’s boat.”

“There is a print going round about it,” Mr. Rennington said. “One of my footmen showed it to me. It is a sketch of the sloop and the duke flailing in the water behind it. Which, I thought, it would be very amusing...if it were not about a duke connected to us.”

“Accidents do happen,” Mr. Penny said, nodding sympathetically.

“There is a nickname going round too,” Mr. Wilburn said, “the overboard lord.”

“Oh, I heard the Duke of Grey-drowned,” Mr. Rennington said.

“Flailing Finstatten,” Mr. Feldstaffer said, “that’s the other one. Flailing. Nobody ought to do it, in my experience.”

“And then the duke and Sir Edward were awarded the Order of the Golden Foot. It is a small statuette of a plaster foot covered on gold leaf,” Mr. Harkinson said. “Sir Edward has been ordered to display it in his drawing room.”

Mr. Browning had heard nothing about a foot statue, though he could not be opposed to it if it inconvenienced Sir Edward. But why were they all talking about this nonsense? It was not to the point. Further, it was not even the duke’s fault—it was all Sir Edward’s fault, as it always was.

“Gentlemen,” he said, “society’s tedious gossip about problems Sir Edward causes are hardly our concern. Sir Edward has always and will always cause a catastrophe wherever he goes. He is a one-person epidemic of trouble. Unfortunately, he is the duke’s oldest friend and cannot be got rid of. Believe me, I have prayed for it. Allow me to steer your minds to the actual problem at hand that needs to be solved and *can* be solved. Miss Fernsby."

He than related how the yellow shawl was switched for green and how the duke did not perceive it as he had the Finstatten distinction of being blind to those colors. He entirely omitted the part where Lady Lucinda had come with the green shawl, as that was irrelevant to the story. Miss Fernsby did not see her yellow shawl displayed. A firm message had been communicated.

"And the duke never discovered the ruse?" Mr. Wilburn asked.

"He did discover it," Mr. Browning admitted. "I believe Sir Edward told him it was green."

"But when I saw the duke, when he was in the water, you understand," Mr. Harkinson said, "there was no shawl at all visible on the boat."

Why were they focusing on the details of the thing?

"He threw it overboard," Mr. Feldstaffer said. "I wondered about that when I heard it, now it makes more sense."

Mr. Browning had not known that. He was not sorry to know it, though. The evidence of the crime was gone, drifting down the river until a scavenger spotted it and fished it out. "The point is," he said, "Miss Fernsby has not been encouraged. She did not see a yellow shawl. It is a critical turning point. Had she seen it, I do not know how the thing would have been turned round."

Mr. Penny shrugged. "It seems as if the duke could clear the whole thing up in a moment, though."

Mr. Browning looked with incredulity at Mr. Penny. Clear the whole thing up? He did not want anything cleared up!

"He'll say something," Mr. Feldstaffer said. "Then she'll know."

Say something? The duke could not be allowed to just go round saying something. The duke and Miss Fernsby were to turn away from each other, saying nothing about the cause, as any normal person would do. They were to both simmer privately, never mentioning the other again, as any rational person would do. What was this idea about clearing things up by saying something?

"And then, what was this I heard about Lady Violet?" Mr. Harkinson asked. "I have a cousin on Portland Place, butler to Lord Hoppington, it is the next door over to Lord Packington's house. He says there was a big to-do on the street last evening with Lady Violet and her brother."

Mr. Browning was far less eager to talk about that particular situation. Nevertheless, he felt rather cornered. "It seems the duke does not prefer Lady Violet. And told her so."

"He *told* her?" Mr. Feldstaffer said. He shook his head sadly. "That was a mistake. A person ought not ever tell a lady a thing she does not care to hear. They get mad about it. The countess did not speak to the earl for a week over the green turban and all he did was frown at it."

Thank you for stating the obvious, Mr. Feldstaffer.

"I wonder if there will be trouble between the duke and Lord Packington over it," Mr. Wilburn said.

Why could not his fellow butlers keep their minds on the topic at hand? The point was to ensure that the duke wed a suitable lady. The Duchess of Finstatten must be everything elegant. She must be stately, a remarkable hostess, a fascinating conversationalist with a reserved and dignified wit, she must be what the old duchess was. She would become a Finstatten, what else could she be? Nowhere in there was Miss Fernsby to be found.

Mr. Browning left the meeting feeling very like how he'd left the last one. He was on his own. He was a rogue butler.

Chapter Fifteen

When Mr. Browning had returned to the house, the duke informed him that he wished to send yellow daffodils to Miss Fernsby and had handed him the note that was to accompany the arrangement.

At that moment, Mr. Browning had been torn. On the one hand, he was accustomed to carrying out the duke's every direction to the letter. But on the other hand, he was now a confirmed rogue butler.

He hurried to his quarters and unfolded the note.

I hope for new beginnings. Greystone.

Mr. Browning had refolded the note and tapped his chin with it. He'd paced back and forth. He'd stood stock still for several minutes. He'd glanced up to the ceiling, wondering how the old duke and duchess would view it. He'd negotiated with God, explaining why the idea circling his mind was actually a good thing. Could it even be a pious thing? No, he probably could not go that far. Righteous, then.

Then, in a fit of daring, a fit of roguishness, a fit of utter insanity, he'd hurried to the florist and arranged to have the daffodils sent to Lady Violet.

He'd left that shop and collapsed into a hackney, his hands shaking as he heaved in breaths.

Going rogue was not for the faint of heart.

~ ~ ~ ~ ~

The moment Finella really dreaded in the season was creeping ever closer. The duchesses' Secrets Exposed party was on the morrow. Gentlemen of the duchesses' choosing would receive seven folded and sealed papers. They were to choose which ladies they would visit from a list of twenty ladies selected by the duchess. Each lady visited would unseal the paper, answer the question posed, and reseal it with her own house stamp. At the party, the duchess would reveal the answers she found most amusing.

The ladies were not to know what the question was until the first paper arrived. Of course, Finella was living in the duchesses' house and so had already been told.

If this gentleman was your husband, what flower would he resemble and why?

It made Finella blush to think of it. At first, her worry had been that no gentleman would hand her a paper. It would be a double humiliation. Any lady would be humiliated to be ignored, but she would have to do it sitting in the duchesses' own house. She was terrified of letting the duchess down.

But then Lucy had pointed out that would not be the case, as she did sit in the duchesses' house. There would be at least some gentlemen who would come to garner the duchesses' approval, or at least not attract the lady's ire.

That was an even worse situation! She would be a pity visit, or a duty visit. It was so embarrassing. And then, what in the world would she write? She was not clever or full of wit like some ladies were.

If she were to write her real feelings on a note, it would read something like "I do not care, my heart is broken though it is my own fault, now go away you stupid asparagus."

Finella had never even believed in the idea of a broken heart. It had always been her opinion that if one's heart was involved that deeply, then the other person's heart would be too. She had brushed off the idea of unrequited love as foolishness and assumed that sort of thing must be only an infatuation that would be quickly got over. How in the world would she ever get over the duke, though? She suspected that she would eventually wed and that she would be very fond of the gentleman, whoever he might be. But she would never feel this. She would always think of the duke.

Much to her dismay, it seemed she'd been wrong about unrequited love. She could not stop thinking about the duke. She'd tried and tried but she could not do it. It would forever be her terrible, and exceedingly idiotic, secret.

Lucy said she was like Juliet, except her Romeo was uncooperative and being wheeled round in a chair by Lady Vile. Finella had scolded Lucy several times over calling Lady Violet Lady Vile, but Lucy claimed that Shakespeare would have approved the moniker.

Finella had also told Lucy she ought not be so pleased over the duke being confined to a wheeled chair as they did not know how serious the injury was. Lucy did not care how serious it was. The duke was the wrecker of her plans and therefore ought to suffer for it.

Finella fretted about it, though. One was not confined to a chair unless a serious injury had occurred. She would wonder if he were paralyzed, but then her common sense told her that if he was, it would be the talk of the town. Something was probably broken though, and that was serious enough. He seemed in good health at the prince's party, but he might take a turn! People took turns all the time. Taking a turn was a common thing. All she could hope for was that the duke's physician was skilled.

The house was in a frenzy of activity, preparing for the party. Even Wagner, so usually composed, seemed a bit harried. The food and drink would be set up in a reception room lined with the duchesses' idea of interesting art. Unlike the rest of the house, that room did not have old ancestors staring down at a person. There were whimsical paintings done by various children in the duchesses' sphere, a rather terrifying mask from

Brazil, and the most interesting picture of all—the paw print of Intrepid, the cat who'd sailed with Captain Cook.

Wagner had been directed to pull the best wines from the cellars. Aside from the usual meats, cheeses, and sundry other items, the duchesses' sideboards would feature mushroom vol-au-vents, which Finella understood the lady was renowned for. The secret, the duchess had told her, was the choice of the German sauterne Cook used in the recipe. Ladies were forever asking her the secret and it amused her to tell them it was a Riesling so they could never get it quite right.

It would all be very exciting if it were not for the Secrets Exposed part of evening.

To take her mind off the whole thing, Finella just now tied on her bonnet. Lucy was to accompany her on a stroll round the square. There was a charming path that went all the way round and it was pleasantly shaded by mature trees. It was the duchesses' opinion that it was the prettiest square in Town.

They had made it a habit to take the walk as it felt to Finella that none of her problems could follow her there. Walking under the trees made her almost feel as if she were at home again.

Gracious, she used to think her day-to-day life in her father's house was boring. She had not appreciated the peace and regularity of the days following one another with no surprises in store. She might drive her curricle into the village and wave at all the same people and visit the haberdasher and examine all the same ribbons she'd examined the week before. In the evening, she would dine with her father. On Sunday, her brother and his wife would come over from their patch, and Finella would listen to the two men drone on about farming problems. As anyone who'd ever owned a farm knew, there was always a problem. When the night drew to a close, she would settle in a particular velvet covered chair in her bedchamber with her latest novel, a cup of chocolate, and her jar of biscuits.

Now that she reflected on it, she'd had a lovely routine at home. Everything had changed once her father was made a baron. Finella did not understand the exact ins and outs of how it happened, but it revolved around her father owning a lot of land and people needing votes in parliament. Her father was supposed to come to Town for parliament this year, but he'd put it off until next year as he had to employ a steward. Whatever had gone on, the duchess seemed to know all about it and viewed it as very usual.

"I think you ought to say something cutting to him," Lucy said, walking by her side round the square.

Lucy was determined on some kind of revenge over the green shawl that had been displayed on the duke's boat. She was determined the duke pay for it in some manner.

"Even if I wished to," Finella said, "which I do not, I am not skilled at those sorts of things. I would only end sounding foolish."

"Asparagus," Lucy said, shaking her head.

"That's it, exactly. I cannot be depended on to say anything sensible, much less witty and cutting, in the heat of the moment. One time, Clara Hilldale told me I looked dumpy in my dress and I said I preferred it. While I was walking home from that encounter I thought, why didn't I tell her I despised her shoes? I didn't really, but it would have been something to say. In any case, I do not want to say anything terrible to the duke. He has not done anything to me. You and I have been foolish in our imaginings. That is all that has happened."

Lucy snorted. "Maybe we ought to say something witty and cutting to ourselves then. I suppose we've been a couple of asparagus."

Finella laughed. "I believe we *have* been two asparagus. Of maybe it's asparaguses."

"Miss Fernsby!"

That voice, that male voice, was behind them and Finella knew exactly whose it was. "Walk faster," she whispered to Lucy.

They picked up their pace, but it was no use. Sir Roger was shortly caught up to them. "Miss Fernsby," he said.

"Sir Roger. I am just on my walk with my maid."

"Yes, I know, I've been watching the house for several hours."

Finella recoiled at the idea.

"Watchin' the house?" Lucy said, sounding very outraged. "Who are you, the London Monster? I thought he was hung in the nineties."

Sir Roger clearly did not care to be questioned by a maid. Or insulted, for that matter. He ignored Lucy and said, "Miss Fernsby, you ought not have to put up with such effronteries from a servant and I can assure you that you will not do so in my household. My servants are courteous, or they are out on the road."

"I'm never going to be in your house," Finella said boldly. It was rather terrifying to defy Sir Roger, but she must make herself clear. This had gone too far. He had gone too far. It was horrifying that he had been watching the house.

She thought he would be very angry. Instead, he laughed. "Miss Fernsby," he said in a condescending tone. "What other opportunities will you have? If I were a younger man, I would not bother to look in your direction. As it is, I require an heir so I must put up with it."

Finella was shocked to her shoes. Put up with it. She was so repulsed by this man. This old man. She stood motionless.

Lucy, on the other hand, did not stand motionless. She used her parasol to hit Sir Roger about the head.

At first, she'd taken him by surprise and she'd landed several sharp blows. She even knocked his hat off and mussed his thinning hair. But then he began to fight back and wrestled the parasol from her hands.

"Run!" Lucy said.

Finella picked up her skirts and ran, with Lucy's pounding steps behind her. Finella was terrified to even look over her shoulder to see if Sir Roger was chasing them. He might be, he really was a monster of sorts.

They reached the doors and flung them open. Finella shut them and slid the bolt for good measure. They turned round, heaving in breaths.

Wagner stood in the hall staring at them.

Lucy said, "That Sir Roger was out there pestering and insulting Miss Fernsby. We had to run away from him."

Wagner's expression grew very dark.

Finella thought they ought to spell out the whole truth of it. "We ran away after we hit him with a parasol, I'm afraid."

"*I* hit 'em," Lucy said, "though kind of my mistress to try to share the blame. I had to leave that parasol behind, too. I was forced to wallop him after he insulted my mistress from here to Sunday. Maybe I shouldn't have done it, but maybe I should have. We'll never know."

Wagner nodded approvingly at Lucy, which rather surprised Finella. She would have thought he'd rather disapprove of a lady's maid hitting a lord over the head with a parasol.

"Miss Fernsby, Sir Roger will never pass through these doors again. If he dares a knock, he will end sorry over it. I will inform the duchess of this new development. Lucy, excellent work."

Lucy bobbed a curtsy at the compliment. Finella thought Lucy was rather outrageous, but she also thought nobody in the world had ever had such a stalwart maid. There had been more than one occasion where Finella had been very glad Lucy was on her side. This occasion had only been the most violent of them.

They had left Wagner to manage things, and Finella was relieved that the butler would outline to the duchess what had occurred. She would be satisfied if she never had to speak of it. She and Lucy jogged up the stairs and looked out Finella's window. They watched Sir Roger come around to their side of the square, dusting off his hat. He gave a terrible look to the house, and got in his carriage.

He was gone. Finella presumed it was for good. After all, there was no coming back with any dignity after being beaten round the head with a parasol by a lady's maid.

~ ~ ~ ~ ~

Hugh was in receipt of the Duchess of Ralston's seven sealed letters and the list of twenty ladies to choose from. If other years were anything to go by, there would be some gentlemen staring at the letters, very much wishing to know what was written inside them. Hugh did not want to know. He did not want to hear himself mentioned at the party. He wanted to slip in and out under cover of darkness like a thief in the night. Like he'd never been there at all.

He had been wrestled into it last year too, as had Seddie. He'd visited ladies he was friendly with, but they were ladies who would not read anything into being visited. At the party, he'd come through unscathed as nothing that had been written about him had been read aloud. The question the ladies were to answer had been what spice or flavor would the gentleman be and why. He never found out what anybody had written about him, but it was not deemed interesting enough to be read aloud and he'd been more than satisfied with that outcome.

This year was different though. He must see Miss Fernsby and see what she would say. The difficulty was he'd have no chance of explaining himself before she wrote something. The rules were specific—the lady and the gentleman were not to speak at all. As Miss Fernsby was in the duchesses' house, that would be strictly enforced. She would answer the duchesses' question before knowing he'd meant to show a yellow shawl, not a green one.

Was she disappointed? Irritated? Angry, even? He'd gone so far as to ask her color and then he'd not shown it. Maybe she thought he'd gone round and asked a dozen ladies about their colors and then just picked between them. She would think him a cad, if that was what she believed.

He'd sent daffodils and a note asking for a new start. Now, though, he wondered how that would be taken. Might she think it meant that he'd gone one way with a green shawl and now changed his mind and went the other way? A lady might think a gentleman very unreliable to do it, as what assurance would she have that the fellow would not change his mind again? A lady could not be comfortable with a man who did not know his own mind.

The other difficulty was the wheeled chair. It was going to be a rather grueling day for the staff attending him. At seven different stops, he would have to be carried out of the carriage, put in the chair, wheeled in, wheeled out, put back in the carriage, and the chair tied to the back of the carriage again. He'd have to give them an extra day off or money or something to soothe their irritation over it. They would not show they were irritated, but Browning had long ago educated him on how it all came out at the servants' table, to be discussed in detail.

If there was one bright spot, Lady Violet was not included on the list of twenty ladies. The Duchess of Ralston had very astute judgment, so Hugh presumed the lady had deemed Lady Violet not quite ready for such a game. Packington had brought his sister to Town too soon, that much was clear. She was a coquettish child who ought to be still under the supervision of a governess.

Of course, Packington might not see it that way. Hugh was

bracing himself to hear from him about what was said at the prince's party.

Hugh had written out the seven ladies he would visit, with Miss Fernsby being the first. His coachman would determine the most sensible route around Town. He did not know what the question would be, nor how Miss Fernsby would answer, but he would find it out tonight. He would bring one of his footmen with him this evening so he would not be at the whim of whoever decided to push him hither and thither. At the earliest possible moment, he would be pushed in Miss Fernsby's direction.

At least Browning had made several improvements to his incapacitated situation. The Merlin chair was being built so that Hugh could wheel himself, though that would not come for another week or so. In the meantime, Browning had re-covered the pink satin chair in brown leather and painted over the pink and green on the back, which was vastly more suitable.

Perhaps the most ambitious of the projects to ease his recovery was due to the prince. Hugh's method of getting up and down the stairs was entirely changed. His Royal Highness had sent members of the Royal Engineers to build and install a chair that used ropes and pullies to go up and down between floors. The head engineer had shown Browning a book that contained illustrations of Henry VIII's stair throne as a model. The men had been all efficiency and had the thing set up in a day.

It was hair-raising the first time Hugh tried it, especially since the footmen had yet to get the hang of it and there had been a drop of ten feet as he plummeted down to the great hall before they got control of it, but it did work well enough.

Now he had gone down to the great hall in the stair throne, been carried to the carriage, and set off. He might not be able to talk to Miss Fernsby as he brought in the duchesses' paper, but he hoped for at least a glimpse. A glimpse of *Finella*, as he'd begun to think of her. He'd recently discovered that her given name was Finella. It was very apt. It sounded soft, just as she was.

~ ~ ~ ~ ~

This was it. Finella was confined to the small drawing room to wait out the Secrets Exposed letters until four o'clock. Either nobody would come and she would be humiliated, or somebody would come and she would have to think of what flower they would be as a husband. Either outcome was nerve-wracking.

The duchess had been kind enough to allow Lucy to sit with her, else she would have been a hopeless mess of fidgets and pacing.

They had a tea tray in and Finella had made good use of the biscuits and petit fours, as that always calmed her and made her more cheerful. Lucy was pouring her a second cup of tea when there was a knock on the door.

Finella felt frozen in her seat. Wagner entered with a letter on a silver salver. One of *the* letters. A Secrets Exposed letter.

"Told ya," Lucy said, hopping up and taking the letter.

Wagner said, "Miss Fernsby, this has been brought by Sir Edward Bromley."

Finella nodded and Wagner closed the door behind him. Finella stared down at the letter Lucy had just put in her hands.

"I reckon you better open it," Lucy said. "The fellow has to wait until you reply, don't he?"

"Oh no, that happens to all the other ladies, because the gentleman has to return his letters to the duchess."

"Ah, so here she just sends him on his way."

Finella nodded.

"Well I suppose you best open it anyway. Got to be done, sooner or later."

"Yes, I imagine you're right." She tore the paper open. It said as she had been told, what sort of flower would this gentleman be as a husband and why. "Gracious, what am I to say about Sir Edward?"

Lucy tapped her chin. "He's the one that tried to drown the duke? Twice? He sounds a dangerous fellow to my mind."

Finella could not help but agree with that assessment. The duke had ended in a wheeled chair on account of Sir Edward.

Lucy suddenly laughed. "He's Wolfsbane, ain't he? If one is not careful around him, they'll end up dead."

"Oh that's very good. So much more clever than anything I could come up with."

She dipped her pen in ink and wrote: *He is Wolfsbane, as he almost killed the duke.* She dusted it and shook it. Once the ink was dry, she refolded the paper and used the duchesses' seal to close it.

Finella let out a breath. A gentleman had come, and thanks to Lucy she had an amusing response. It was the best outcome she could have imagined. Nobody else need come, one was enough. She'd done her duty by the duchess. She laid the letter in the little basket the duchess had provided for completed letters.

"There, that was not so hard," Lucy said.

"Not for you, perhaps. I cannot think up things like that. Especially not so fast."

"You'll be the queen of the quips the minute somebody needs to be called an asparagus, though. Nobody will think of it quicker. Or at all."

They both devolved into giggles as it really was quite ridiculous. Finella Fernsby would never be an acclaimed wit unless naming a person an asparagus was suddenly deemed the height of it.

There was another knock on the door. Wagner entered with another letter. Finella stared at Lucy. She was not certain she had been hoping for more than one visitation.

"From the Duke of Greystone, Miss Fernsby," Wagner said.

Chapter Sixteen

Mr. Wagner had just brought in another letter for Secrets Exposed. From the duke.

Finella did everything she could to avoid falling off her chair. As it was, she leaned back and peeked out the window. Sir Edward stood next to the duke's carriage, while the duke himself sat inside it. The duke caught her eye and waved. She weakly waved back and shut the curtain.

"He's right outside," she whispered.

"Where else would he be?" Lucy asked.

Wagner had watched this whole ridiculous operation expressionless. He bowed and let himself out of the room.

"Let me get a look at this wrecker of plans," Lucy said, leaning over her to peer out the window. "Well, he's fine-looking, I'll give him that much."

"He is the finest man in England, everybody knows it," Finella said.

"Everybody knows it, do they?" Lucy said with a snort.

"What is he doing now?" Finella asked.

"Talking to a gentleman that I imagine is Sir Wolfsbane and looking at the window." Lucy took that moment to wave.

"Oh Lucy, do stop!" Finella said.

Lucy sat back down. "By the by, he waved back. He seemed very jolly about it, not like that Sir Roger what hates to hear from a maid."

"Of course he would be jolly," Finella said. "The duke

is everything kind and friendly, which is how I allowed my imagination to run away with me to begin with."

"Well, there is nothing for it," Lucy said, "what kind of flower is the duke? We could make him Wolfsbane too, for killing you with kindness and friendliness."

"No, the duke cannot be a poison. Despite my injured feelings, which is entirely my own fault, we must think of something that really represents him as a gentleman."

"It's gonna be hard for me to think of anything cheerful as he is the wrecker of my plans. You know me, I got a charitable disposition, born with it, but wrecking my plans is a step too far. He's Wolfsbane to me."

Finella unfolded the paper. She must think of something on her own. She thought about the duke, his handsome looks, his kindness, his cheerfulness. Then of course, whatever she wrote would be confidential, she would never be identified as the author. She could just write what she really felt with nobody the wiser.

She dipped her pen in ink. *The duke is a daffodil, all smiles and sunny temperament.*

It was not a work of genius, but it would have to do.

"Well?" Lucy asked.

"I named the duke a daffodil."

"I suppose he's daffy enough to not perceive your worth," Lucy said, "so I'll agree to it."

Finella sealed the letter. Yes, she was right to describe him so. He was a very kind sort of person. She would not be at all surprised to discover that the duke had visited her this day because he was afraid nobody else would. He really was that kind. He'd probably talked Sir Edward into it for the same reason.

She could not fault him for being kind. She could only fault herself if she ever again allowed herself to read something more into it.

As the time ticked by, getting ever closer to four o'clock, nobody else came. That rather confirmed to Finella that the duke had taken pity on her. It was uncomfortable to know it. To understand that a gentleman felt sorry for her.

Nevertheless, she could not in any way denigrate the duke's kindness. She was not meant to understand that he'd come so that she would not be humiliated. He was a good man, he was simply not her man.

What a shame that was.

~ ~ ~ ~ ~

It occurred to Browning that he was getting rather used to going rogue. Roguish ideas came to him faster now. They seemed to almost fall into his lap. It was as if they'd always been there, unseen, and now his roguish eyes made them apparent.

It was a longstanding habit that he managed the duke's calendar, just as he had managed the old duke's and duchesses' calendar. They had never seen the need to employ a secretary when Browning was so reliable. He would alert the coachman that he would be needed and when, he would inform the valet of what type of evening it was, and he would alert the cook of what was wished for. From the kitchens, sometimes what was wanted was nothing at all, sometimes it was a light dinner before departing, sometimes it was a cold plate left for the duke's return. All information flowed through Browning. He was the lifeblood of the house. He was the lifeblood of the Finstattens.

Mr. Browning was, of course, well aware that the Duchess of Ralston's Secrets Exposed party was this evening. He'd already told Cook to prepare a light plate of food for the duke to consume before he left, as the duchess would not do a sit-down dinner. As well, the duke's valet was prepared to dress him, which these days took two footmen to help. Getting the duke into his clothes and down the throne chair and out to the carriage was a regular military campaign.

What Browning had not done, however, was alert the coachman that the carriage was wanted. The stables would think nothing of it. They might know about the party through the usual household gossip, but Sir Edward so often came and took the duke places, and Browning was so reliable, that they would not question it.

It was a very roguish thing to do. It did take some time to hitch the horses, after all. He had come up with a plan to delay the duke's departure to the very house Miss Fernsby resided in. Further, the plan did not implicate the coachman as being at fault. After all, he might be a rogue butler, but he was not the devil.

The duke had come downstairs via his Henry VIII throne chair. Mr. Browning made a great show of opening the front door and looking about. Then he'd turned and said, "The carriage is not yet outside."

"I wonder what's keeping him," the duke said.

As well he might wonder it. The duke's coachman was never late in arriving.

Mr. Browning then dramatically clutched at his chest. "It is my fault," he cried. "I've forgot to tell him!"

The duke stared at him strangely and Mr. Browning began to wonder if he'd overplayed the performance. He did not have any experience treading the boards on Drury Lane. It was hard to know how it came off.

"All right, all right," the duke said, "no need to have an apoplexy over it. Go tell him now, as quick as you can."

"Yes, Your Grace, deeply sorry."

Mr. Browning hurried out the doors and shut them behind him. Then he very leisurely walked down the mews to alert the coachman that he was wanted.

He felt as bold as any highwayman. Any *rogue* highwayman.

~ ~ ~ ~ ~

Hugh had been dubious over whether he'd get a glimpse of Miss Fernsby that afternoon. He had, though. He'd met Seddie coming out of the house and while his friend was outlining all the reasons he thought Miss Fernsby would be kind to him, Hugh had seen a curtain flutter. Then she had peeked out. He'd waved. She'd waved back.

She'd pulled back as if she were embarrassed by her own daring, the darling lady. Then another face had appeared; a maid he presumed. She'd been so forward as to wave at him and he'd waved back because why not? She'd seemed amused by it. His mother would have called the girl "pert."

"I will call on Lady Genevieve, what do you think she will say about me?" Seddie asked. "It's a risk, I know, but then if I do not go to her, it might look cowardly. She'll think so anyway."

"You'd better face it," Hugh said distractedly. He was too busy wondering if Miss Fernsby and her maid sat in the room with the daffodils he'd sent to pay much mind to his friend. He wondered what she thought about it. Did she keep the note? He understood ladies kept such things if they were favored. Hopefully, she'd somehow understood the meaning of his note regarding a new start and had not concluded he was unreliable and prone to a changing mind.

"Yes, I will go to Lady Genevieve's house," Seddie said. "And who knows, maybe she'll say something complimentary. She has to give up eventually."

"Don't you ever worry that Lady Genevieve will wed somebody else?" Hugh asked.

"No, we're meant for each other. Always have been."

As the curtain in the window did not flutter open again, Hugh had left Seddie ginning himself up to visit Lady Genevieve.

He'd gone home and wiled away the hours with a book. The time had finally come to depart for the Secrets Exposed party and somehow, his carriage was not ready. Browning was acting so strangely these days. Hugh had already seen him fall on the floor, and now he'd forgotten to alert the coachman of his calendar.

It was not at all like Browning and Hugh hoped he was not beginning to suffer from old age. He seemed young for it, but those sorts of mental maladies could strike younger than expected. He could not imagine another butler in the house. Browning might be grim-faced on even the best days, but he was a veritable Finstatten institution. Hugh suspected the house ran as smoothly as it did because nobody who worked in it wished to come up against Browning's grim face. He was especially good at looking disappointed, so much so that Hugh himself preferred to avoid causing the expression.

Finally, the carriage had arrived to the front of the house. The coachman was scowling so Hugh imagined Browning had got an earful over his not being informed ahead of time. There had been the whole operation of getting him into the carriage and his chair tied to the back. Frederick, the senior footman, climbed into the carriage after him, looking very alarmed to be on his way to a party in a house owned by a duchess.

To put him at his ease, Hugh had said, "Frederick, there is not much of a trick to this. Just wheel me in the direction I say to go."

"Yes, Your Grace."

"And if you hear the name Lady Violet, wheel me away immediately."

Frederick's eyes widened. "Yes, Your Grace."

Hugh supposed his footman was now wondering what went on at these parties his employer was always going to, what a Lady Violet might be, and why they were to run the other direction if they encountered her. Poor Frederick was at an age where all women seemed mysterious and possibly dangerous.

Hugh remembered embarrassingly well how he and Seddie had gone through it. Lady Genevieve had been just a girl. They encountered her often at this event or that in their tightknit neighborhood. They'd ignored her as she did not like to do fun things like build something or shoot something. And, if he were forced to admit it, they'd considered themselves superior because she was just a girl.

But then during the term break one summer, she had been different. Very different. She was no longer just a girl. She was turning into a lady. He and Seddie had approached the situation with a very false bravado, trying to act like grown gentlemen, with very little success. He still felt red in the face when he recalled the lawn party at Genevieve's father's house where he and Seddie spent the entirety of it talking loudly of various conquests of the shooting birds variety. To hear them tell it, they had shot every bird in England out of the sky. Seddie called it the year they'd tried out a Corinthian savoir-faire and managed only to produce boyish grandiosity. Lady Genevieve referred to it as the summer they were insufferable.

Now, Hugh finally arrived to the Duchess of Ralston's house very late, on account of Browning failing to alert the coachman that he was needed. Had it been any other moment, he could have just saddled his horse and been off, but that could not be. For the next month, everything he did took an inordinate amount of time. He tried not to be aggravated over it, as that would solve nothing. Nevertheless, it was aggravating.

After the wheeled chair had been untied from the back of the carriage and he'd been helped into it, Frederick wheeled him in.

There was nobody in the great hall but a footman. The festivities must be underway already. Hugh directed Frederick down the corridor and into the ballroom.

The duchess stood on a raised dais at the top of a crowded room. Everyone was turned toward her with their backs toward Hugh. Being low in a chair, he could not see much. He did not know where Miss Fernsby was. She was short and he was even shorter at the moment. It was impossible.

"Frederick," he whispered, "look for a lady short in stature with marvelous blond curls. She has dimples too, but look for the hair, you cannot miss that lovely hair."

The footman looked terrified to asked to look for a lady with lovely hair. Nevertheless, he stood on his toes and peered round. As the footman was tall to begin, he must have a very good view. He bent down to Hugh and whispered, "Will she be the shortest lady in the room?"

"Yes, very likely."

"She is near the front and to the right."

"Excellent. Get me there."

Frederick nodded, though he looked dubious over how to get him there.

"Be bold, Frederick," Hugh said.

Frederick began to weave him round people, whispering, "Excuse me, pardon me, His Grace coming through."

At the front of the ballroom, the duchess said, "I always do hope to be amused by the responses I receive from our chosen ladies, and this year has been particularly good. You are all to know that the question posed to the ladies was if this gentleman was your husband, what flower would he be and why?"

There was general laughter over the question, Hugh supposed from those people who had not been roped into the duchesses' entertainment. He could not imagine what flower anybody would think him. But then, the duchesses' question was always nonsensical.

"The first offering is this: This husband would be holly,

pretty to look at but coming to a sharp point."

The crowd laughed. Someone called out, "It is Lord Farragut, surely."

"But it might also be Sir Richard," someone else called.

"Come now, it must be Brummel."

"Brummel was not even included in the game, though."

"It still must be Brummel," the accuser said laughing.

Frederick continued weaving him through the crowd, his strategy seemed to be bumping a gentleman with the chair until they turned around, much to the annoyance of everybody.

Hugh did not care. He must get to Miss Fernsby. He would not be put off it. As for the husband who would be holly, it seemed that there were more than a few gentlemen who were pleasant to look at but had a sharp point. He was satisfied that he had not been named amongst them.

The duchess said, "Here is an interesting one. He is Wolfsbane because he almost killed the duke."

The crowd roared with laughter. One after another, people called out "Sir Edward." Hugh was not surprised someone had written it, though he was surprised that they'd included the identifying information. It was tradition that the lady should attempt to cover anything that would lead directly to the gentleman in question. The answer might have been constructed as something like, the gentleman is Wolfsbane, as he can be dangerous to his friends. That would lead everyone to guess, rather than make it so obvious that it was Seddie.

On the other hand, Seddie had well-earned it.

"Pardon me, excuse me, His Grace coming through," Frederick whispered.

He'd just bumped Lord Garrity, who gave Frederick a very dark look but moved aside.

Finally, he saw Miss Fernsby just ahead.

Frederick leaned down. "Is that her?"

"That is her," he said. All he could see was her back, and her glorious fair curls. She wore a soft velvet dress the color of claret, everything about her was soft. He had a great urge to come up behind her and hug her around the waist. Which he would never, ever do. "Forward, Frederick."

"Yes, Your Grace," Frederick said, bumping Lord Harvey as the last person to get out of the way.

He rolled up to her side and said, "Miss Fernsby."

She practically jumped and he supposed he ought not have snuck up to her like he had.

"Your Grace," she said in a tremulous voice.

Hugh thought he instantly understood the situation. Miss Fernsby was not the type of lady that would glory in all these mocking jokes. She was too much of a soft touch to enjoy someone else's discomfort. This particular party must be difficult for her to enjoy.

There was a sudden jostling to his other side. Hugh looked in that direction and gritted his teeth. Lady Violet had managed to push her way to his side.

Why? He had been more than clear with the lady.

"Your Grace," she said.

"Lady Violet," he said, and he did not think his tone sounded very friendly.

Upon hearing the name Lady Violet, Frederick jerked his chair back. Hugh had forgotten he'd instructed his footman to go the other direction if he heard the name. He held his hand up to stop him. "It is all right, Frederick," he said over his shoulder.

Lady Violet gave his footman a strange look, as if she wondered why he needed to be reassured in her presence.

Hugh was trapped. If he took himself away from Lady Violet, which he very much wished to do, he would be taking himself away from Miss Fernsby, which he was not going to do.

"Ah," the duchess said, "I did chuckle over this one, and I did find it very apt. This gentleman is a cuckoo flower, as he has just as much sense."

"That must be Sir Edward too," someone called out.

Hugh imagined that was right and probably written by Lady Genevieve.

"No need to debate," Seddie called from the other side of the room. "I'm sure it's me and equally sure I know who wrote it, Lady Genevieve."

This prompted laughter throughout the room. Hugh took the opportunity to say, "Miss Fernsby, how do you get on since the regatta?"

Why had he asked that question? Why could he not think up a graceful way to mention the mistaken color of the shawl? Why would Lady Violet not go elsewhere, as it would be far easier to talk about it if she were not there. He was already waiting for Packington to say something to him about what he'd said to the lady at the prince's party. A brother would not like to hear of a slight to a sister. Anything he would say now about positively not intending to show French verte would seem to her another slight she could take back to Packington.

"Now here's one," the duchess said. "The duke is a daffodil, all smiles and sunny temperament."

"Hah! We do not even need to guess who that is then. I believe only one duke was included in the exercise," Lord Harvey called.

Hugh supposed it had to be him, though he could not complain about being called a daffodil. It was better than Wolfsbane, holly, or a cuckoo flower.

"Speaking of daffodils," Lady Violet suddenly said loudly, "perhaps that same duke has sent exactly that to me, requesting new beginnings. Naturally, I will consider it."

What on earth was she talking about?

To his right, Miss Fernsby moved quickly away, disappearing into the crowd. "I did not send daffodils to you," he whispered to Lady Violet.

"Yes, you did," she said, staring at him.

By her expression, he did not get the feeling she was lying. And then it dawned on him that she could not know the contents of the note if she had not received it. What had Browning done?

"Lady Violet, I did not intend to send those flowers. I believe my butler has gone mad. I apologize on his behalf for this unforgivable mistake."

"I see," she said coldly. "I will, naturally, inform my brother of this *mistake*."

Hugh thought he would be very lucky if he did not face Packington on a green at this point. "Frederick, wheel me in pursuit of Miss Fernsby."

Frederick stood on his toes and looked around. "I can't see her, Your Grace, on account of she's so short."

Lady Violet laughed bitterly. "Indeed, she is."

"Wait," Frederick said, "I think I just saw the top of her head."

"Forward, in all haste. Lady Violet, my deepest apologies regarding this unfortunate confusion."

Chapter Seventeen

The evening Finella had dreaded had finally come. The house had been readied and after all the activity to prepare for it, Wagner had assumed his more usual calm and unruffled demeanor. The duchess said that her butler always adopted a 'surrender to the fates' attitude at such moments. He'd done everything possible to prepare and now the party was in the hands of destiny.

Finella wore a dress of lightweight velvet in a claret color with a silk lining which she very much favored. In fact, she very much favored the material in any color at all. Though the dress was undecorated with anything to draw the eye, the nature of the fabric meant that it draped well on her. It had a little more structure than silk alone. It also had a lovely soft feel to it. It felt comforting, which she needed just now.

It had occurred to her as Lucy helped her into the dress that she might have made a mistake with answering the duchesses' question about husbands and flowers. She recalled that the duchess had said the fun of the evening was her guests attempting to guess who a particular answer referred to.

She had written her answers so that there could be no doubt as to who it referred to.

Lucy had soothed her by pointing out that if there was anything wrong with her answers, the duchess would simply not read them. In any case, who wrote those responses would be forever a secret. Nobody would know it was her unless she told them.

She would see the duke and she must be cheerful about it.

She had every reason to be cheerful. She was an extraordinarily lucky young lady who had been given the rare opportunity to be sponsored for a season in Town by a duchess. Had she allowed certain things to go to her head? Yes, of course she had. But it had been a learning experience and she felt a deal older and wiser now.

Certainly she did feel that way.

Finella could be further cheered by knowing she would not see Sir Roger at the event. It was just as well, and she had no idea what one would say after one's maid had beat a person round the head. Wagner had apprised the duchess of the events that had occurred during Finella and Lucy's walk around the square.

Finella had worried that the duchess might be angry with Lucy for striking a lord, but the lady had found it hilarious and claimed she always did like a spirited lady's maid. She'd then written Sir Roger a sternly worded letter and told him he was never to approach Finella again and he was not to set foot in her house, despite any prior invitations. He was to go away quietly, lest he invite her more public ire. She reminded him that he would look very foolish if it became known that he was bested by a lady's maid's parasol.

Finella did feel relieved over the whole thing. Sir Roger had not seemed to take her opinion seriously, but she did not believe he would dare cross the duchess.

She'd since gone downstairs and stood in the receiving line with the duchess, steeling herself to see the duke with a friendly smile on her face. He would say something nice, as he always did, and she would read *nothing* into it. It would be just the Duke of Greystone being pleasant, as he was to everybody.

And who knew what else might happen? She might very well meet a gentleman more suited to her. She must keep that in mind too.

People came and came and came some more. The Secrets Exposed party appeared to be very popular. The duke did not come though. This began to frighten her. She was certain the duke would not purposely let down the duchess by failing to appear. Had something happened? Had he taken a turn? She had been worried about a turn and now she could not think of what else would keep him away.

The duchess did not like to dawdle and so after three quarters of an hour greeting people at the door they made their way into the ballroom. The duchess took her by the hand and led her toward the top of the ballroom. Finella might have had trouble making her way that far through the crowd, but the duchess had the ability to part the seas, and they made their way forward easily. Wagner was already there to meet them, and he helped the duchess up to the dais.

As the duchess spoke from her stage, the duke suddenly appeared by her side. Finella felt both a thrill, a very stupid thrill, and relief. He'd not taken a turn, he was just late. She supposed going anywhere was a complicated operation for the duke now that he was confined to a chair.

If she was to flatter herself, she might even believe he'd arrived to her side intentionally. After all, how did he get through that crowd in a wheeled chair? It must have taken a lot of effort.

She had experienced the disastrous consequences of such assumptions and had learned her lesson with them. As she was no longer subject to ridiculous fancies, her fact-driven mind instantly concluded that his footman had pushed the chair with determination, forcing people out of the way. It would be necessary for the duke to be near the front to be able to see anything from his location in a chair. That was the rational explanation.

Finella noticed how easy it was to come to a rational conclusion once a person became determined to do it.

Her conclusion that he'd not sought her out *was* very rational, too. Lady Violet was just as fast by the duke's side. One might almost imagine they'd planned to meet and she'd been waiting for him. It was very right, of course it was. Those two glorious-looking people certainly belonged together. Nothing more usual.

Gracious, she was really getting experienced with looking at the world through fact-filled glasses. It was becoming almost natural. One might not always see what one wished, but one would see what actually was. That was important, she thought. The truth must always be faced, even if one did not like it.

The duchess had read the comment she'd made, or rather the comment Lucy had composed, about Sir Edward being Wolfsbane. Finella stared straight ahead so she would not give herself away as the author. Then the duchess had read what she'd written about the duke. He was a daffodil for his smiles and sunny temperament. Finella was quite certain she'd turned purple while attempting to look unconcerned. If the duke asked her about it, if he asked her if she had written it, what could she say? She could lie, but then she was a very bad liar.

She did not wish him to know. It came too close to her feelings and the duke would be embarrassed to know her feelings. Any gentleman would be mortified to know they had caused disappointed hopes, even if the hopes had been absurd to begin.

Before she had a moment to decide on anything, Lady Violet loudly claimed the duke had sent her daffodils and spoke of new beginnings.

It was too much. Finella might have transformed herself into a rational sort of person, but she was not unfeeling. Her heart had not had a chance to catch up to her mind. She turned and hurried away. She could not leave the event though she wished she could. She'd much rather run up the stairs and be with Lucy. But the duchess would be offended, and she would never knowingly offend the lady. She could at least get away from the happy couple. Accepting the truth was one thing, but a person did not need to stand around and stare at it.

Finella hurried toward the reception room. It would be devoid of people as of yet, but it would have the sideboards ready for the crowd. As a usual thing, a biscuit might soothe her, but just now she thought wine would do better. Or both together. Her body felt as if she had been struck by lightning, her fingers and toes tingled almost painfully. She dearly hoped it was not a precursor to a faint. This night was bad enough without being discovered splayed on the floor like an idiot.

She found the room empty and poured herself a generous glass of Riesling. Then she took an almond biscuit and dipped it into the wine.

As she was chewing, the duke sailed into the room in his chair. He flew by her at an alarming speed, barreling toward the far wall. He leaned forward and took the crash into the wall with his hands. His chair bounced backward under the force of the collision and the pawprint of Intrepid crashed to the floor.

"Sorry, Your Grace!" the footman said, chasing after him.

It seemed that, somehow, the duke's footman had been pushing the duke too fast and then lost hold of the chair.

"Turn me round and then get out, Frederick," the duke said.

Finella was frozen at the sideboard. Why was he here? Did he need a glass of wine? Had he chased after her?

But no, her rational mind must rule. He needed something. Of course he did.

The footman hurried to the duke and turned him round. "Am I dismissed from service, Your Grace?" the footman asked in a low voice.

"No, no, just dismissed from the room if you please."

"Very good, Your Grace." The footman, looking happy to have flung his employer across a room without losing his place, fled the room.

"Might I get you some wine, Your Grace?" she said. Or whispered, as it sounded to her ears.

"Wine?" he said in an incredulous tone.

"Tea, then?" she asked, not entirely certain why he sounded so appalled by the mention of wine.

"Miss Fernsby," he said. He used one foot to slowly push his chair forward. "Ah, I cannot get far in this manner. Do come over here."

Finella set down her glass of wine and biscuit and she slowly walked over. She still did not know what he required.

"Now, I have to clear a few things up. Mostly, about the shawl. I am blind—"

"Blind!" she cried.

"No, not entirely blind, I am blind to colors. Certain colors. You might as well know it. I know it is a deficiency and I probably ought to have told you before now, but there it is."

"I see," Finella said quietly. She did not actually see at all. It was a shame, she supposed, that the duke could not see colors as other people did, but as a deficiency it did not seem the worst thing in the world.

"I am afraid it could be passed to my children. Male children, in particular."

Why was he talking to her about children? Should not that conversation be had with Lady Violet?

"So that's what happened with the shawls," the duke said. "The shopkeeper told me it was yellow, and I could not tell the difference."

Did he just say he went to the shop for a yellow shawl? Yes, he did. She was sure he did. He said he went into the shop to buy a yellow shawl.

Finella pinched herself. Rationality, Finella, rationality! There will be a rational reason why the duke went to buy a yellow shawl that has nothing whatsoever to do with you. Do not be fooled by your feelings!

He grabbed her hand and said, "Miss Finella Fernsby, I have been besotted with you since you took my hand while I was lying on the road. I cannot say what your own feelings might be after...well after all this."

"My feelings?" Finella said. She had just told her feelings not to fool her. But he'd just said words, direct words. He'd said he was besotted, that was a very direct word...there could be no rational explanation for that word.

"Also, the daffodils were supposed to be delivered to you, not Lady Violet. I do not know what has come over my butler, but he is making a lot of strange mistakes. He might be ill."

Finella felt she was struck dumb. No, not just felt like it, she really was struck dumb.

"What I am saying, Miss Fernsby, is would you consent to wed me despite...recent events."

"Really?" Finella said with a sob. It was overwhelming, she did not know what to do. She was not entirely sure it was real. Perhaps she'd lost her wits and was even now on her way to bedlam, babbling about the duke.

"Yes, of course really," the duke said.

If she *were* on her way to bedlam, which felt like a distinct possibility, she might as well enjoy the delusion and play it out until someone informed her that she was insane. "Well I would. Also, I think I might faint."

"Sit down, Miss Fernsby. Sit down so you do not injure yourself in a fall."

"Where?" Finella said. There were no chairs.

"Sit here," he said, patting his lap.

Under no circumstances that she could have imagined would Finella Fernsby have sat on a gentleman's lap. She really did feel woozy though.

Before she could positively decide what to do, he'd pulled her down and she found herself on his lap.

"There, that's better," the duke said. "Now was that a yes? I cannot kiss you until I am assured of it."

"Yes, assured. Be assured," Finella whispered.

Then he did kiss her, very softly. If this was bedlam, Finella was happy to stay for the rest of her life. His lips were different from her own. They were somehow rougher, and she liked it very much.

Out of the corner of her eye, she saw a head pop into the room. It was Sir Edward. He winked, pulled his head back, and closed the doors.

The duke kissed her again and it was really very marvelous. Then he traced his finger up her neck and cheek and that was even more marvelous. He ran his hand down her bare arm and gently removed one of her gloves. If she'd not been sitting on his lap, she would have fallen over. His hand wrapped round her bare hand.

"Ever since The Strand, I wondered what your little hand would feel like with your glove off," the duke said.

His hand was so much larger than her own, but hers felt very safe wrapped in his.

"And look at those curls, they are perfection, and dimples too," the duke said, kissing her once more.

"I'm very short," Finella said. She did not know why she felt compelled to point that out but it seemed somehow necessary, as if the duke might not have noticed.

He laughed. "Yes, I know. You can be difficult to find in a crowd, especially when I am in a chair."

"I am more rounded than other ladies?" Finella said. Why on earth was she directing the duke to look at all her faults? It was as if she could not stop herself.

He wrapped his arms around her and said, "I know, and very soft. As for me, you won't mind my current situation? That I am stuck in this chair for a month?"

"Gracious, no. You have a lovely lap, Your Grace."

"You'd better call me Finstatten. Or Hugh if you like it better."

The duke kissed her again. It became very much settled in Finella's mind that she would like to spend forever kissing the duke. Or Finstatten or Hugh, as she would know him. It really was the best thing to do that she could think of.

The doors to the reception room were flung open. The duchess stood in the doorway. It occurred to Finella that the lady would not appreciate finding the lady she sponsored wantonly sitting on a gentleman's lap. She wrestled herself out of the duke's chair and to her feet.

"Took you long enough, Duke," the duchess said. "I presume from this display that you are engaged to wed?"

"We are, Duchess," the duke said. "As for Miss Fernsby's position on my lap, she was feeling faint and there was no other place to sit."

"Yes, yes, very convenient," the duchess said with a snort.

"I really was woozy, Your Grace," Finella said. "I did not expect..."

"You did not expect?" the duchess said with a laugh. "I've been expecting it for weeks. The two of you are very well suited. Perhaps too nice to run a sensible household, but very well suited nonetheless."

Since the duchess had opened the doors, more and more of the people in the ballroom began to gather round the doorframe and peer in.

The duchess turned. “You will all be delighted to know that Miss Fernsby has accepted the duke. Now do avail yourselves of the refreshments I have provided.”

The duchess, as always, was very astute. If there were one thing to distract people from gossip, it was food and drink. The lady then directed the duke’s footman to his chair and led them out of the room as the rest of her guests spilled into it.

“You may spend a quiet hour in my library,” the duchess said. “I will direct Wagner to bring you wine and a tray. I feel confident that it is safe, as you are engaged and the duke is, at this particular moment, incapacitated.”

She led them through the ballroom and Finella saw Lord Packington leading his sister out, rather than into the refreshment room. Finella could not imagine what the lady thought, as she had received daffodils and she had thought the green shawl was meant for her. Lady Violet was not to know of all the mistakes that had been made.

The library was quiet, the duchess left them there, and Wagner was efficient with the wine and a tray. The footman helped the duke onto a sofa and was sent away.

Finella sat next to him, very close, and admitted that she had assumed the duke and Lady Violet were a match. The duke said that Lady Violet had thought the same and he did not know if he would have trouble from Lord Packington.

“On no account are you to meet him on a green to settle it,” Finella said. “I really feel strongly about that. Perhaps I should not have an opinion on what gentlemen choose to do, but I really am against it.”

The duke had laughed. “Have all the opinions you like about me, Miss Fernsby. Well, he cannot challenge me at the moment, in any case. Nobody ever shot at somebody in a wheeled chair. In time, I hope he will see the true situation and realize that his sister was never ready for a season."

"That's what the duchess says," Finella said. "Also, you should call me Finella."

"Ah, I have been calling you Finella in my thoughts for some time. Sometimes I have even called you Finny."

Finella laughed at that, as those close to her at home often called her Finny. Then the duke stopped her laugh with a kiss. Their hour alone together went by surprisingly fast.

It did go by though, and the duchess returned to them. She said that while she was exceedingly liberal, she did still have to report to Finella's father and the baron counted on her to protect his daughter's honor.

The duke was helped back into his chair and his carriage was called. Finella walked out to the pavement and waved the duke off. As his carriage trotted away, he hung out the window and waved. She waved back. Goodness, they had done an awful lot of waving through this courtship that Finella had never been convinced even was a courtship.

The duchess stood next to her. "Well now, I cannot think of another two people who deserve to be happy as the two of you. Your father will be most pleased with my efforts, I think."

Her father. The baron would be more than pleased. He would be positively bowled over. His parting advice was to avoid wedding a vicar. He would hardly imagine she'd wed a duke instead. Perhaps what the duchess and her father would never understand was that her fiancé was a glorious gentleman and she would have accepted him even if he was a vicar. He could be a pirate for all she cared about it. Who could refuse Finstatten?

Finella fairly floated up the stairs. In her bedchamber, Lucy was peering out the window, watching the carriages coming for the duchesses' guests. Her maid turned and said,

"There you are. See? You survived the night just fine."

"More than fine, Lucy. I am engaged."

"Engaged?" Lucy said, staggering back. "To who? Is he poor? Is he in the straits you've talked about? Can he afford a lady's maid?"

"I am engaged to the duke. I am engaged to wed the Duke of Greystone."

Lucy tossed back what was either water or gin. "My dream is coming true. I'm to be the lady's maid to a duchess. I can hardly believe my luck."

Finella laughed. "Yes, I am feeling rather lucky too."

Chapter Eighteen

On the night of the Secrets Exposed party, Mr. Browning had been told he need not wait up for the duke's return. After having forgotten to call the carriage, though he had not forgotten at all, the duke had said Browning clearly needed to rest.

He did wait up, though. He needed to discover if his roguish moves had paid off. He'd allowed the switching of the shawls to go forward, he'd delayed the duke's carriage, and he'd sent the daffodils to Lady Violet instead of Miss Fernsby.

He supposed it was how a highwayman felt when making off with the goods he'd stolen out of a carriage. It was time to have a look at what his efforts had produced. Was it diamonds or was it paste?

After the party, the duke's carriage had arrived home and he'd been wheeled inside. For once, he did not have Sir Edward trailing behind him.

"Browning. I did not think you would be up, but as you are, would you care to explain how the daffodils I ordered for Miss Fernsby ended up being sent to Lady Violet?"

Mr. Browning stared unblinking at the duke. He was caught. The magistrate was at the door! How? It was only meant to encourage Lady Violet in her efforts at landing the duke. She was not supposed to say anything about them. She was meant to be flattered, silently, and then redouble her efforts to charm.

What was this new English habit of discussing every single thing that happened? He really did not find it very dignified. People ought to keep their own counsel, not go round allowing their thoughts to leak out of their mouths in a willy-nilly fashion.

He would be dismissed. What then? He had no other skills aside from butlering. Nobody would ever hire him if the duke dismissed him. He'd end up a laborer. He was not cut out for laboring! He could not go round digging holes and hauling things around and doing whatever people did in wheatfields. Or, heaven help him, he might be sent down to the mines. He could not be a miner! The lack of cleanliness alone would kill him.

A hundred thoughts ran through his mind. Reasons and excuses, maybe he could even act surprised, as if he had not known he'd done it.

The duke's eyes were boring into him. "Browning?"

"I believe I may be going senile, Your Grace," Mr. Browning said. He did not know if it would be believed, but it seemed as good an excuse as any.

The duke frowned. He was frowning. What did it mean?

"I think you are just overtired, Browning. Take a rest, Frederick can manage things while you do. Going forward, maybe think about writing things down so you do not get confused."

"Writing things down, yes, very good, Your Grace. I will write everything down. Absolutely everything."

Was that it? Had he got away with it? Was he the highwayman who had escaped justice? It seemed that he was. He was a regular Jack Sheppard. That fellow might have been hanged at Tyburn, but that was only because he kept robbing people. He did not know how to quit when he was ahead. Browning was not so foolish. He'd never try the daffodils gambit twice.

"By the by," the duke said, "I have engaged myself to Miss Fernsby. You are to have a new duchess in the house."

Mr. Browning woke some hours later in his own bed. As Frederick told it, he'd fainted dead away at the news of a new duchess to be installed. He'd hit his head on the banister of the bottom stair on his way down. They'd all stared at him for a few minutes, hoping he'd get up by himself, but he didn't. They'd hauled the duke upstairs in the throne chair and got him squared away. Then they came back down and he was still lying there so the footmen and the grooms in the stables had carried him to his chambers and Sir Henry had been fetched.

That gentleman agreed with the duke's assessment—Mr. Browning was overtired, and now the fall had jostled his brain and given him a lump on his head too. Quiet days were recommended until he felt recovered.

Recovered. How was he to recover? He'd been meant to lead the duke into a glorious match. One that would be talked of as the match of the season. Privately, he'd been hoping for the match of the decade. The duke was meant to wed a diamond, not the short daughter of a new baron.

He'd put so much work into it! He'd even gone rogue, all to no avail.

He'd stayed abed for a few days. He did not do so out of any physical need. He did so for two reasons. One, he did not care to hear from the duke about banns or a special license or St. George's, or solicitors drawing up the contract. It almost felt as if he did not hear it, it was not true. The other reason was that he preferred to hide from his fellow *League* members during this tragic interlude in his history. Oh, they had all pretended that Miss Fernsby was perfectly acceptable, but they could not really think it. Even if they did think it, perfectly respectable did not exactly cover him in glory.

As he lay there, day after day, the staff was quite solicitous. As if they could perceive that he needed cheering up, they all did their bit. Cook sent in marvelous little cakes and plenty of tea. Frederick assured him that all was running smoothly in the household. The maids even sent him a card, urging him to good health.

It was all very nice, but he still had *The League* to face. He, Matthew L. Browning, butler to the illustrious Finstatten family, had fallen below the mark. Oh, how he had privately laughed over some of the other members' adventures in matchmaking. But none of them had ended with the short daughter of a new baron.

It could not be avoided longer though. The usual *League* meeting was this very day. As Mr. Browning was currently at his leisure, he did not even have to invent another supposed accident happening to one of the many of his invented old aunts who had nobody to rely on but him.

He'd fairly dragged himself up the stairs into the club's set of apartments in Cheapside.

"It is said that Miss Fernsby was discovered sitting on the duke's lap," Mr. Harkinson said gleefully.

"Oh yes," Mr. Wilburn said, "they were in that room with all the strange pictures. Nobody is entirely clear how Miss Fernsby ended in that particular location, but it is said that there may have been some sort of scuffle."

"A *scuffle*?" Mr. Wilburn said, sounding scandalized.

Mr. Wilburn nodded gravely. "The famous pawprint of Intrepid, the cat who sailed with Cook, was even knocked off the wall."

"Bad business, knocking things off walls," Mr. Feldstaffer said, to no purpose whatsoever.

Mr. Browning had not been privy to the idea that Miss Fernsby had been discovered sitting on the duke's lap. Or worse, that there had been some sort of a scuffle. How very typical of a newly minted baron's daughter to be involved in a scuffle and leap into a gentleman's lap.

But if Miss Fernsby had instituted this scuffle... For the first time in days, a small glimmer of hope began to light in Mr. Browning's breast. "Gentlemen, could it be that the duke has been trapped? Has Miss Fernsby maneuvered herself into a compromising position to trap him?"

He did not know how to get the duke out of it, but it would be something to work with. The duke was trapped against his will.

"No, no," Mr. Penny said. "Sir Edward has been telling all and sundry that he knew how it would be, as the duke has been besotted for weeks. Ever since the encounter on The Strand."

And just like that, Mr. Browning's glimmer of hope was snuffed out.

~ ~ ~ ~ ~

While Hugh was not an overly formal sort of gentleman, he did recognize that his wedding could not be a run to Gretna Green. He'd rather it could be, but he was the Duke of Greystone. In any case, he was just this moment confined to a wheeled chair so there was plenty of time to plan, and he would not insult Finella's father by something less than splendid.

The Duchess of Ralston had taken everything in hand and seemed to know what was required. It was lucky she had, as his butler was still abed and only taking a few jaunts out of doors to take in the air. Poor Frederick had been left running the household and he would not know the first thing about how to proceed with a wedding. The fellow seemed alarmed enough over the idea that there would be a duchess roaming round the house and asking him for things.

Hugh had written to Finella's father, asking for permission to go forward with the engagement and introducing the name of his solicitor for a drawing up of a contract, should the baron agree to it. That gentleman had written him back giving his approval. The letter was so filled with good cheer and good sense that Hugh was sure they would get on famously. He did not see how it could be any other way, as Hugh intended to be ridiculously liberal in the terms. Finella could spend what she liked with no discussion with him about it.

He rather hoped she would buy more of those velvet dresses that looked so well. Jewelry too. He'd already visited Rundell & Bridge and purchased a delicate platinum and topaz ring for her little hand. He'd seen she owned a topaz necklace and it would match very well. Then, of course, there were his mother's jewels. Lucinda had inherited some pieces, but what was left was extensive. There were some very good tiaras in the collection. He'd already sent one over to Finella, in case she wished to wear it to the wedding.

While the duchess planned the nuptials, and she did not seem to require any opinions from the couple to do it, he and Finny went on famously. He knew his first instincts were right. She was not just pretty as a picture, they had so much in common. As they rode through the park in the duke's open carriage, they discussed it all.

For one, they both did not care to rise early, as some people did. They were not "up with the sun" sort of people. They were closer to "up for a midday meal" people. As a married lady, Finella could have her breakfast served in bed. She proposed that he should do so too so they could breakfast together. After all, he was a duke, could he not make up some of his own rules and traditions? So that had been settled—they were to dine in bed each day, likely around noon. He did not know what else Finella thought they might do in bed, but he had some ideas of his own.

Another thing they had in common was they both liked to ride and they had matching greys. They planned to ride all over the duke's land, which was extensive. Kestrel would be sent for and be waiting at the family seat.

The only difference of opinions regarding food and drink they discovered was that his fiancée preferred a Riesling or other sweet wine, rather than anything dry. He'd contacted his wine merchant that very day to have both of his houses well stocked.

But most of all, they had very similar outlooks on the world. They both preferred to be happy, and that everybody else be happy too. They did not like gossip or mean spiritedness. They did not see the point of it, as it just made people unhappy.

Hugh had, of course, had to warn his fiancée about his sister, who never wished to be happy. Lucinda had rushed to the house when she'd heard of the engagement. As he'd been expecting her, the door had been bolted and Frederick was told to keep her out. His footman had done it too, but he looked as if he'd been to the wars and back after she finally left his doorstep.

Lucinda had then sent a letter, which he'd thrown away without reading. He informed the duchess that his sister was not invited to the wedding service or the breakfast that would follow, as she could not be trusted to behave in any rational manner.

The duchess did not seem surprised, nor disappointed. Hugh got the idea the lady had never liked his sister.

All of that had transpired even before Finella had told him what she overheard in the ladies retiring room at Almack's. He'd been positively incensed and had written Lucinda a letter, barring her from his house, and his life, forever. He should have done it long ago and she would not be missed. He did not expect any trouble from her husband, Lord Gaddington, as that fellow probably wished he could bar Lucinda from his life too.

One person who was not barred from the house, but who Hugh dreaded seeing, was Packington. He had expected to see him sooner, but a full week went by before he turned up.

The first thing he said was, "I've taken Violet home."

Hugh did his best to outline how things had gone, including the wrong color shawl and the misdirected daffodils. Packington had not even known about the flowers until Lady

Violet had shouted out about them at the Secrets Exposed party. Even then, he had not known if they were real. He told Hugh he'd had several direct conversations with her about her behavior and that if the duke had an interest in her, he surely would have mentioned it to her brother. She could not be convinced until word went round the ballroom that Hugh had engaged himself to Miss Fernsby. Considering how fast her feelings had gone from distress to annoyance, it had only been a youthful infatuation.

In the end though, Packington blamed himself. He'd been sure she was not ready for a season and had allowed her to push him into it. He'd spoiled her, ever since he'd become head of the family and she'd become headstrong without the maturity to manage it. She was home now, and she would come back in a year or two, with a deal more sense.

As much as Lady Violet had irritated him and got in the way of his plans, Hugh did not hold anything against her. It was only the folly of youth, and he and Seddie were well acquainted with that particular brand of folly. In any case, what right would he have to hold anything against anybody when he found himself in such happy circumstances? He had been blessed, backward and forward, and he wanted everybody to be just as happy as he was.

~ ~ ~ ~ ~

For the first few days of her engagement, Finella had felt a bit off kilter, or woozy, or dizzy, every time she saw Finstatten. He took her breath away and she was going to marry him. She grew more comfortable over time and the thrill felt more manageable, but the beginning had been nearly overwhelming.

Still, every time she thought about walking around as a duchess and people calling her Your Grace, she felt woozy again. Finstatten had sent over a tiara that had been owned by his mother, and of course she would wear it, but it seemed too grand for Finella Fernsby.

She had at least got past her insecurity about her height and her Rubenesque figure. It had seemed impossible that the Duke of Greystone would be at all interested in her person. But he was. He most definitely was. She had thought she would not be for everybody, but she might be for somebody. The duke turned out to be the somebody. A very enthusiastic somebody. The night of the Secrets Exposed party was not the last time she'd sat on his lap.

Lucy had entirely changed her opinion of the duke, now that she was to be lady's maid to a duchess and he was no longer the wrecker of her plans. Finella had written her father about taking Lucy with her, as she had been one of the baron's housemaids and he'd been expecting her back at some point. He wrote that the housekeeper and the other housemaids were delighted, as they all thought she was a shirker of duties. The housekeeper even mentioned that Lucy could have a very pert attitude and was far too prone to speaking her thoughts as they arrived. The lady was thrilled that the girl would not be returning. So, a happy ending all round on that front.

The wedding, the actual day, was another thing that made Finella woozy. The duchess was planning it all. Finella had on occasion imagined her wedding day through the years. It had been a small affair in her home church, to a gentleman with a modest estate.

Now she was to wed in St. George's. She was marrying a duke. All of society would be there. The duchess said even the queen would be there. The Queen of England. At her wedding.

It was best not to think of any of it. She would not think about it and just depend on Finstatten to hold her up at the altar. She had already warned him that she was terrified and there was every chance she might faint in view of the queen. He assured her that she would be all right. He would be right by her side. Then he advised Finella to have a glass of wine and some biscuits ahead of time.

She could not wait for it all to be over. She would be married to Finstatten and they could go away and be alone. They'd had extensive discussions about where they would go after the wedding. They might stay in Town, they might do a tour of various relations, they might go to Suffolk so she could see the estate. One of the difficulties of all of those places was that there were a lot of other people there too. Where could they go to be alone?

Then Finstatten had an idea. He had not been there in years, but his family owned a very small lodge in the Lake District. More of a camp for his father, who'd been a keen fisherman, than anything civilized. It sat on a very small lake, hemmed in by hills. Nobody lived within view and nobody but his father seemed to think the lake worth fishing. Hugh sometimes thought his father liked it so much because he could go there alone and there was nobody asking him for anything.

One could even swim in the lake, if the frigid temperature could be tolerated, though he did not recommend it. Hugh had tried it once and it was really awful. A quarter mile down the very lonely road that led to the camp, there was a caretaker and his wife who could cook meals and take in laundry.

He'd almost forgotten he owned the property. The last time he'd been there was years ago. He and Seddie were determined to become expert fishermen when they were on a term break. They had not become expert. Like a lot of their suddenly hatched plans, it did not work out the way they'd imagined. They were either terrible at it or there were not any fish in the lake.

The fishing not turning up anything, one day Seddie wandered off into the woodland to have a look around. That had been in the morning. By the late afternoon, Hugh was fairly confident that he'd got himself lost. Hugh and the caretaker spent hours looking for him. When the sun began to set, they decided to return to the lodge and set out again in the morning.

They'd ended up finding him on the way back, sitting by a small stream. He said he'd walked for hours and then decided all was lost so he would stop and die next to the stream as he was bound to get thirsty while he was in the process of perishing. He'd been about two hundred yards from the lodge.

Finella had no intention of wandering off into a wood so it sounded perfect to her. It would be the perfect antidote to the frenzy of the wedding. The duchess had shielded her from the frenzy as much as possible, but now her part had come. The duchess could not shield her from standing at the altar in front of a crowd.

Lucy helped her into her dress, which had been specially designed by Madame Beaumont. It was a lightweight velvet in a very pale and soft yellow with very subtle daffodils embroidered round the neckline. It felt like spring and sunshine and everything happy.

"Gracious, now look at that dress," Lucy said. "Not like the bows and ruffles and sparkles you started with."

"I am done with trying to distract the eye, Lucy. The duke prefers me as I am, and the duke's opinion is the only one that matters."

"Aye, but there'll be ladies sittin' in them church pews what are wantin' to kill you for that hair. Mark me, I know women."

This was the first Finella had heard about Lucy knowing women, but she was cheered by the idea nonetheless.

"Your pa is downstairs already, he's dressed very fine, he looks every inch a baron," Lucy said. "I told him I was sorry I could not act as a housemaid in his house now that I am lady's maid to a duchess. He was very kind about it. He went so far as to say he would not try to keep me from the opportunity for all the world."

Finella pressed her lips together so she would not laugh.

Lucy had no idea that the baron was delighted to see the back of her. Her father had arrived in Town three days ago and stayed with his old friend, Sir Robert. He'd met Finstatten and reported he liked him very much and he was confident that he'd put his daughter in competent hands.

Lucy placed the pearl encrusted tiara on her head.

There was a quick knock. The duchess let herself into Finella's bedchamber. "Ah, you look perfection, Miss Fernsby. I have brought you a posy to carry, as well as a glass of wine and a biscuit, on the duke's orders."

He was really a darling to think of it. The duchess handed her the loveliest little arrangement of daffodils, tied with a pale yellow ribbon and set the wine and biscuit on the dressing table.

"Now, Miss Fernsby, you are not to be nervous. Remember, Middling Margaret once tread the same steps you will take today."

"Middling Margaret?" Lucy said softly.

"Middling Margaret is me, Lucy," the duchess said. "I came through it to rule the *ton* with an iron fist and so will Miss Fernsby. It is the purview of a duchess and a great deal of fun if one manages it right."

~ ~ ~ ~ ~

As Hugh was well aware of Seddie's habits, and as Seddie was to act as his best man, he'd sent a carriage over for him and given him the wrong time. Thanks to that planning, his friend arrived to his house early, rather than late. Seddie took the opportunity to complain about the trickery, but Hugh explained he would have had to drown him in the Thames if he was late. His friend thought about it and then agreed that arriving early was the better option.

Seddie had handed him a flask in the carriage on the way to St. George's. Hugh had no intention of being drunk for his wedding, but he took a swig. He was to be stared at by hundreds of people, including Queen Charlotte, and he did not like to be the center of attention like that. He'd hinted to the duchess that perhaps they would not need to invite everybody in the world. She was distinctly against that idea. He proposed holding the ceremony in his house. He had a special license so they could have it wherever they liked. He thought the house would set a limit on how many people. The duchess was against that too. She insisted on St. George's. Hugh was not exactly sure how many people that church could hold, but the duchess seemed to know it. Aside from the pews, it had a gallery, so probably quite a lot of people.

She told him he was a duke and therefore had obligations. Furthermore, anybody left off the list would privately seethe over it. The point was not that anybody would so much like to see him marry, it was that they wished to casually mention to their acquaintance that "the queen was looking very well at the duke's wedding." To not be able to mention it would sting.

He'd said nothing to Finella about his discomfort, as she was already a ball of nerves over it. He had to pretend at viewing it as nothing at all and had promised to hold her up if she looked faint. Hugh hoped she'd had that glass of wine and biscuit that he'd advised.

"So this is it," Seddie said. "Remember when we were eight and we cut our hands, mixed our blood, and swore we'd never marry? I guess that's off."

"That is definitely off. In any case, have you not been attempting to sway Lady Genevieve's opinion of you for the past two years?"

"Yes, but after the regatta fiasco, I'm probably going to need another year. I think she needs to see a months' long streak of what she calls 'maturity of judgment.'"

Hugh thought Lady Genevieve might be waiting longer than a year for that particular streak.

The rector of the church, Mr. Hodgson, met them at the doors. They had arrived well ahead of time as Hugh would not risk being late on account of a horse throwing a shoe or any other delay.

The rector himself would deliver the vows. Hugh had expected nothing less, a rector would hardly pass up the opportunity to perform in front of the queen.

The man led them in and Hugh got his first look at the duchesses' handiwork. It really looked very good. The outsides of the pews were decorated with arrangements of daffodils and white roses, running all the way up to the altar. The altar itself was adorned with tall vases of white roses.

"Just this way, Your Grace. There is a small anteroom to wait in until the time grows near. It is my experience that a groom can do without standing at the front of the church while his guests file in. It can feel uncomfortable."

"Clever," Seddie said. "Maybe I'll get married here too."

"When are the expected nuptials to take place, Sir Edward?" the rector asked.

Hugh snorted. Seddie said, "It's hard to pin down when, at this juncture."

They sat down and the rector left to supervise whatever needed doing before it was time. He was getting married. The idea had always been a bit of a haunting thing, because as much as he looked, he could not find the lady he wished to wed. Until he met Finella.

Now the only haunting thing was the ceremony in front of all those people. He hoped she was doing well and not dwelling on it.

As the time passed, Hugh could hear the hum of people filling the church. Then there was a sudden silence and the sound of shuffling.

“That will be the queen,” Seddie said.

The organ outside the room began playing a piece by Handel. The rector poked his head in the door. “It is time, Your Grace.”

Chapter Nineteen

The rector had come for him. It was time.

Hugh rose. He walked, one foot in front of the other. He would not look at the crowd, not even the queen, who was bound to be at the front. He would just think about Finella.

After what seemed an hour but was probably a few minutes, Hugh heard the crowds rise behind him. There she was. Finella Fernsby.

Her father and the duchess accompanied her, one on each arm. Hugh hoped they were not actually holding her up. He hoped Seddie would not have to hold him up.

Whatever her nerves were, she was looking positively smashing. There could not be a lovelier lady in London.

The duchess took the bride's bouquet and removed to the empty seat by the queen. Finella stared at Hugh. He stared at Finella.

The rector began the solemnization of marriage from the Book of Common Prayer. The man talked and talked. Then he got to the part inquiring into any impediments. Hugh's heart froze over the idea that Lucinda might be out in the pews somewhere or hiding in the gallery, intent on making trouble. Though what reason she could give against the marriage, he did not know. The church would not have an opinion regarding who was or was not a mushroom.

The moment passed. Then they said their "I wills." Finella's voice trembled and he could see that a glass of wine and a biscuit had not entirely settled her.

The rector asked who giveth this woman, and the baron answered. Finally, Finella's hand was placed in his own. He felt better instantly and he thought she did too. From then on, as she squeezed his hand, they said their vows. Just between them.

They had done it. The rector had droned on with some homily or other, dragging it out in Hugh's mind. However, it was to be expected. That part of it was the rector's performance for the queen and he would not cut it short. He'd finally run out of steam and Hugh and Finella had practically run out of the church. They'd done it and neither of them had fallen over.

Inside the carriage, Hugh closed the curtains. They would have twenty minutes of privacy before arriving at the duchesses' house for the party. He pulled her close. "You see, you have nothing to worry over."

Finella laughed. "Really? I believe I went blind for a few seconds, then the church seemed too hot, then it seemed too cold. I am sure those in the last pew could see my heart beating through my dress."

"I was rather a wreck myself," Hugh admitted. "I did not tell you how I dislike being the center of attention in a crowd, as I thought it would make you even more nervous than you were. It makes me very uncomfortable."

"We are a couple of asparagus," she said.

"Asparagus?"

Finella nodded. "It is the most devastating mockery I have ever been able to come up with. As you can see, I am not very clever with such things."

"We should keep asparagus to ourselves," Hugh said. "It will be a secret word. That way, if we need to use it around other people, nobody will know what we're talking about."

And so it was. As the years went by, whenever the rare situation occurred where they were inspired to criticize or mock a person, that person was instantly named an asparagus. They did not think they were too unkind about it, as they named each other an asparagus far more often.

~ ~ ~ ~ ~

Finella walked into the duchesses' house, no longer Miss Finella Fernsby. She was Finella Finstatten, the Duchess of Greystone. No matter how ridiculous it sounded to her ears, that's what she was.

As the Duchess of Ralston had planned the luncheon and as the queen attended, it was an elaborate affair. There were select guests at the dining table and the rest of the guests were in the ballroom, which had been transformed with tables and chairs.

Finstatten whispered to her that they could leave as soon as the queen departed. They were to set off for the Lake District this very day. It would take them four days to get there, and they were eager to be on their way.

They would take two carriages, one for her and Finstatten, and the other for Lucy. Her husband's valet would ride ahead, ensuring the inns were prepared for their arrival. The bags were packed and the staff would be ready to go at a moment's notice.

Lucy had not been exactly bowled over by the arrangements that had been made for the wedding trip. As the lodge was really only two rooms, a main room and a bedchamber, Lucy was to bunk up with the caretaker's wife, while the duke's valet would bunk up with the caretaker. Finella did not know how her husband's valet viewed it, but she supposed it was just as grimly as Lucy did. Her maid felt the accommodations as they had been described did not suit a duchess, and most certainly did not suit a lady's maid to a duchess. She would not be able to regale the staff regarding their luxurious accommodations when they returned home. Finella had soothed her by mentioning that she'd already arranged for her maid's wages to be increased.

The luncheon passed with toasts, even the queen said a few kind words. That lady was particularly kind to a newly married couple, as she'd ended with, "I will take my leave now. I understand the duke and duchess will set off for their wedding trip this afternoon and heaven forbid anybody leave before the queen."

Once her majesty had departed, she and Finstatten made quick work of getting out of the house. Finella kissed her father and thanked the duchess profusely for all her efforts and they were on their way. They were to stop at Luton at The Old Bell for their first night.

Finella supposed she ought to be nervous about the wedding night. Perhaps she was, at least a little bit. But nothing could approach her nerves in church. All those people, the queen among them, staring at the back of her head. She would be forever grateful that she did not faint in a heap. Finstatten had been there, holding her hand, and she imagined he always would be.

The Old Bell was a fine establishment and Finella was tickled to know that Finstatten had made extensive preparations for their first stop. They arrived in time for dinner and the private dining room had been reserved. It was candlelit but rather dim with just two places set. The innkeeper proudly brought in two bottles of wine.

"As your staff requested, Your Grace, a Riesling from the Schloss-Johannisberg vineyards and the Haut-Brion claret."

"You remembered I prefer a sweeter wine," Finella said.

"I will always remember your preferences," Finstatten said.

They had their dinner and Finella was certain it must have been very good, as the innkeeper kept saying, "As you requested, Your Grace." It was very hard to keep her mind on it, though. She was married to this wondrous man and they spent most of the dinner staring at one another.

She had drunk three glasses of the wine, which was far more than she usually would. As she had, she fairly floated up the stairs.

Then, the door was shut and they were alone. There would be no further interruptions from anybody. Finstatten undid her buttons, which he found a surprising number of. Then he got to the petticoat and was further surprised to find stays under that. By the time he got those undone and found a chemise underneath, they were both laughing.

"This is like an unending maze of buttons and ties and mysterious configurations," Finstatten said.

Finally, the chemise was on the floor. Finella did feel the littlest bit self-conscious. After all, she had never particularly admired her person.

But then the duke had took her in and whispered, "Marvelous." He was out of his own clothes far faster and they fell into bed with each other.

Finella had no experience at all and the duke had very little. She was an innocent lady, and he most certainly was not a rake. Sometimes, that is best. Two people can discover what they like without any preconceived notions about what they ought to like.

Through much practice, which they were happy to do, they did discover it.

They woke late and ordered breakfast to be sent up and did not set off from the inn until after one o'clock. This habit, carried on from inn to inn, turned their four-day journey into seven. They did not mind it, though the duke's valet and Lucy may have had other thoughts.

They finally did reach the lodge in the lake district. It was small, as had been described, but it was lovely and private. The caretaker's wife, Mrs. Parker, came up every day around noon to make their breakfast in the rudimentary kitchen. It was always a large one, as they would not eat again until dinner. Fresh country eggs, bacon from the caretaker's own pigs, fresh-baked bread, pots of tea and coffee, it was heavenly.

Mrs. Parker usually had some comment to make under her breath regarding the onerous task of having Lucy as a houseguest. In retrospect, Finella realized she could have left her maid at home, as she was little needed. Finstatten had become very expert with her buttons and ties.

They spent their days reading or walking along the shore of the lake and wandering the woodland. At night, after Mrs. Parker had left them with their dinner, which was always a very simple stew or a roast, they would eat in front of the fire. They talked of everything under the sun. They spoke of children, but even before that they had decided that Finella must have a dog. She'd always wished for a small lap dog, but her father was of the opinion that a dog ought to be able to go out on a hunt with a pack. Then it came out that Finstatten had always been interested in having a cat. He did not have one, as he wondered if it was a particularly manly sort of pet. It was decided he must have a cat immediately on their return.

After important questions such as those were settled, they would let the fire die out and find warmth between themselves.

Finella thought there could not have been a better way to start a marriage. If she would have to go home and act a high-flown duchess, it was well that everything had started so simply.

They did eventually have to return home, if for no other reason than Mrs. Parker's comments about Lucy began to grow very dark. By that time, they had firmly settled that Finstatten would be called Fin and Finella would be Finny, and so they were, all their lives. They made their leisurely way to Suffolk just as slow as they'd come. The duke's staff would have closed the London house for the season and it was time to take up day-to-day life. And get a dog and a cat.

And what a life it turned out to be. The house might feel too big, the servants too many, and her title too grand. None of that mattered though. The one thing that fit just right was Fin.

The following year, Lady Violet did return to Town under the closer supervision of her brother, Lord Packington. What a difference a year could make. Sometimes, a young person just needs to push things as far as they can go, and be chagrined over the result, to make a leap in maturity. She came with a far more sober outlook and found success with Viscount Rareton.

As for leaps in maturity, Seddie did take a bit longer. Several things did help him along though. The duke, his primary partner in stupidity, had wed and was no longer willing to try out any harebrained idea. And then, he caught wind of a certain gentleman pursuing Lady Genevieve. These two things appeared to have hit him over the head. Or as he told Finstatten, "It occurs to me that I must change or die alone, an old man who never grew up." After a monumental effort at self-control, Lady Genevieve was finally convinced she might safely wed the man she'd always preferred.

Seddie and Finstatten still went regularly to the Devil's Den, but they did not stay until dawn anymore, to the approval of both of their wives.

The Duchess of Ralston carried on as she always had, teasing the *ton* and ruling with an iron fist. She and Finella saw each other often during the seasons and wrote each other regularly when they were at home. The Duchess of Ralston was a font of advice for Finella, though she did not have the nerve to carry out half of the lady's suggestions.

Lucy was as loyal a lady's maid as anybody could wish for. If she made free with the duke's wine cellar because she felt she'd become too elevated for gin… If she drove the housekeeper mad with her high opinion of her position… If she somehow had Finella doing half her work for her… Well, everybody had their peccadilloes.

Sir Roger was not as lucky, but perhaps he got a just fate. He had no success finding a wife that season. When the next was coming to a close just as fruitless, he offered for a vicar's daughter. Miss Gerhard did produce him a son, but she also came to his house with an iron will, as a clergyman's daughter can be stalwart indeed. Such were their battles, as she was absolutely unafraid of him no matter what he did, he finally dropped dead of apoplexy. His widow went on to be a very merry widow, raising her son, the new baronet. Sir Roger's staff were very merry too, as the lady was far more liberal than he had ever been.

Lucinda went on as she always had—annoyed, bitter, and complaining. The duke might have banned her from the house, but he could not ban her from Town. They did encounter one another from time to time. It did not help her temperament that she was forced to address Miss Fernsby the mushroom as Your Grace. It further did not help when she had attempted to assert her authority and called the lady Miss Fernsby and then pretended it was just a slip up. The new duchess had answered the slight by naming her an asparagus. The duke had found it hilarious, for some reason. Lucinda did not know what it meant, exactly, but she was afraid to ask anyone as she assumed it was something terrible. Lord Gaddington had overhead heard it, though, and took to regularly calling her an asparagus, though he did not know what it meant either.

Mr. Browning had dreaded His Grace returning to Suffolk with his new duchess. How was he to take orders from a mushroom? As well, she would be a constant reminder that he had failed in his matchmaking efforts.

To no surprise to anybody but Browning, Finella won him over in time. One of the things he liked most about her was her unfailing faith in his judgment. It was very hard to continue to dislike a person when they were forever saying things like, "You will know best, Browning. I trust you implicitly."

As well, Mr. Browning could not deny that the duke was exceedingly happy with his choice. The couple were forever calling each other Fin and Finny, which he did not find dignified. However, the duchess had produced a girl, and then the blessed boy heir. He must give credit where credit was due.

One could not say that the duke and duchess showed themselves to be particularly strict sort of parents. They hired all the right tutors, but were forever interrupting their children's studies to do something else. That something else was usually taking out the horses. It became a common sight in their neighborhood to see the duke and the duchess on their greys leading their children on ponies. The consensus of the neighborhood regarding these four people was that they were all very nice. It was not a usual compliment for a duke and duchess, but it was precisely what they were.

Of course, all that was yet to be. The next season, Mr. Feldstaffer would take the lead in *The League of Butlers* matchmaking adventures. He was dreading it, but then Mr. Feldstaffer generally dreaded everything.

Lady Beatrix Bell, the daughter of the Earl and Countess of Copperstone, was to make her debut in society. Mr. Feldstaffer was not entirely certain what sort of disasters she would create, but he was sure she would and he thought he could guess what the root of them would be.

When he attempted to cheer himself up over it, all he could come up with was he might be dead of natural causes before the season even started.

The End

More Books from Kate Archer:

Come visit The League of Meddling Butlers Series Page https://amzn.to/3UKfVF7

Book One: A Confounding Regency Romance

Book Two: A Baffling Regency Romance

Book Three: A Mystifying Regency Romance

Book Four: A Befuddling Regency Romance

Book Five: A Perplexing Regency Romance

Book Six: A Vexing Regency Romance

Connect with Kate:

Follow Kate on Amazon to get notice of new releases! https://amzn.to/3V3d5eD

Come visit Kate at https://www.facebook.com/KateArcherAuthor and https://katearcher.weebly.com/ and https://www.instagram.com/katearcherauthor/

Want news from Kate? Sign up at: https://bit.ly/katearcher

Email Kate at mailto:katearcherauthor@yahoo.com

Other Regency Romance series by Kate Archer: The Dukes' Pact, A Series of Worthy Young Ladies, A Very Fine Muddle and A Series of Senseless Complications.

Statement on the use of Artificial Intelligence in Fiction:

Dear Reader:

I received the following in my inbox regarding authors' use of artificial intelligence (AI):

"Many of us have been using these tools for more than a year already, and attitudes have shifted as it's become clear they are here to stay. I hope more authors will define themselves as AI-Assisted Artisan Authors in the year ahead."

I do not know whose attitude has shifted, but that's about the stupidest thing I've ever heard. Not one word, not one plot point, not one description, not one sentence of dialogue, produced by me will ever have any assistance from AI. I will not use AI to produce cover art, but will pay an artist to use their art.

If I choose to produce an audiobook, I will use a real narrator. Period.

As a member of the Author's Guild, I have pointed out that approving the use of AI for "some" things and not "other" things is a slippery slope that requires self-discipline that many will not have. Further, it does not create firm boundaries for what is being pushed on readers. Already, people who are not writers and do not put any work into it are churning out AI books that were built on the backs of real authors. Publishers and online platforms are being inundated with them.

So what's the problem? If some idiot wants to try their hand at producing an AI book, it doesn't mean anybody has to read it.

The problem is, AI did not think up whatever it regurgitated. It used my books and every other author's books. It stole them, in fact. Most AI systems were trained by being fed books from pirated sites. Needless to say, authors were not asked for their permission despite holding copyrights, and authors were not paid for this theft.

For any author to use AI is to feed the beast that is stealing from them.

If that were not bad enough, writing is a skill. If a person does not have the skill, they should try to develop the skill. Depending on AI will result in book after book that lacks originality and fails to surprise the reader. People with more IT skills than writing skills will be sure their rankings are at the top of the web page and readers will find themselves swimming through a vast ocean of mediocrity. Suddenly, it will feel as if all historical romances are the same now. Because they will be.

And most importantly to me, the arts are a human endeavor. Not something to be produced by a machine, where the most successful are the best marketed. If Andy Warhol had used AI, there would be no Andy Warhol. AI does not produce any new ideas, it just steals and recombines from those humans who do. It is a false imitator and the companies owning it are in receipt of stolen goods, which they are selling for their own profit.

I believe we are, as usual, becoming the victims of a bunch of bros (gender neutral) who are determined to make money regardless of the consequences. This happens to us all the time —think the 2008 recession, the A bomb, the oil industry/climate change, taking advantage of inflation, shrinkflation, etc.

This time, I think we will discover far too late that AI has robbed our lives of meaning. I do not only refer to the arts here. Lawyers will not need to lawyer, pharmacists will just watch a screen, social workers will be tied to algorithms, nearly every job will be affected in some way and many will be completely lost. I was once an entry level file clerk in a court office. I kept myself engaged all day by inventing faster and more efficient ways to file. I was really into it. We're humans—we create things, we think up things, we accomplish things.

With AI in the future, most of us will just be watching things.

Those are going to be some long days.

For now, online platforms are requesting that authors who use AI say so. I'm thinking they will not say so.

I WILL say so, though. All Kate Archer books have been written by Kate Archer and only Kate Archer. That means, from the original idea to the final product there has been no interaction of any kind with AI. Not research, not plot ideas, not outlines, not editing, not ANYTHING.

I became a writer because I like to write. You became a reader because you like to read. Not everything in the world needs to be "disrupted" or "hacked." Sometimes, the next new idea is just a Rube Goldberg Gordian Knot that makes a thing more complicated than it needs to be.

Now, my dear reader, I hope you are enjoying this

meddling butlers journey with me. Those six gentlemen are expert at causing a lot of trouble for everybody, including themselves. Never fear though, the ladies and gentlemen in question are well-prepared to face any ridiculous obstacles thrown in their paths.

Kate

Printed in Dunstable, United Kingdom

68586951R00141